Madison

God's Fingerprint 1.618

By A.V. Smith

Book Cover: Eric K. Marshall, Cornerstone Graphics & Imaging

Consulting Editor: Kristin Reeg

Editor: Charita Laurice Sullivan

Editor: Tricia Barnes

Warped Writing and Publishing LLC, Columbus, Ohio

ISBN: 978-0-578-49627-6

Dedication

To my children, Devan, Naiya and Christian:

My prayer to The Universe for you has been sent. You are my life source; greatness awaits you.

I Love You.

ACKNOWLEDGEMENTS

"To God The Universe I hear the words you send. I submit."

To the Jefferson, Burton, and White ancestors: Because of you, I am.

My parents, Diane and Irvin: a child grows best in a stable foundation. Thank you for pushing us to be better every day. I love you.

Fred Jefferson"Pops": Your support and love spreads through me and your grandchildren.

To the memory of departed father Roger Smith, life lessons are learned sometimes in the strangest circumstance.

Auntie Charlotte Burton: Our elder, I have always known our history and love through your voice.

Aunt Candy: Your energy and appreciation of life inspires me... and those cakes!!!

Auntie Eileen: Words move through me as music does you.

My siblings: Portia White; Rod Smith; Irvin White III; Troy Smith; (Donald, Cameron and Marcette): I can't imagine a day of my life without seeing the greatness of you.

Greg, Gazelle, and Nehgel Pickett: It is true that cousins are really just extended siblings.

William,Bruce; Rob Lewis; Dave Johnson ;Solomon Cole; Darren Drake: We still pour a little out for Eric Vaughn and Michael Gardner.

Cousins: Kathy Mayfield; Dave and Charles Moss; Terence Jones; Kyle Jefferson; Chantel Jefferson; Henry Jackson II; Matthew Burton: Our family branches grow upward and outward, sometimes touching briefly, but the roots hold strong.

Shawntel and Nicole for the gifts of our children.

Wiz; Hot Rod; Holmsey; DC Thrill; Country D; Phazer; Speedy; Anton; Toy; TLynch; DoDirty; Cricket; Sweet Ced; B Hill; Robb G: We shared the most important years of our young lives together-Ay Ziggy!!!!

Beverly: Darlene; Gisela; Scott; Raymon: Much of the lessons learned from a boy to young man was influenced by your friendships. Thank you.

Michelle Hardgrow; Carlitha Canady; Donita Watkins: You've been My eyes, My family, and My first Book Club "We ain't done."

Tracy Shavers; Sonja Carsey; Michael Armstrong; Michael Cundiff; Marcietta Wilson-Coleman; John Plymak; Cedric Woodard: Thank you for all the feedback during the process. Invaluable.

(The Hunt family and The Wentz family)

Charita Laurice Sullivan: Editor

Eric K. Marshall: Cornerstone Graphics & Imaging

Lee Krumlauf & Big Rich Miller: You're good men.

Mary Hoffett; Richard Higgins; Cynthia Stocksdale; Brandon McNeal; Erin and Tony Myers; Valerie Jenkins: Thank you for shining a light in my dark hours - I haven't forgotten about you

Amy M.: "You're alright with me, lil dude."
Wali C: Thank you for putting me on stage @ Long street live, keep doing your work.

Ron Reese: "GoodKarma Radio" for helping my voice be heard.

Ed Mabry and Barbara Fant: Sometimes you never really know who you inspire, your words and presence bring light.

*...and so many more.

Special acknowledgment: April Michelle: Whether It's "A reason, a season, or a lifetime," in each step you are deeply loved.

Table of Contents

Introduction

He walked up the stairs, after drinking a beer with neighbors who were playing late night spades and listening to the mix party on the local radio station. His navy-blue wind breaker hung off his shoulders as he stumbled up the first step. With nearly a half a case of beer and half a liter of tequila in his system, he leaned up against the steel guard rail attempting to balance, as each foot alternated upward. He finally had a reason to exhale after leaving the service. He had bartered a deal for his employer and returned from Panama with five additional keys of cocaine for himself and his partner. Searching for his house keys, two eight ball packets of cocaine; his product, fell onto the floor in front of the door and as he bent down, he hit his head on the door knob.

"Fuck," he touched each pocket of his blue jeans, falling back into the wall as he picked up the packets. He could feel himself meshing deeper into intoxication brought on by hard liquor, beer and the combination of marijuana mixed with 'crack'. He had lost his sense of perception as he faded back and forth into consciousness. He squinted to locate his keys and he fell backwards, sinking onto the cold brick wall. Painted green for appearance it was solid brick and although this was one of the final units built in this grouping, it was still low-income housing.

He lost his train of thought and tried remembering all the things he has done that night, but in just the few minutes he struggled up the stairs, he wasn't even able to recall how he had gotten home or who was just downstairs. He slumped backwards and was poked as he rolled onto his knee; he had found his keys. He grabbed the steel railing and hoisted himself but was still unable to comprehend which key to use to open the door, as he tried several until he got it right. He placed the packets of cocaine back into his shirt pocket, turned the door handle and staggered into the living room.

"Fuck… pot…potpourri," he smelled the scent of cinnamon in the air. His wife had transformed into a homebody since his return from serving. She was a woman who continued everything he had begun with his daughter, for that he was grateful. He wanted his child to be able to defend herself against the evils in the world he had seen. He felt bitter towards his wife after hearing rumors that she had stepped out on him while he was away serving, and he dealt with it by numbing his pain with narcotics. She was into a phase of 'trying new shit' ever since he commented on how everything was always the same and she needed to do something to break up the monotony. Her every attempt at his requests only deepened his anger believing she was only trying to make up for her infidelity.

His mouth was dry and the little bit of saliva that he did produce added to his frustration. He stumbled into the kitchen, tossing his keys onto the counter. He grabbed a yellow plastic cup from the dishwashing rack, and poured some water in it, unable to hold onto the cup it fell into the sink splashing water back onto his face. The stack of mail caught his attention.

"Muthafucking bills, gon be gone soon," knowing with the extra product his family's life would be changing soon, but right now he was still parched. He held onto the kitchen counter as he moved towards the refrigerator. A plate of food with a note scribbled with a heart on it had been left for him. He mustered a smile only to be replaced with a vision of his wife being unfaithful. Holding onto the refrigerator door he focused in on a forty-ounce bottle of Colt 45 Malt Liquor and cracked it open.

Mixing the weed and crack was a new way to smoke his marijuana. It was the feeling that made his mouth numb and took away all the pain of being a so-called miscreant to society, even after serving his country loyally. Had it not been for his connections he made in the military he would never have met his employer. Only the fifth trip he had taken on behalf of his employer, who had his sights on controlling the Midwest flow of drugs. The initial investment was only the risk and pulling five extra kilos of cocaine using their employer's money even riskier, but only he and his partner knew. He took the note off the plate of food and threw it into the trash.

"Fuck that cheating ass bitch," he said. These were the same five words he thought when he was told about her infidelity followed by the first laced joint, he had smoked over nine months ago. He knew he had spiraled out of control but couldn't keep the anger from forcing his hand with his wife. When he took his first toke of the joint, he knew better, 'a hustla don't get high off his own supply' but the sweet taste of the joint and the high kept calling him back. He closed the refrigerator door and walked slowly to the living room sofa. He drank more of the Colt 45 before breaking one of his two packets of cocaine down into six lines. Snorting two lines quickly, he reached for the bottle of malt liquor, lost his grip and it slipped out of his hand to land on his foot.

"Muthafucka!" he said out loud as the bottle rolled onto the tiled floor.

"Fuck it, I ain't gon feel none of this," he snorted another line before picking up the bottle.

...

The noise in the kitchen woke her out of her sleep. She had been dreaming of winning her first martial arts tournament. She was just fourteen years old but knew more than most adults. Her father had pushed her hard, she didn't know if it was because he wanted a boy or if it was just in his nature. She would never have a brother, or sister for that matter, because her father had abused her mother so badly, she had been damaged. She hated when he drank, and recently she noticed he was doing more than that. Many nights she prayed for her mother to find the strength to pack and take her away. She loved her father, but she hated the man into which he was transforming.

She didn't know how he could say he loved his wife and would never hit her again, but now the physical violence seemed to be happening more often than naught.

She heard him walking down the short hallway; stopping at her bedroom door, she could sense his foreboding presence but didn't want him to know that she was awake. His personality was Jekyll and Hyde when he drank, and she didn't want to be yanked out of bed and whooped for not doing one of her chores; so, as he walked into her room and stood over her bed, she kept her breathing shallow to make him unaware that she wasn't sleeping. It felt like minutes had passed as he stood there watching her. His wife opening their bedroom door helped him realize that he had 'zoned out'. Hearing the footsteps, he walked back to the entry of his daughter's door before his wife approached his side.

"Baby you need anything, anything at all?" she tried to lessen his burden that he always talked about, being a veteran and black man in America. He didn't know why the question had aggravated him, but it did.

"Take yo ass back to bed and turn the TV off you just wasting electricity around this muthafucka My name ain't Thomas fucking Edison," he stared at her expecting to be obeyed. He went back into the living room after hearing her turn the bedroom television set off, still wired from the drugs he couldn't sleep if he wanted.

He separated the rest of the cocaine into four smaller lines and snorted one before rolling a joint mixing it with the 'crack' he had sold to someone to teach him how to make the new drug. It was a bigger profit margin to be had and less expensive, supply and demand was simple economics. The sweet taste of the joint gave him a new appreciation for narcotics. He had tried heroin overseas while in the military. He had also engaged in acts with female minors that would be illegal in the States, but the motto was 'When In Rome Do As The Romans Do.'

He felt highly aroused, thinking back to the times he only had the comfort of a female because it was an exchange of products and services. He put an X Rated movie into his VCR and picked up the remote and before long he retrieved lubricant from the bathroom. Although his wife was in the other room, he wanted to feel like he was somewhere else in some other time. He loved his wife but believing another man had been with her calloused the joy of the emotion. He blacked out as the scene advanced on the television, when he woke, he rolled another laced joint and snorted another line.

"Primo," in reference to what he had heard one of the people smoking with him earlier called it when it was mixed with crack. Smoking half of it he snorted the rest of the cocaine and plopped another porno tape in to watch. His eyes glossed over and barely open, any sense of identity had been lost.

"Home," was the only thing that flashed in his mind, but it didn't feel like home. He was burning hot with sweat profusely pouring down his body, so he took off his shoes, wind breaker and shirt followed by his blue jeans.

...

She thought that she was dreaming when she felt the arm go around her, but the smell of alcohol and dope filled her nostrils... she was awake now, trying to move away from her father who was pressing his naked body up against hers. She had never been with a boy, but she knew that this was wrong.

"Daddy," she pushed him away, but she was no match for a grown intoxicated man's strength. She saw him looking at her with his eyes glazed and didn't recognize him, and Mattie saw that he had no recognition of their familial bond.

It wasn't the look of a proud father who told her 'good

job' when she won her events in club track. It wasn't the supportive look of a parent watching her break wooden boards in karate, or when she placed in a Jiu Jitsu tournament against purple belts who were higher status only because of her age requirement. What she saw frightened her and she rolled off the bed opposite of over where he slouched.

"Come here you little egg shh…shell," he tried saying but his mouth didn't quite form the words; however, his actions of trying to pull her boxer shorts down spoke huge volumes of the tragic act taking place in the darkness of the night.

"Daddy, No, please Daddy!" she screamed loudly, crying as tears rolled down her face; hoping he would recognize that what he was doing was wrong and bring him back from the place he was now lost.

The door to her room flew open and her mother stood with her eyes and mouth wide open. She was shocked and distraught to see her husband attempting to molest their daughter.

"What the fuck are you doing?" she moved quickly towards the bed to stop the sickening assault, but he was still able to react quickly with his fists raised. The first punch halted her advance, the second punch opened wounds with blood gushing out her nose and mouth. The momentum forced her backwards into the hallway.

"Mama…Mama!" The daughter screamed watching her father in his nakedness advance on her again.

He stumbled into her bed as she backed away into the corner, there was no way she would be able to get around him and out the door. Reaching out he took hold of her arm; even in his intoxication he was strong, and she had no way of breaking free.

"Daddy…Daddy Please…please!" she begged, but it had no effect on him. He didn't recognize the dreadful act he was about to commit or who he was violating; the drugs and alcohol had erased any sense of morality.

"You still young so I'm gon get it…and get it good," He tried to pull her into him. She tried fighting him off with what she had learned in self-defense, but the problem was he was her teacher.

"Oh God no!" she yelled at the top of her lungs watching his manhood come closer.

"Get away from my daughter you sick fucking bastard,"

her mother was standing in the door way again with a copious amount of blood streaming down her face, but there was resolve in her voice.

"I told you wait yo' fucking turn, I'm gon kill yo ass this time," he let his daughter go, turning towards his wife. Even in his blackout, he was dangerous, and without compulsion the night would be covered in darkness.

Everything was happening so fast and all she could of think were her father's words drilled into her since she could understand language, "always survive". The daughter reached onto her dresser to grab a trophy. She moved toward the door with the trophy raised, she was done watching her mother get beaten and she knew they were going to have to fight him together to have any chance of survival.

"Pop…Pop…Pop," the daughter heard the familiar sound as each echo followed. The blood sprayed across her blue and white boxer shorts, she saw drops of blood on her forearms and she stumbled backwards watching her father fall to a knee and then to the floor.

Her mother swayed back and forth with the gun still pointed on her father's naked body as he trembled and bled out onto the floor. Her cotton nightgown was highlighted with blood splatter and her expression unreadable. The gun shook slightly as her hand quivered, but it was still locked on him. He was still alive and from the blood pouring out of his left leg and abdomen he had been hit twice.

"I had no choice…I…I had to protect you, I had to protect you, you're my daughter, my flesh and blood," she repeated while he moaned on the floor. The mother was rationalizing her actions not understanding the full trauma of tonight's actions.

"Call 911," the mother told the daughter, who still stood by the dresser with her trophy in her hand, staring down at her father bleeding into the carpet. She lowered the gun to her side and began shaking her head. She knew life would never be the same for her family. Realizing her daughter had not moved she was even more firm the second time she spoke to her.

"I said go dial 911!" she yelled, startling her to move away from the dresser.

The daughter walked to the side of her father's body as her mind was being torn apart, being thrown into adulthood sooner than any teen should. She stepped over the blood like it was a deadly virus, walked to the kitchen and picked up the wall phone to call the emergency number.

The mother walked into the kitchen behind her and placed the gun onto the counter before going back to sit down on the floor outside her daughter's bedroom to stare at her husband, crying because he had once been a good man.

"I'm sorry, but she's my daughter, your daughter…she's your daughter," she repeated with emotion moving closer applying pressure to his wounds as they waited for the police to show with paramedics.

Shortly after, the ambulance took her father away fighting to save his life. Even with the young daughter's account of what happened and the narcotics they found in his clothing, the police placed her mother in handcuffs after admitting to shooting him, and took the daughter to Franklin County Children's Services. This department in Columbus, Ohio wasn't concerned with the young daughter, as she passed in and out of foster care until her grandmother was awarded custody nearly a year later.

CHAPTER 1

CIVIL ASSET FORFEITURE

"You only take our fuckin plata, filthy abogado!" a Hispanic woman yelled with a heavy accent as she held onto a new born baby. Another child in blue jeans and t-shirt; appearing to be about eight years old was pushing the baby carriage as they followed an older white man dressed in a bland gray suit.

This wasn't the first time Mattie had overheard clients not satisfied with the legal representation they received. She knew all too well the emotions this woman was feeling because it ran along the same line of anger and loss she felt when her mother had been sentenced to nearly two decades in prison.

For those from Spanish speaking countries, the fear of deportation since the new President of The U.S. had been sworn into office, caused them to be the last to seek justice from the courts.

The halls of the courthouse hadn't changed in over twenty years except for newer chairs in the waiting areas before entering the courtroom. The building always smelled the same. Old and musty, and it was always cold in the ante room.

Mattie found herself sitting in on certain trials over the years, and especially after being moved around in the foster care system, she vowed to watch and learn more about the criminal system because she would not fall victim to it again. She omitted the term "justice' system because she knew it was also corrupt and governed by backroom favors and individual biases aimed at the poor people of this country, but most precisely poor people of color.

Whenever Mattie had time, she studied the case, and both the prosecutor and defense attorney. She saw good people who had no criminal history, and good law-abiding citizens having sentences being set at maximum for a first offense, while actual criminals were being set free because of some simple breakdown, misspelling, or wrong time entered on legal documents. Mattie had witnessed some of those set free on technicalities return to court later for different charges. It was a criminal system and not a justice system. She couldn't fathom how people couldn't see the disparaging actions taken against the less fortunate man compared to them.

Mattie viewed, on many occasions, that poor people received terrible representation from the public defender's office, and knew that money was becoming the great equalizer as a gun once was.

"We should just learn to be good human beings," the thought faded as she read court dockets on the media screens stationed outside each court room. Mattie knew that was an oversimplification as she pulled her hoodie back and removed her hat.

She wore a black corduroy blazer with a matching black hoodie and khaki pants, over the years a few of the bailiffs had come to know her.

"Madison," a voice called out. She turned towards the voice and recognized her friend Henry walking towards her, dressed in a dark navy-blue suit. He had been the only real male influence in her early life, but right now Mattie surmised he was a witness in one of the court proceedings.

She had seen less of him and his wife Michelle since his promotion to detective, but she often saw his son when they played with the children of one of her closest friends.

“Calling me Madison is gon get you stabbed Hank,” they greeted each other with a hug.

“Point taken Mattie, point taken,” he responded. He hated being called Hank except by family, fortunately Mattie was considered family, by both he and his wife.

“Michelle just asked about you this morning, she said you’ve been trying to get her out to some wine and painting event. Don’t blame her. Honestly, it’s all my fault, I get called on cases and never really know when I’ll be home,” he paused staring at her with one brow raised.

“You’re just down here canvassing nothing of a personal nature, right?” he asked. He understood her affinity for sitting in and observing, but he also knew the troubles she had as a juvenile. He had kept her from harm’s way when he was a rookie police officer after she had gotten into a fight with a mother and daughter who tried robbing her. The case turned against the women because Henry secured footage identifying the women being the aggressors. They ended up healing behind bars after pleading guilty to attempted robbery charges with fractured orbital bones for the mother and a broken knee cap for the daughter.

"I've given up most of the craziness, but I may catch a case against you if you don't find some time for Chelle to hang with me and the girls, are you testifying today?"

She had never set in on a trial he had participated in, except her own. He was a fair officer. He was born and raised in the same neighborhood Mattie had been. A promising high school athlete offered collegiate scholarships to mid and major universities. He remained home to take care of his ailing mother who passed nearly seven years ago.

"I'm here for a child neglect case, a mother left her child for two days," he said hesitantly, realizing it may resurface memories for her. He remembered the broken teenage girl who sat in the courtroom listening to accounts filled with lies and speculation as the prosecutor only sought to gain another notch on her belt.

"It's ok Henry," Mattie interjected feeling his uncertainty.

"A, uh, mother had left her son unattended for over two days. There is a bunch of circumstantial shit surrounding it, but I honestly think the mother had set arrangements for his well-being. Anyways I am on the witness list because I spoke with the child in passing once before, after she had overdosed on heroin three years ago. She has been clean since and did not test positive when they arrested her."

Mattie heard the conflict in his voice. He knew that many times there were underlying themes to behavior. He skirted a fine line between common sense policing and strict adherence to the law.

"Where was the mother for two days though, I am not a parent type of person, but leaving a child for two days?" Mattie asked as the doors opened from the court room.

"Henry," a woman waved at him as she approached. She wore a beige pant suit with a white blouse. Her leather, sling back, blue shoes matched the leather attaché hanging from her shoulder.

"Natalie," he extended his hand to her.

"This is Madison, the sister I never had," knowing Mattie would take notice to the introduction.

"Natalie, my pleasure. I am going to leave you and Hank to business," she paused as she and Henry laughed.

"Funny, very funny," they hugged each other before Mattie departed.

"So, we dropped the charges against the mother. Turns out the aunt was there initially to watch her nephew; but left the child alone to get a fix. Somebody called in a tip that Children Services followed up on," Natalie's voice trailed off the further Mattie walked away from them into the courtroom she had originally planned. Her attention was drawn because it was a case of assault. She recognized the name on the docket. It was one of her foster brothers. One of the better ones. "Samuel Lewis," she read taking a seat in the back of the court room.

Mattie marveled at the fabric of people present. A collection of ages, colors and class. She scanned the room towards the rear where the attorneys and judges were allowed entry. She saw the officers before the males in orange jumpsuits. A group of prisoners, linked together by a chain, stood against the wall facing the judge.

The judge sat staring at her computer reading the charges levied against the defendant. Her black robe was in stark contrast of her pale skin and red hair. The bailiff approached the bench with papers he had retrieved from the prosecutor.

Someone laughing had gained the attention of the judge who was now staring at those gathered.

“I do enjoy a good joke from time to time, but right now is not it. Anymore disruptions will be met at my full discretion,” she finished before readjusting her attention to the documents in her hand.

Mattie had seen Judge Emily Radcliffe in action before. She was as fair as Mattie thought a judge could be, sometimes giving strong recommendations to both prosecutor and defense attorney based on the merits of their case. Mattie also knew she meant what she said, and hoped people had borne her warning.

“Mrs. Kersey please rise. Have you read your plea agreement and agree to waive your right to a jury trial and to allow this court’s judgement based on plea?” Judge Radcliffe asked.

“Yes, your honor I do,” an older black woman stood next to her attorney facing the judge. Her sandy colored business suit spoke volumes of the wealth she had. The platinum watch band hanging loosely from her wrist was an indication that she could afford her attorney; Clayton Monroe III. Mattie had seen him work before, and knew his retainer was five thousand dollars and if the case went to court, he billed another five thousand dollars; then billed at five hundred dollars per hour.

"Regardless of your intent, Mrs. Kersey, the law is the law. This court sentences you to twelve months of basic probation with an exception at six months in addition to court fees," Judge Radcliffe paused as she looked the defendant squarely into her face.

"Please do not let me regret my leniency," she finished.

"Thank you, thank you so much your Honor," Mrs. Kersey answered, as her attorney gathered her belongings on the wooden table.

"We have to sign a form, and then we can get you set up downstairs with your probation officer, with time to spare to make your appointment Sandra," he told her.

Mattie knew that the one thing that could make the playing field more level dealing with the court system was money and Sandra Kersey had it.

Movement from the rear of the courtroom caught

Mattie's attention as Mrs. Kersey exited through the doors with her attorney. An officer was walking one of the prisoners to the table Clayton and Sandra had vacated. The male in the orange jail garb kept his eyes down as he walked. Mattie knew instantly it was her foster brother Sam. The city prosecutor was conversing with a very young public defender who seemed more anxious to make pleasantries than to speak with his client. Mattie felt uneasy, as he approached Sam who was still standing at the wooden defendants table. Sam sat down before his attorney.

When the young defense attorney began speaking with Sam, his whole demeanor began to shift. Where he had been somber and meek, he began showing signs of agitation.

"Mr. Jardin, do you need time with your client?" Judge Radcliff asked as she looked up over the brim of her glasses.

"No, no your honor. I apologize we have come to an accord," he answered. Sam was still visibly upset, and began speaking with more force to his attorney.

"Those muthafuckas attacked me without warrant, they came into my house with guns and tried to rob me, why the fuck do you want me to plead guilty? They found no narcotics, only cash that I earned, and now they wanna keep my money and you letting them. Civil asset forfeiture is bullshit!" Sam said loudly.

"Mr. Lewis," Judge Ratcliffe spoke out to gain his attention.

"Mr. Lewis, I am going to allow you and counsel to speak privately before reaching an agreement. You have rights and I want you to completely understand them before moving forward."

"Your honor that is highly abnormal for your courtroom." The prosecutor addressed her.

"Whose courtroom?" she asked the prosecutor.

The relaxed posture that the young dark-haired prosecutor had was quickly replaced with attentiveness. "Forgive me, I have no objections your honor." he replied as Sam and Attorney Jardin walked towards an unoccupied room to speak.

"I saved all that money over three years of working and they can't have it, they found ten grams of marijuana that I use medicinally, but because I had money, I am considered a drug dealer and my earnings are forfeit, and on top of that there was no identification until after I snuck him. Fuck that shit!" he was irritated.

Mattie didn't make eye contact with him as to not embarrass him. She followed behind them with some distance and watched them enter a room set aside for attorney-client privacy. She understood that whatever Sam decided was set in stone once he made up his mind. Passing by the room she heard the attorney say,

"But you assaulted a police officer with a baseball bat!"

Mattie chuckled as she walked towards the elevator, knowing for Sam it was always the principle of the matter. She would secure better counsel for him because she took his word as truth.

Mattie left the court house shortly after, she was supposed to meet her friend Cindy at a car dealership in case the negotiations went terribly wrong, and knowing how sanctified her friend could be, she hurried.

When she arrived at the dealership, she was hounded by car salesmen, but that quickly changed when she told them she was here for a friend. Entering the building she saw her friend Cindy who waved her down.

CHAPTER 2
A FAIR DEAL

"Ok, here's the deal, we can get this done right now at that monthly rate, but we just need a little more money for the down payment," the salesman named Charles said. It was the way he said it, so casually, that told Cindy there was something else that was being kept hidden from her. He had on blue polyester slacks and a white shirt. Like the rest of the sales people in the dealership, he wore a tie and a light brown sports coat.

"More of a down payment?" she sat upright in the chair. She glanced at her friend who was up getting a bag of popcorn from the car dealerships machine, wiping a few salt crumbs off her corduroy blazer.

One manager sat in his chair staring out the window. He was a brown skinned, dark-haired man, wearing glasses and an eggshell colored shirt with a multi-colored tie, predominantly emerald green. He seemed to be paying attention to everything the salespeople were doing outside. The other manager was sitting down with a white short sleeved shirt with the top button undone, and his tie snuggly pulled up around his neck. He kept staring back towards Charles' desk and his computer.

"You know in the old days, they'd ask for your signature and a handshake to commiserate a deal," Cindy paused as Mattie sat back down next to her at the desk. Cindy had deliberately taken an Uber to the dealership. She dressed in deep colored blue jeans with black ankle high -boots and a layered black crew top. Her hair short styled with rose highlights was accented by the red shawl draped across her shoulders. Cindy knew how negotiations went, and was often fair when she bargained for personal items like homes and cars.

"So, what you're saying to me right now Chuck, is that the little short guy told you to come back over here to me and try to get more money out of me?" she asked sounding slightly amused.

Mattie set back in her chair waiting to see how far her friend was going to push the situation to get exactly the deal she wanted. Cindy had learned it was always best to deal from a position of power, and only rarely did she ever bluff.

"When I came in, I told you just to be straightforward with me and I'd give you all the information you would need so we could make this as simple as possible. I was clear when I told you that, that's exactly why I didn't sign the application. Did your boss run my information Chuck?" she abruptly leaned forward pushing the sales paper back towards him across the desktop.

Mattie raised her eyebrows knowing what was coming next after her friend had invaded the salesman's space. Cindy was the number one realtor in Central Ohio and didn't hesitate to take control of the negotiation.

"No…no I don't think he did, I told him you didn't sign the card." Charles responded, trying not to frown before removing the sports coat off his back to hang it across the backside of his chair.

"That's good; I don't want my credit pulled. So, here's

my counter offer Chuck," Cindy said reaching out for the sales paper which had sets of numbers scribbled all over it. She turned it over and began writing her terms, Cindy then laid it back out in front of Charles and smiled before sitting back in her chair again.

"I'll need you to okay this, or whoever is writing the deal, on that line," Cindy finished. Mattie smiled and shook her head. Her friend never ceased to amaze her with her wit or "smart ass mouth" as many had described.

Charles stood up and walked over towards the sales tower. He thought there would be no dealing to be done between the two parties. "She uh, she countered your deal Bob."

Bob sat back in his chair and squinted at the paper. His lack of hair made wrinkles start at his eyebrows and move upwards to what was left of his hairline.

"What the fuck is this? This woman ain't buying shit from us. I'm not selling her shit!" Bob threw the paper onto the desk.

"Watch your language Bob," the other manager staring out the window had been listening.

"Peter, this fucking bitch," Bob paused to lower his voice taking the cue from Peter frowning at his language.

"This uppity ass bitch wants a price on the vehicle, and for every ten minutes she has to wait she's deducting another five hundred dollars off any final price. Then she crossed that shit off and marks an "X" for buying the vehicle with six thousand dollars off the listed price. Her friend rode the bus in, and she took a fucking Uber or some shit. Charles you should've controlled that better you fucking idiot. I'm not getting paid. Peter isn't getting paid. Do you like working for free you fucking moron?" Bob was clearly upset.

"Uh, excuse me but I hope you didn't run her credit, I told you she didn't sign the card," Charles said leaning over the sales tower he didn't like Bob speaking to him in that tone.

"Charles, I want you to go back over there and keep her company. If she asks, tell her your boss is looking at banks, but to make sure we can do her deal, we need her permission to run her credit, and I will give her an out the door price as well," Peter handed Charles the welcome card to get her signature.

“This is pretty good but how much longer is this gonna take? I’m starving, and all this popcorn is doing is making me thirsty,” Mattie said questioning both Charles and Cindy as he returned. Cindy took that as an opportunity to take the lead.

“I’ll get you something, do you want a pop Chuck?” Cindy stood up with her small, vintage, check, Burberry wallet in her hand.

“And Chuck don’t worry, you’ll get an A plus review because I don’t expect you to work for free. My original offer, according to my research, would’ve paid you a little less than twelve hundred dollars. Your greedy boss is causing you to lose money Chuck, so if you can have him come over to give me the best offer, I would appreciate it, or when I come back from getting soda we will be leaving,” she finished before asking Mattie what she wanted to drink.

As Charles and Cindy went their separate ways, Mattie sat at the desk wondering why Cindy always pushed the envelope a little more than others.

Friends since junior year in high school, their journey began in the school choir. Cindy was voted most likely to succeed, she was after all in a professional singing group at age fourteen. "Gemstones" was the name. They were featured in 'BreakOut Magazine", a journal that looked for the next superstars in a variety of genres. Gemstones got air play on regional radio stations and broke the top ten with their single "Not As Young As You Think". Unfortunately, the manager of the group was also the father of one of the singers and mismanaged the group's money. Following several lawsuits, the group disbanded.

That same year over the summer, Madison moved in with her grandmother. She had listened to people saying a family is the best way to raise children with the entire nucleus present. Often, she laughed inside and thought how adamant people could be about their beliefs.

Madison met Cindy in music class. Cindy was boisterous and confident walking onto the auditorium stage; Madison was quiet but very observant. When their music instructor told the students to pair up to sing harmonies, no one wanted to sing with Cindy so when the dust cleared Madison was left. Madison had no idea who Cindy was, but no one knew who she was either. Their instructor, Mrs. Pugh, told them to pick a song and find the right range. Cindy began singing "I'll Be There" an old Jackson Five song, very simple but harmonious. When Madison joined in the song Mrs. Pugh and the rest of the class sat back and listened to these two harmonize a perfect soulful rendition. When they had finished singing the two girls hugged and had been best friends ever since.

Cindy was returning with the soda in her hands.

"I don't know how you can still eat and drink all this crap and keep that figure, and he hasn't come back with his manager yet?"

Mattie who shook her head no as she twisted the cap off to her pop.

"Well let's go, they're gonna chase us down, his greedy ass boss ran my credit, so they need to gauge how pissed I am right now, I ain't no spring chicken." As if on cue, Charles was calling her name walking quickly across the showroom floor with his boss trailing.

"Ma'am, Ms. Champion, hold on if you will. Please, my name is Peter Hanford and I'm the General Manager. For any inconvenience you and your friend have endured please accept my apology on behalf of my dealership. Would you mind if I make sure that I've done everything possible to earn your business right now?" he asked motioning for them to have a seat. He had put on his jacket before leaving the tower and was much taller than she had expected. He was a handsome man.

Cindy hesitated before taking the few steps back to the desk. She sat down and crossed her legs with her arms folded on top. Charles pulled an additional chair from his co-workers' desk so he could sit down, but Madison decided she was tired of sitting and walked the showroom. She stayed within earshot of the desk to listen to the manager. However, it was Cindy who dove right in.

"Did Mr. Greedy Mceady run my credit Pete?" she sounded slightly condescending.

"My given name is Peter, Ms. Champion and yes, he ran your credit. If we are able to meet the criteria of your counter offer can we finalize this deal Ms. Champion?" He was straight forward. Cindy said yes because she only had a few ways to push back with him. He had corrected her about his name, something that told her he was a confident person, unlike Charles who accepted being called Chuck. Peter met her head on about her credit being run and got straight to the point, the deal.

"Then give me a few more minutes," he paused as he stood up,

"Yes, I realize we are still on the clock, I do need your signature please," he finished sliding the welcome card toward her. He pulled an ink pen from his sports coat and handed it to her to sign. Excusing himself he walked towards the sales tower passing Madison along the way.

"She's one tough cookie huh?" he asked with a smirk on his face, but he wasn't being offensive.

"You have no idea," she replied before she had thought the words.

"Well let me get to work, I'm Peter by the way," he said offered his hand to shake

"Madison," She returned the grip firmly.

"Mattie you just cost him another five hundred dollars," her friend approached them swaying her hips. Peter smiled again at both women and walked away.

"His fine ass gon give me a good deal Mattie watch," she slipped her head into the half-ton pickup truck that was on the showroom floor. By her estimation Peter was handsome. He was tall and broad shouldered. His hair was tapered cut, very low. Peter stood around six foot three, and as he walked away, he moved with a purpose but not in a hurry.

"I don't know… he alright, he seems okay, but this is a car dealership," Mattie hopped into the driver seat, reminding Cindy that a car dealership was in the top five of the slimiest places to work.

Mattie looked to where Peter was sitting and saw the balding manager who Charles had originally gone too, was now standing with his arms crossed. Peter had moved him out of the chair. From Bob's expression he didn't like what Peter was doing. Peter stood from the desk with papers in his hands and headed back towards Charles desk.

"Ladies," he said motioning them to sit down. Peter waited until both women were sitting before taking a seat and extending the sales paper back across the desk towards Cindy.

"This is the overall price of the vehicle if you are to finance with us, and with three thousand down, your payment would be $812.77 plus tax, have we earned your business Ms. Champion?"

Cindy leaned forward to look at the sales form. She saw all the numbers clearly and the price was even lower than she had expected. It was a fair offer.

"Yes, we have a deal, I will put fifteen thousand down

and allow the half point in the interest instead of doing my own financing, you earned that Peter," nodding affirmatively.

"Charles will you take Ms. Champion's Infinity QX80 to clean up, tell them I said to detail it like it's my car, and what I'll do to make this seamless Ms. Champion, is prepare all the paper work to get you in and out within the hour," he extended his hand to shake Cindy's.

"An hour, I'm starving, let's go eat and come back," Mattie said. She was hungry, she hadn't eaten since four o'clock the previous day and the popcorn was more fluff than sustenance. Peter smiled and this time it was to Mattie he responded.

"I can treat for lunch if you like, nothing all fancy though. We typically order from "Star's Restaurant" across the street, have either of you ever eaten there before?" he shifted his attention to Cindy and then back to Mattie whom he responded.

"No," Mattie answered as Cindy shook her head.

Peter began scooting his chair back. "I'll have Charles show you the menu, and anything over thirty dollars that you order you two will get the difference, fair enough?"

Peter excused himself after saying something to Charles who's whole demeanor lightened.

"Thank you, thank you," he said pausing as he reached into a desk drawer scrambling through menus. "Write down what you want to eat so I can get it ordered. Excuse me for a sec, I left your owner's manual and warranty information, its' still in the glove box."

"Charles what do you want to eat?" Mattie called out to him. Slightly taken off guard by her question, he turned around to face them straightening his tie.

"Uh, I don't think Peter will buy mine, that menu is for you two," but Mattie interrupted him.

"I am buying yours Charles for putting up with my sister without blowing your cool. A lot of people can't tolerate her when she gets like this. So, what do you want to eat?"

"Fish and Chips if it's not too much, and thank you, but honestly you don't have to do that," he headed back to the detail portion of the dealership.

"Tolerate me when I'm like what Mattie?" Cindy looked over her shoulder at the menu. Mattie slid the pen towards Cindy, so she could write down what she wanted to eat.

"Don't play with me Cynthia," she paused taking another sip of her Pepsi. "And make sure you apologize to him. His name is Charles," as her phone rang.

"It's Geri."

"What's up, did you slay in Chicago?" Mattie knew her friend had worked hard building her business, and had positioned herself to be relevant in the magazine business.

Geri was just as much of a sister to Mattie as her other two close friends. The only difference was she was white. They met in college and ran track together, but Geri became an ally, first fighting injustices against people of color before she had become a friend. Being a child of two attorneys she was familiar with the law, but never wanted to join in the legacy.

"Mattie these dry ass men thought I was an idiot, I'll tell you all about it when I get back tomorrow, because I fly in close to midnight. One of the executives was a creeper too. Anyways did she get her car?" Mattie put the conversation on speaker so as not to have to repeat anything.

"Girl you know I got my car." Cindy said loudly.

"And did you bullyfoot em again?" Geri asked as her

laughter came through the cell phone.

Mattie laughed along with Cindy. These friends shared nearly everything, along with the fourth friend Sheila, who was an assistant nurse manager with two children and divorced.

"Mattie I won't be at the gym in the morning, but you already knew, right?".

Geri had been a long-distance runner in college, filling in on the 4x400 meter relay, which Mattie ran, when a substitute was needed. Geri stayed in shape and allowed Mattie to train her over the past three years. She had shaved her head in college before Amber Rose made the style fashionable. Strangely, she was built like a model, except she wasn't skinny, but fit. She was never afraid of a challenge and understood that people weren't just one single thing but always had layers within their identity.

"Yeah, I know so I am going to work out tonight at home and be ready for event night," Mattie finished.

"Is this all you want?" Cindy asked after finalizing her food order before walking it to the sales tower.

"Geri, let me go. This heifer is about to flirt with the car guy," Mattie said, Geri needed more information.

"Is the man at least handsome this time?" Geri asked laughing again. Cindy didn't have a certain type of man she dated, the last guy barely spoke English but had built a reputable construction business. In the end Cindy needed a man who accepted her freedom and remained a challenge.

"Uhm, he's ok but definitely more of a looker than the last one," Mattie couldn't help but join Geri in talking about their friends' dating choices.

"Diallo worked hard and treated me good, he just couldn't give me what I wanted sexually, it's only so much eating 'chocha' can do for a sister. Now this one right here look like he working with something," Cindy replied, looking back over her shoulder at Mattie as she walked towards the tower.

Mattie smiled knowing she had been blessed with true friends and she would do anything for them.

Chapter 3
Cinnamon 'Burn' Rolls

"What do you mean the loan isn't going to get bought? He's a first-time buyer and he fits that category undeniably. I've had people with less credit, job history," Cindy was on the phone speaking with the loan manager about her client as she drove home from the dealership. She was still high off her negotiation with the manager from the dealership, that she was trying to bully the bank for one of her clients.

Mattie had heard Cindy at work countless times before and she had no doubt that by the end of the conversation her friend would have this home loan closed. The fact at hand,

Cindy was great at her career.

Drivers blowing their horns attempting to force their way onto and off the exit ramps to the interstate intensified the noise Mattie was hearing, but as she sat in the passenger's seat, she kept to herself staring out the window.

"Watch out!" she suddenly shifted in her seat, as a city vehicle merged from the entrance ramp into their lane without signaling. Cindy shifted in her lane to avoid being hit.

"Damn," Mattie stared out the window as the driver held up his hand, whether he was apologizing or saying thank you, they couldn't tell.

Cindy responded by 'flipping him the bird' before putting her blinker on to exit the congested highway, still holding a conversation with the banking agent.

"Gary, Gary, we've done business for over ten years and you're telling me you can't get the loan bought as is? Work your magic," Cindy paused.

"The appraisal, what about the appraisal?" A frown came on her face. Mattie's cell phone went off from a text message sent from her grandmother asking her to pick a few items up from the mall, before noticing the exit Cindy had taken was to the neighborhood she grew up in before her tragedy as a teen.

Looking at the homes and brick apartment buildings brought back visions of playing on the jungle gym and see-saw…running around the small play areas which seemed much larger when she was a young girl, but now all her flooding memories weren't simply the joyful ones of a child.

Cruising near the four-unit brick apartment she last lived before her grandmother was awarded custody, Mattie's stomach felt like it had butterflies, and she felt sick. The traumatic ordeal of 'that night' tried to surface, but just in time Cindy was close to wrapping up her call but she quickly muted it.

"This muthafucka Gary is trying to run his little game on me, acting like my client can't get a loan on a one hundred and ninety thousand -dollar mortgage loan with eight percent down," Cindy paused.

"Damn what exit did I take, oh okay I know where we are. This is your old neck of the woods," she finished.

"Yeah, it looks way different than when I grew up, or

maybe I've just grown up and can see it for what it is now," Mattie responded without emotion in her voice.

"See it for what it is, it's the hizood girl, you grew up in the ghetto," she sat back and laughed.

"Yeah but everything ain't always bad in the hood and still, I don't know nobody who ain't trying to move up and out the hood," Mattie paused,

"And don't act like you grew up in the suburbs with a white picket fence," with a little sarcasm in her tone.

Cindy laughed because until 'Gemstones' had a little success Cindy's family struggled and received assistance from the county.

"I can't lie, you right, I still remember my hand me down pink Chuck Taylors, I wore those hoes out," as she stared at her cell phone to make sure she still had Gary muted.

Off in the distance police sirens were heard, a very common occurrence in this portion of the city, and as Cindy turned down a side street, attempting to take a short cut, they were stuck behind three police cars.

"It never fails does it?" Mattie asked rhetorically.

Four officers had a group of young men lined up against the side of a store front business patting them down, while another policeman was directing traffic at the intersection. Drivers in all directions were slowing down to watch what was going on.

Mattie stared at the teenagers wondering if any of them would make it out of the cycle of poverty. One teen, who was being patted down began to resist the officers, and as another policeman went to assist his colleague, two of the other teens decided to make a break for it, heading towards Cindy's car.

"Marvin, stop them!" an officer shouted to his partner directing traffic, as he pursued one of the fleeing teenagers.

He turned and was able to apprehend one of the juveniles because the young man's sagging pants kept falling, slowing him down with no real chance of escape. The other suspect had fled, throwing something out of his pockets to land next to Mattie's passenger door.

"Who was your friend?" The officer asked the apprehended teen now in handcuffs. He walked with the suspect towards Mattie's door and retrieved the plastic bag with smaller plastic packets of crack cocaine in it.

“That dude ain’t my friend, I don’t even know him,” the handcuffed teen tried to say.

“Shut up, this is your bag then. Is this what you threw before I tackled yo ass?” the cop asked.

“Hell naw, that ain’t mine, I ain’t even make it this far. That shit ain’t mine,” vehemently denying possession being forced back to the police cruiser.

Mattie shook her head. It was a shame to see the same cycle perpetuating.

There had been open aggression between law enforcement and gang members since the murder of a father and his two children at the beginning of the summer. The Mayor’s office made it a priority to find the murderer because those killed were family members of his life-long friend; Bob Fredericks. Bob had taken a different route to generate his family legacy and divert criminal activity into community action plans to rebuild the city. It was a strenuous process as not all members of his family agreed to leave behind the criminal foundation their family was built on, but with the Mayor’s support, he had helped improve the perception of good being done within the city.

“I would’ve got out and whooped some ass if they

woulda put one little scratch on these wheels," Cindy said as they were able to maneuver through the blockade and drive away.

Mattie didn't reply because she was thinking back to the night her father was put on a gurney and rolled away. That night police had found two ounces of crack, a half- pound of marijuana, and two handguns with their serial numbers filed off when they searched the home. The charges filed against Mattie's mom relating to the cocaine were dropped later, but they had to make an example by having her plea to the marijuana charges and those charges against using a firearm unlawfully during the course of committing a felony.

For nearly two months as her mother's incarceration and trial went on, young Madison was back and forth between courtroom and hospital visiting her father. He apologized repeatedly over and over. Each time Mattie always said, "It's ok daddy," but she was unsure about what she felt for him. He was her father, but she had not completely forgiven him for tearing her world apart and couldn't see a time she would.

Young Madison felt the full emotion of her mother's circumstances as the prosecutor's revelation that her mother was on cocaine and had been using it the night of the shooting.

"You're an addict Mrs. Parks, isn't that why you shot your husband, not because he was attempting to molest your daughter, but because you were high on cocaine and jealous of her?" She questioned.

The same prosecutor was now a judge who handed down sketchy decisions from her bench, and who had been brought before the review board when overriding the sentence recommendation of someone found guilty of aggravated robbery and bodily injury.

Mattie sat in her courtroom once, and could see that Judge Olana Johnson was more about her own ambition than justice.

Mattie knew that her mother shot her father to save her from an ultimate sin, and she also knew her mom wasn't the person being described in the courtroom as a junkie and mentally unstable with grossly impaired judgment, suicidal ideation or the inability to distinguish between reality and non-reality. Yet the knowing couldn't erase the words. In the end Mattie's mom was sentenced to eighteen to twenty years in the State Penitentiary, leaving young Madison in her own prison of sorts. Her father pled guilty to the possession of the cocaine and unlawful use of firearm as well. This ensured that the real tragedy would not have to be re-lived by his daughter in a courtroom full of strangers having her recount of that night. His life was short-lived, but he had set Mattie up financially for life without her knowledge.

"You alright?" Cindy asked in the awkward silence.

"Huh, oh yeah I'm good. I need to stop and get grandma some sweets from the store. Can you drop me by the mall, and I'll catch a bus home. Let me just run in and grab some stuff really quick," Mattie answered as they pulled up in front of her property.

Mattie ran in and came back changed into a hoodie, sneakers and carrying a book bag. The rest of the drive to the mall Cindy was back on the phone speaking with Gary, who had suddenly found a way to get the loan bought. As they pulled up to one of the anchor stores Cindy put Gary on hold.

"See you later sista," she hugged Cindy before closing the car door as she exited. She put her back pack across her shoulders and situated her .380 Smith & Wesson Bodyguard under her hoodie.

"Call me later, this dude is about to ask me out again," waving bye to Mattie.

Mattie decided to be quick. Her grandmother could ask

for anything and Mattie would make it happen. Fortunately, Grandma Redd's requests came sporadically like this one. She wanted a half dozen cinnamon rolls from the 'store at the mall'. It always made Mattie smile because her grandmother called the store Cinnamon Bum Rolls.

The parking lot was an indication of how full the mall was. Families were beginning back to school shopping, as the stores bore multiple sales, and some groups of teenagers walked the mall as she once did. Mattie thought about a few items from Homage and Victoria's Secrets, she could pick up. As she left the blue jean store, she nearly was knocked over by two women seemingly in a rush. Mattie allowed it to slide without addressing them. She still had a mat workout with a three-mile run at the end of it. Her day had been easy, and she wanted to keep it that way.

She overheard conversations between parents explaining to their children to put certain items back not included on their shopping lists. Mattie wondered how different her life would've been without the darkness of 'that night' over a decade ago. She understood that life was more than structured paths taken along the journey.

It was being prepared for the unexpected, something her father had drilled into her.

The mall was still new, bright with themed décor throughout. Large open spaces on each of the three levels allowed people to see a large portion of its grandeur.

Mattie rode the escalator down to the first floor, passing more specialty stores and a Jeweler with displays and sale signs on an extended number of items.

"I can't right now," Mattie thought causing her to laugh out loud. A few people stared at her; she was uncertain if it was because she had chuckled, or because she was wearing sunglasses inside with her hoodie pulled over her head. The only moment she had lowered her hood was when walking into the two stores she had just shopped, only to pull it back upon leaving.

She could smell the variety of food being served and she was grateful she had eaten at the dealership, because she would have a hard time deciding from all the choices.

Mattie saw that there were only a few people waiting for cinnamon rolls. Whereas many of the other food places had substantial lines. The smell of her surroundings helped her decide to eat a few mini rolls with coffee before walking to the bus stop.

There was a small rush towards the pizza shop which had

brought out free samples of pizza, as she waited in a shorter line to get the baked treat. A few people tried to skip people in front of them, but a young burly man spoke up and told them to wait.

Mattie saw the two women who had nearly knocked her down earlier walking around the food court separately. She thought about approaching them about bumping into her earlier and decided it wasn't worth her breath. People could be single minded when they shopped, but there was something odd about them, as they never made eye contact or looked at any of the food courts menus. A young boy of caramel complexion, about the age of twelve, was arguing with his mother about needing better shoes than what he had been bought and it caught everyone's attention. He argued that the one hundred- and fifty-dollar shoes she purchased would make him look cheap because he told his friends he was getting the brand-new version.

"Spoiled ass kid," someone said out loud causing a few people to laugh as the mother, embarrassed, moved her son along towards the exit of the mall.

Mattie speculated that the boy's behavior was another sign that younger parents wanted to be friends with their children first, instead of being parents first. Mattie was content being god-mother and proverbial aunt to her close friend's children.

A young Indian mother pushed a two-carrier stroller to stand in line behind Mattie. Two young babies were nestled comfortably in each seat. One slept while the other fidgeted with his pacifier. He dropped it, so Mattie picked it up and handed it to his mother, who thanked her in return.

"I could use a nice ring," the thought flashed into her mind after seeing the mothers wedding ring. Mattie chuckled, knowing she had just experienced envy and knew that was no reason to purchase anything. But watching groups of people carry bags of sale items Mattie thought again about going back to the Jewelers and seeing if there were real bargains, knowing that the markup on their items was often four times the amount people should pay. The two women had regrouped close enough to where she stood, and that's when Madison overheard them speaking in Spanish.

"Se agarrarla en el estacionamiento," the hair on the back of her arms stood up and as she ordered the desserts, she kept an eye on the women. Roughly translated 'grab her in the parking lot'. She hoped that they weren't in pursuit of a victim as the news had carried stories about the increase in crime along with human trafficking.

After paying, Mattie decided to sit closest to where she could view most of the eating space.

The women walked back and forth never moving far from the food court, with their attention drawn towards a lone female.

Mattie saw a young, biracial, teenage girl she figured to be about the age of seventeen, who had several shopping bags at the side of her table, as she ate rice and talked on the phone. She wore a catholic school skirt with blue leggings underneath. Her Gucci purse wasn't the only indication that she came from a wealthy family. Her matching Gucci watch and expensive Import car key fob dangled from her purse. She was oblivious to the fact of her surroundings and clearly not understanding she seemed to have been targeted.

Mattie debated staying out of it, catching the next bus and going home. She wondered, if she was just speculating about it all. She needed to stay away from confrontation because it caused an imbalance that she had to maintain control over. The adrenaline of conflict was seductive and addictive.

The teenager walked to get extra napkins from one of the near condiment tables. One of the women casually approached her and began speaking with her. She had quickly gained the young girl's attention by handing her a business card. The teens posture relaxed, as they continued conversing, but she kept looking toward her table because she had left her belongings. A few positive head nods relayed to Mattie that they agreed on some accord, about what Mattie was unsure of.

"Lord have mercy, I must be paranoid," she checked her cell phone for the time of the next bus arrival.

A group of college aged students walked into the dining area with three large pizzas creating a stir and drawing attention.

Mattie noticed the woman's partner was standing near the teen's table. She appeared to have fidgeted with the drink left on the table. Unfortunately, the group with the fresh pies had blocked her access to the woman's actions while moving tables together to form a larger eating area.

She didn't have incontrovertible evidence but Mattie's agitation grew. If these women had boldness like this in a mall full of people, then they had done this before undoubtedly. It infuriated her and she knew her mind had been made, but she had to be patient because there had to be another accomplice, it would require a vehicle to assist in the robbery or the abduction attempt.

The girl returned to her seat and made another call to tell someone about what the woman had said to her. Her excitement could be heard in her voice.

"She said they are having auditions for modeling this weekend and gave me her business card, she said she loved the ethnic look of my braids," the girl paused as the person on the other line interrupted.

"I know, I know a modeling agency wants me, I get a shopping spree and a hookup on my birthday. Okay yeah I'll meet you in thirty minutes I'm finishing now," when she finished the call, she took one last sip from her drink.

Mattie noticed the partner walking towards the exit as the woman who spoke to the teenager hung behind in the food court. She was sitting at a table where she had a clear view of the teenager's action. Seemingly using her cell phone, but Mattie could see through her sunglasses that the brunette-haired woman had not taken her eyes off the girl. She drank the last of her coffee and put the napkin from the mini rolls she ate inside of it to discard.

The girl gathered her tray, and placed her purse under her

arm. She tucked her phone into the button cardigan sweater she wore, and pulled her hair to the side. Mattie could see why a modeling agency would attempt to recruit her. She was nearly five foot ten inches tall, and she had almond skin, and it was true her braids gave her a beautiful look.

The teenager cleaned her area but wobbled a bit adjusting her shopping bags. She began walking towards the exit and that's when Mattie followed carrying the cinnamon rolls. She tossed her trash and unzipped her book bag before placing her grandmothers request inside, keeping the multicolored bag slightly opened.

The teenage girl swayed again, almost losing her balance, as she got closer to the mall exit, that's when the first woman who spoke with her approached her side and asked if she needed help. People walking by them glanced but offered no assistance or sought information about what was going on, their concern was on the items they came to buy.

The brunette woman took hold of her firmly as the corridor narrowed and moved her swiftly towards the exit into the parking lot.

Mattie could see people staring at the girl and woman as

they ate, but they only pointed towards the two through glass windows after the two had passed.

Mattie knew most humans shied away from confrontation, she wasn't angry. She was without emotion, she was focusing on on her environment.

"Be prepared for the unexpected," she heard her father's voice in her head. Mattie had no intention of allowing them to abduct this teenager, nor did she have any desire to take an unnecessary risk becoming a victim.

"Here let me help you," the woman's partner emerged by the door. Had Mattie not known the two women were together she could've overlooked what was happening, as it appeared a Good Samaritan was assisting a mother helping move her daughter along.

Mattie closed the distance as she saw a van parked by the curb. She had decided to engage the moment the girl wobbled, confirming that the girls drink had indeed been spiked.

As the two women struggled to carry the girl to the van, a male exited the vehicle to assist from the driver's side, ordering the two women in Spanish.

"Prisa prisa puso en la espalda y dejemos!" he yelled, as two of the shopping bags fell to the ground. Mattie knew for certainty it was an abduction after he had ordered them to put her in the van so they could leave quickly.

The young girl was losing control of her body, Mattie could only see the back of her braids as the women, one on each side, hauled her away. She did notice the teen girl struggle, attempting to yell, but she had lost the power to do so.

The closer they got to the van, the angrier Mattie got as she slid her book bag from her shoulder. These weren't human beings, they were exploiters and killers of dreams. They weren't just trying to rob her they were attempting to darken her soul. Kidnapped and sold into slavery or being ripped away from parents the same way her mother was taken from her, it was all the same, but now she could fight back. Now she had the tools to bring about a positive outcome and change the fate of this girl, not much older than she had been when her life was uprooted.

She decided not to use lethal force. Mattie reached into her book bag, and felt for her equipment as the man retrieved the fallen shopping bags. Mattie slowed to ask him if he needed help, and quickly surprised him by using the stun gun she retrieved from her bag. The women still approached the back of the van not seeing what had just happened to their male counterpart.

She slipped the stun gun back into her bookbag before moving her hand under her sweatshirt.

Mattie closed the distance and struck the woman who spiked the drink with her gun, before smashing the other woman's face into the back of the van twice. Her motion, fast, the girl only brushed against the rear door before Mattie caught her. Zip ties were spread throughout the vehicle, and rusted chains bolted inside of the van. Dried blood could be seen in the uncovered metal floorboard.

Mattie pulled her away from the van and propped her up against the side of the building in view of people entering the mall, making sure no harm could come to the girl as she finished with the three abductors.

The man still writhed from being shocked, but Mattie approached him again and set off another volt of energy. The woman she pistol-whipped was still face down on the ground, while the other was screaming with blood streaming down her face. Unable to stop the blood from the deep cut above her eye, she couldn't see when Mattie approached her for a second time. She swung and cursed at Mattie, who grabbed her by the neck, drug her next to the man, and secured them together with handcuffs they were set to use on the young girl.

Onlookers had originally walked by, but now seeing people in handcuffs they slowed to ask how they could help.

"Call 911 or get mall security. They tried kidnapping her, they spiked her drink and she needs an ambulance," Mattie finished with her hood covering most of her face.

"God she's so lucky an undercover police officer was here." An older white woman said, making Mattie realize that she didn't want to be around when law enforcement showed.

The older white woman walked to the teenager and checked her vitals as she explained that she was a doctor. Mattie heard sirens coming and decided to make her exit. She secured her book bag at the back of the van as it slid off her, she then placed the stun gun back inside. The woman she had cold cocked was stirring awake, cursing in Spanish that she had no idea who they work for and that she is going to be hunted down, so as Mattie walked to leave, she bent down and whispered in Spanish. "My reach is long, you should worry about who is going to watch your back."

Mattie quickly left the scene without looking back, as the ambulance and two patrol cars passed her. If she hurried, she could catch the next bus and be gone before anyone started asking questions. The adrenaline was familiar, especially after the things she had done for her Colombian family. She enjoyed bringing justice to those who deserved it, but she knew it could become an addiction. It was the reason she trained in at least one discipline daily. Boxing, Jiu Jitsu, Muay Thai, and for the last three years Krav Maga, an Israeli self-defense art form.

Mattie had received formal gun training from her father from the age of five, and continued into her present long after his death. In fact, by the age of twelve she had shot thirty three out of forty targets administered by her father; the same testing he did to receive his Expert Badge in sharp shooting. If there was anything besides the money he left behind, Mattie attributed her skill set to him.

She made it to the bus stop just as it approached. Without having exact change, she folded two single dollar bills into the fare box. She caught the driver staring at her and when he pointed to her face, she looked in the mirror and saw a few blots of blood. She thanked him and wiped it off and found a seat. She opened her book bag and noticed the bag of cinnamon rolls had been smashed.

Her grandmother would not complain, it was her way, and it was Mattie's way to minimize what happened without lying to her.

"Some people were scuffling at the mall and I bumped into them trying to get home," she thought, before using her camera to check for any more blood splats. She pulled her hoodie back to check her hairline and the side of her face before checking social media.

When Mattie got in, she spoke with her grandmother briefly, and then took a hot shower. As she put lotion on, she felt compelled to read the only letter her mother had written to her after being convicted, probably after realizing how fast life can change from her recent interaction. She opened her nightstand drawer and pulled out her journals. In the back of her oldest one she found the envelope containing the letter, the ink had faded but she knew each line of each page and began to read:

"This ordeal has revealed more to me than ever expected, no matter how I try to rationalize my behavior or my thoughts. In the end I know I have

failed as a parent up until this point. I know as a woman I have run short on showing you that 'our strength' lies in the knowledge of self. Your father was not always a bad man, before his tours in the military he had promise, the promise of tomorrow. But for him, like many others, war has changed him. War has changed me. These things you had to bear witness to in the court room were not all entirely true, but as my mind has become clear from withdrawal and detoxing, I am able to come to certain truths.

I was addicted to cocaine and no matter how well I functioned daily, I didn't recognize the effects it had on protecting you...protecting you from 'him'. Now I must be a mother to you. Now I must protect you from me. I have considered the prosecutor's words and I have relived 'your' dreadful ordeal. I question everything now Mattie, I question how much of it is true. I defended you in that blink of an eye and in that moment nothing else mattered but your safety. I will never lie to you again, and thus I struggle to write. Is it because holding an ink pen as my hand shakes from withdrawal or of the nervousness I am not sure. I am now a convicted felon, a role model I am not. You should never have seen your mother beaten and degraded, you are worth more than that. You should have never been intimidated by the man who gave you life. His forms of discipline were emotionally driven by ego and not love. I am ashamed to have been more frightened of him than I showed you love.

Mother, your grandmother, taught me better, she showed me better, but the lesson wasn't learned and now...now you suffer on levels I can't understand. I was a drug addict; I found comfort in cocaine and weed. I allowed it to take away my ability to think and rationalize. I allowed my addiction to keep me in a marriage that was toxic. I am a lost soul asking God for redemption. So, I pray to Him to protect you in my absence. Decisions I make now are of my 'choice', they are being made to keep you safe. Things I have done while 'high' as I think back were things that grew me into depression, and in the back of my mind I knew my ways were wrong. Perhaps this is why "he' hated me but loved me and why I loved but hated 'him'. I was afraid, and even as I write this, fear is attempting to push through my being, but I know what I must do to ensure your wellbeing. What you may see now as cowardice I can only pray that in time you will know the strength that it takes. I will not seek a retrial or early release. I will serve every day of the sentence as a means to show you that I love you enough to set you free. This will be the first and final letter to you, this, my gift to the daughter I love.

You still have goodness inside of you, purity untouched. I have no doubt that you will succeed in whatever endeavors you choose to make in life. I will have no visits from you while I'm enduring my sentence, a choice that I am willingly taking. A choice...the choice a mother makes out of love and to protect the only good piece left inside of me. I love you Madison Imani Parks."

Mattie held the letter in her hand and stared at it. Her thoughts traveled to the brief foster homes she had to stay in, as Grandma Redd was forced to get better living arrangements before the court awarded her custody of young Madison.

The foster homes were a terrible stay as she was forced to sleep on the floor with only a sheet, and only fed once per day. One day the other foster kids in the home called her names as they held her down and cut all of her hair off. She tried to fight them off, but four teenage males and one girl were too much. She cried for hours and when everyone was sleep, she took a frying pan and beat two of the older boys who had instigated her trauma. The next day she was sent back to the county with charges filed, only later to be dropped because her one foster brother spoke out and verified her story that she had been assaulted.

Mattie thought back to the males she let disrespect her during her junior and senior year because she had seen the same behavior in the home of her parents. She sat on her bed shaking her head reliving the moment she didn't find the strength to tell her date 'no' when her virginity was taken in the back seat of a car during 'homecoming'. He forced her out of the vehicle when he was done and made her walk home because she could not stop crying. From the memories of wearing clothes from the Goodwill or Cindy's hand me downs, Mattie sat on the bed and stared at the letter. Her life had been tumultuous until she escaped to college where she learned to live the semblance of a normal life.

The first two years she dove into her studies, maximizing the amount of credits she could take each semester while running track to maintain her scholarship. Cindy and one other friend were her only outlets her first two years besides an occasional trip home to see her psychiatrist. She had put all romantic notions to the side, apart from kissing a female psychology graduate student who saw her vulnerability and took advantage of it…the only secret she had ever kept from her friends in college.

Her phone vibrating drew her back. It was a text message from Geri letting her know she just landed. Her friends and Grandmother sustained the goodness in her, but sometimes it wasn't enough to erase everything.

As Mattie folded the letter and placed it back in her nightstand, she felt the 'emptiness' inside herself trying to force its way out, so she got on her knees and prayed before crying herself to sleep.

CHAPTER 4

BEING OUTLAWS

Geri had been to Chicago before, for the Taste and other events. Mattie and she had even bought courtside tickets for the Cleveland Cavaliers playoff series against the Bulls when they were in the playoffs. This trip, however, was quite different. Most national printed publications were centralized under one umbrella company, and with their support Geri was ready to move her magazine out of the Midwest, and onto the national stage. Cindy had urged Geri to take legal representation that had background in conversations such as this but Geri, being the daughter of two prominent attorneys, decided she could handle any negotiable terms.

As she stared out the windows of the airplane window, with a half empty coffee mug in front of her, Geri knew from the earlier discussion they were offering to buy her magazine for a hefty price, but she would no longer have any determination on what was published. She would be giving up building her "dream" for $1.5 million dollars, but what tilted her was the discloser she would not be able to continue any new publication for five years. Geri's departing excitement was an act, as she had told them she would have to think on it. She made her cordial departures and said something funny as the elevator doors closed behind her but internally, she already made her decision "No fucking way!" The flight home was over before she knew. The time in the air had been spent going over the entire meeting.

"Ms. Marcom we have great respect and admiration for what you have built. We believe with appropriate funds and a shift in target demographics we could be onto something big. Our vision," she thought back to earlier but all she heard was "blah blah blah" after realizing they wanted to buy her publication because on a regional scale, she was outperforming them per every ten thousand. She knew this but from their presentation they thought she wasn't as educated in the matter; their mistake.

As Geri rolled her luggage to short term parking, she knew she had to slow down and figure out what good the money would do for some of her charities.

"I'm not pressed for money," she had thought about completing law school, but she wasn't looking forward to the pressure of becoming her parents' legacy.

"Nice boots," an older woman said. She was wearing a cowboy hat, a white blouse and blue jeans with a huge silver belt buckle with a turtle insignia.

"Thank you, I love yours too," Geri replied genuinely with a smile. She had caught the woman's voice softly as she had been deep in thought. With the brief compliments passing, Geri loaded her car and exited the airport parking lot.

Geri detoured as she got off the highway exit going home. The face to face in Chicago had her emotions running high and she was too wired to go home. Geri understood she had to regroup and look at her obstacle to national publication a different way. It would take a night or two to figure out what the next course of action would be to take. She needed a drink, and ended up at her local neighborhood bar, she grew to know a few of the regulars over the last few years.

Mostly younger professionals, they were the reason the city had undertaken such a large measure to renovate. With a steady influx of graduates from The Ohio State University, and other local colleges, a plan was set in motion over twenty years ago to keep as many of the highly qualified graduates within the city. They were the reason that two global companies had recently moved headquarters to Columbus, and the city welcomed them along with their money with open arms. A mixture of ages and culture were present when she walked in, and Geri loved seeing this type of group dynamic.

Mirrors was larger and a step up from a dive bar, but nothing fancy. It catered to the new millennial, but it kept a lightly intimate atmosphere that drastically changed on the weekends to something resembling more of a club, as these same patrons let loose. The owner, Benelle, was helping the bar serve drinks, since they were hosting a well-known local band, along with open mic for musicians and the crowd was unusually large. Geri liked the way he ran his bar and treated people.

"I asked for two shots of Jameson, neat, but I don't think

she heard me," an older man was speaking with Benelle reaching into his sports coat for his wallet, but Benelle waived him off.

"Calvin, these are on me, just make sure you tip Barb. She's been doing a good job with all things being considered," Benelle said addressing the older white man who shook his hand and laid a twenty-dollar bill onto the bar counter.

"Thank you, Cal," the female bartender said, as she passed them by with two pitchers of beer in her hands hurrying down the bar to serve them. She stood out with fresh Herringbone braids and a dark green tank top with Bob Marley on it.

Geri found Benelle attractive in many ways. He had qualities of openness surrounding him. He was kind, but at the same time firm, and although he was a gentleman, she recognized he contained an aggressive side. Once he carried two men outside after they were rude and began harassing a group of older women who were sharing a drink to their recently departed friend. He tried reasoning with them, they tried fighting him, but they soon realized he was more trouble than not after he knocked one man out with a single punch, and choked the other man out as he tried to take up for his buddy. Women enjoyed his slight flirtations, but he kept his personal life close to the vest. Geri had heard a few rumors over the years about a couple of women he dated. Women flirted with him all the time, even lesbian women. Geri thought it ironic that the same sex couple who invited her over to get more acquainted with them were coming on to Benelle.

"To each their own," Geri thought. She had considered it because they were very attractive. The talkative one was shorter than the other. Standing about five foot three, she had long auburn colored hair and green eyes. She was fairly-light skinned with freckles. Voluptuous was an understatement. Her breasts were natural, as she let it be known each occasion she got drunk. She was firm in the waist and was the only woman Geri knew who was built like Sheila; naturally. The other was Geri's height but more of a slender build. She had long legs and wore low cropped shirts to show her abdominal muscles, nearly as perfect as Mattie's, but in the end, they told too much of their business and Geri was turned off by that.

"Benny, you know you're the only man I would let touch her, right?" The short voluptuous woman said.

"I know Carol, but you guys are my friends and married.

You know I can't do that, morals, morals you know," he answered jokingly as he hugged them both.

"I know, I know. Plus, you might want to move in with us afterwards," Carol replied kissing him on the cheek.

"Hi, Benny," the slender woman kissed his other cheek.

"Hey Reyna. Am I gonna have to hire bodyguards tonight?" He asked with a smile on his face.

"Benny, Benny!" The second bartender was trying to get his attention yelling above the many conversations going on. She was waving at the beer on tap, one of the kegs needed changed.

"I've got to go, enjoy yourselves ladies," he paused.

"And behave yourselves," he said laughing out loud as he walked away.

Geri hadn't noticed but she watched the whole conversation and realized Carol and Reyna were headed her way.

"Geri with a G," Reyna approached openly waiting for Geri to hug her. Carol's eyes lit up when she saw Geri.

"Geri, Geri, Geri," she said giving her a hug too.

"So, I see y'all scared Benny away," Geri laughed as they made small talk.

"He's scared of us just like you are, we just like messing around," Reyna excused herself, telling the other two ladies she was going to order drinks.

Geri watched as Reyna walked away and started to flirt with Benny again as she forced her way to position herself to be next in line. She laughed as Benny shook his head in disagreement to her tactics.

He had never directly flirted with Geri, but something in his eyes were always speaking to her. The full capacity crowd was a large assortment of professionals, and musicians. A few bikers with their colors had come in and mingled with the crowd. The collection of people was how Geri wanted to see the world.

"This represents the growth of the city," she thanked both women for the Martini as the musicians were assembling for what was their third set and she felt like dancing. When they began playing "Killin Me Softly"; Lauryn Hills' version, she found herself dancing by herself amongst a group of about twenty others. Carol and Reyna had zeroed in on a graduate student who had moved into the area recently.

Benelle snuck up from behind Geri and began dancing with her. She turned around feeling his hand on her waist. "These guys are afraid of you."

"They should be, it's too much for them to handle," she turned her back to him rotating her hips seductively as she continued dancing. The band went from Maria Maria by Santana to Havana by Camila Cabello. Geri was enjoying herself and had slightly forgotten about her setback earlier in Chicago.

Benelle got called back to the bar to help again.

A couple of Martinis got sent to Geri. She didn't know if it was from the girls or someone else trying to gain her attention, but she accepted it while the second bartender was flagged down.

"Thank you Ally, I'll tip you. Who sent it over, so I can thank them?" It wasn't uncommon to have drinks bought for her but typically it was followed up by an approach.

"They asked not to share, but honey you know those two don't stop," Ally replied with a smile on her face. She didn't tell but insinuated and Geri knew it was from Reyna.

"Send them back whatever they're drinking and pour a double," Geri replied pulling out forty dollars and handed it to Ally.

"Keep the change," Geri paused. "Can I get a big mug of water with lemon squeezed in and not,"

"Don't put it in the glass, yes we know Geri with a G," Ally laughed knowing that's how Geri always ordered her water.

"You guys know me so well," Geri drank her Martini down handing Ally the empty glass.

Geri stayed unusually late, but she enjoyed herself, especially after being in a room full of vultures earlier trying to minimize her ability to become a national publication by offering to buy her business. She caught herself staring at Benelle as he changed out one of the kegs on draft. His muscles flexed under his shirt. As he walked the empty keg towards the stock room, she overheard two women talking about him.

"Chandra said he was all that," one of the women said louder than she intended.

Geri acted as if she didn't hear what was said, and headed

to the restroom. She realized she was more than buzzed and would need to take an Uber. When she exited the ladies' restroom, she lost her balance, stumbled and fell into Benelle who was rounding the corner wiping his hands off on a towel tucked in his belt.

"Whoa, I got you," he grabbed her by the waist firmly to secure her.

"I see you keep trying to put your hands on all of this," flirting with him, feeling the effects of the alcohol racing through her bloodstream.

"I told Brigette to cut you off. Here come with me and sit down for a second, I'll get you some water," he said as he walked her into his office and set her down onto his mahogany leather sofa.

"I'm really fine, but that water would be amaaaaazing," she knew she was drunk, as she slouched backwards into the soft leather couch. She looked around the office as he left and was staring at the ceiling when he walked back in.

"They're wrapping up out there and I am going to be taking off in about twenty minutes. I can drop you off at your place if you don't want to Uber. It's on the way." Benelle paused as he heard his name being called over the bands PA system.

"I will be right back. Drink all of that," he pointed to the Steiner size glass of water in her hands rimmed with lemons halves.

She regained her composure and left his office as he said thank you to everyone who came out and asked the band to play two more song before wrapping it up.

"That was cool B," Geri said after he shook a few hands, gave out a few hugs and made his way towards her.

"Thanks, yeah I think we are on to something," his voice was drowned out as the as the band struck up again.

"I can leave my car here and it will be ok?" she accepted his invite to drive her home because she was still tipsy.

"Yeah it will be fine. Let me check with the girls and see if they need anything and then we can bounce," he made his way to the bar counter before walking out.

The night breeze hit them both as they left the bar. It was warm but it felt like rain was in the air. The music could be heard faintly, but it was Geri's cowboy boots sounding off as she walked onto the concrete pavement.

"You ok, you need some help Calamity Jane," Benelle laughed out loud.

"Does that make you Wild Bill Hitchcock, wait, wait, wait a minute," Geri stumbled over her words "They weren't kind to Native Americans. So not them but we can be outlaws tonight," Geri finished.

Benelle walked towards his car, remotely unlocking it and opening Geri's door. Geri sat down and reached over and opened his before sitting back.

"You can drive me to your house and then home in the morning," Geri couldn't stop the words before they came out as she strapped her seatbelt across her lap. Now after a fifteen-minute drive she was sliding off her cowboy boots in his living room.

Benelle had already poured bourbon into a Glencairn whiskey glass he had warmed and was now making Geri a Martini upon her request.

His complexion fair, but his features were dark along with his dark hair. Benelle's arms and chest were full, his shoulders wide. His legs strong but the way he moved he seemed nimble. His physical characteristics were attractive, but it was his soulful interaction and openness to people and life that had Geri walking towards his balcony. She was also wondering if the rumors of his sexual imagination were true.

"The latch; push up on it. Do you need water?" he asked seeing her fiddle with the door handle leading to his overview patio of the city.

"I'm trying to have you take advantage of me tonight, water is counterproductive," Geri looked back over her shoulder flirting again, as she stepped onto the wood laminate. She could see the Scioto River and downtown Columbus along with the massive amount of construction work rerouting traffic.

"I will be taking advantage of you tonight Geri Marcom so I thought I should hydrate you before I drain you of everything you came to give me," he said stepping onto the balcony. He said it with a grin on his face. She was uncertain if he was joking or being serious, but what she did know is that it made her get warm inside.

"You must make a killing with your bar, I looked at these properties when I first came to Columbus but back then, the way my account was set up."

He shook his head as he smiled understanding her

reference to a Kevin Hart comedy special. "I see you are also witty on your feet," fidgeting with his cell phone. Music started playing from speakers mounted along the wall. Maxwell's "Whenever Whatever Wherever," came out smoothly. Although it was over twenty years in the past, Geri thought it was the perfect song, at the perfect time.

"I do ok, my regulars keep me above water. Now that we have local musicians coming in, it's driving business during the week. I bet you're wondering how I can afford this place," he said, extending Geri the martini to stand behind her overlooking the river.

"I invested with a group of friends and now I have enough to have a few of the finer things in life," he moved to stand behind her. The energy could be felt as he approached her.

"I've always noticed you Geri, quiet and strong when you need to be. Fierce and feisty when in boss mode. I love your publication, but I've always loved this ass more," Benelle pushed his crotch up against her rear, grabbing her by her hips while bending down to kiss her neck.

"What catches your eye looking out into the dark sky?"

he paused, running his hand up her back to touch her lowly shaven head. He kissed her neck again.

Geri heard the question and took a sip of her martini and tried to reach backwards to grab his waist, but he stopped her.

“I asked your sexy ass a question Geri,” he said pressing his crotch against her ass more firmly.

Geri liked the directness in his question. “The stars, the inordinate brightness of each. Is it the vast darkness that is the contrast or is it the other way around? Both must exist for either to exist,” she then took another sip of her martini.

Benelle took her hand and placed it on his waist.

“That wasn’t such a hard question, was it?” whispering into her ear as his manhood began pressing into her rear. He kissed her neck again and then her shoulders.

“I see how everyone looks at you, your mouth when you talk, your legs and ass when you walk. I try not to because you’re more than this,” he took her hand from his waist and extended up to her breasts, controlling the movement. He was touching her, making her touch herself and she was highly aroused.

"I bet," he paused to push his lips gently into her ear, "Most men don't push you," he finished by biting her ear softly and squeezing her breasts at the same time.

Geri moaned. It felt good to be led without being overwhelmed. Benelle was right, most men didn't push her. She didn't have sex as much as she liked, but when she did, she was more disappointed than not.

Benelle took a step back and placed his glass onto the balcony table. He sat down and waited for Geri to sit opposite of him.

"I have heat vents out here to help keep your beautiful legs warm," he said leaning forward to kiss Geri before sitting back.

Geri smiled and felt the heat on her legs.

"That feels good," he leaned forward a second time to kiss Geri more passionately.

"That tastes good," Geri replied as their lips unlocked.

The moon allowed their shadows to fall into the floor and she found a sexual energy tracing through her. She had indeed come to have sex with him. Most men would've tried to handle her by now and she appreciated the fact that there was no apparent rush.

"You do taste good, I've wondered so long how your mouth would feel pressed against mine, or what your lips would taste like. You are one of the few women that I have thought about after years of owning the bar. I just know you're about your business and I always want to make sure you feel comfortable at my place and I want you to be the same person in the future."

Geri understood what his subtle request and offer to her was. 'Let's not be all weird and shit after tonight, when you come back into my bar,' Geri laughed uncontrollably before she responded. "Two things I've never been, a stalker and I don't want anybody up in my business either."

"I can tell you're grown," he stood and walked behind Geri and began massaging her shoulders.

"You've got knots on top of knots baby, just relax," as the music played through his balcony speakers, his touch eased her tension. Geri took another sip of her martini. Slowly he began kissing her neck. "Your skin is softer than I imagined it would be, it excites me to have you here. I've crushed on you."

"I would have never guessed it until tonight, you're

always cool and cordial with everyone," Geri paused holding her breath as he pushed more firmly against her knotted shoulders and back.

"What kind of man would I be if I didn't have discipline, if I let my big little head direct me?" He pushed his crotch up against her arm, before he pulled his chair closer to her to sit face to face.

"Kiss me Geri," she hesitated and then leaned forward. The kiss exuded passion. Benelle ran his hand up the side of her face and held it while they kissed. His left hand traced the side of Geri's arm, up to the shoulders and across her clavicle.

"You are stunning," he added while standing to lead her by the hand back inside. "Do you need another? "I've been working all day and need to shower."

It was a matter of fact statement Geri thought, handing her glass to be refreshed. She felt comfortable and that made her more at ease with sharing herself. "You're different than I thought, I mean that in a good way."

"Well thank you, come here beautiful," Benelle led Geri into another portion of his home, walking past an office and guest bedroom. There was another large entertainment room opposite of the living room and kitchen. It had several arcade games, an eight-foot billiard table and a projector screen on the far wall with five stadium recliners.

"This is nice B, did you design all the extra space?" Geri asked.

"I did, I did," he answered stepping into his bedroom before pushing open the door to the master bathroom. It was full of mirrors accented with black and white accessories. The towels were deep red along with the rugs in front of the sink and toilet.

On the walls were paintings of volcanoes and oceans, forest and stunning aerial views. The all had similar vibrant primary colors dominating each theme.

Benelle turned the lighting down and started the shower. "Hotter, or colder?"

"Hot," Geri answered as she walked behind him, she wrapped her arms around him and laid her head on his back. He turned around and began kissing her again. Pressing his body and hers against the wall. His hands began unbuckling her belt and skirt. He pulled her shirt off and took a step back.

"I wanna look at you, your face and eyes are perfect. The

way your shoulders meet your breasts," he said pausing as he began to undress himself.

Geri grew weak in the knees as he pulled his pants off. He reached out with one hand and unstrapped her bra, before sliding her skirt and panties off. Benelle took her glass and sat it on the counter before kissing her again with naked bodies pressing into each other.

She gripped his arms as he stiffened against her skin, kissing her neck and shoulders before leading her into the shower.

"Is it hot enough for you?"

She stepped into the shower with her hand extended and ran it across his chest.

"Absolutely," she stood face to face, staring into his eyes.

Benelle found a wash cloth and mango scented shower gel, lathered it up and began washing her gently as he kissed different parts of her body. He whispered how beautiful she was not only in the physical sense, but mentally. The genuineness of his words melted her, and when he turned her away to wash her backside the washcloth moved from her neck and back to her legs and feet.

"Baby arch your back," he said as the hot water beads splashed them both.

Geri moaned as he spread her cheeks with lathered cloth in hand.

"Is that too much?" He removed the wash cloth to replace it with his fingers, tracing the outside of her hips before sliding his hand into the crack of her rear.

"Hmmm no it's good," she took the wash cloth to return the favor. She marveled in the fact that he had still been a complete gentleman. She leaned into him and kissed him as she moved the soap filled washcloth across his neck and shoulders. She took her time as she washed him, his hips were strong and although he didn't have stomach muscles, he was firm. His forearms were chiseled along with his chest. He was a man in every sense of the word and as she moved the wash cloth back and forth across his groin she asked,

"Is that too much for you?"

Benelle rinsed off as they began kissing more passionately. He pushed Geri back against the wall, so she could maintain her balance holding onto the top of the sliding shower door and the towel rods inside the shower. Benelle was turned on by looking at her, but the softness of her skin and the power in her body had his mouth watering so he bent down and kissed her stomach.

The water and his lips hitting her skin forced goosebumps across her body. When he pushed her legs further apart, she felt his tongue slide across her sweetness causing her to moan loudly.

She felt intoxicated again but not from liquor. She stared down at his light chocolate skin and the muscles in his back. Geri watched the rotation of his neck as he got a better position to taste her.

"Honey you taste so damn good, even better than I imagined," his tongue pressed against her, causing her hips to jerk forward, muting what he was saying.

Geri pulled on his neck as he reached up to massage her breasts with one hand. With the other Benelle found her ass and gripped it like a vice, causing Geri to jerk forward again.

"God that's so good, your lips, Mmmm… that tongue. Oh Fuck!" she gasped because he slid a finger inside her and pressed his tongue across the stem of her fruit.

"I've wanted you for so long, to taste you, to know what your skin felt like against mine," he slid another finger inside her and squeezed her nipples together.

"Eating your sweetness is making me so hard," he was devouring the sweet cream beginning to flow from Geri.

Geri could feel the tingling build in her stomach, she could hear his words, and each time his fingers moved inside she could feel herself becoming more wet.

Benelle started to hum and push his tongue deeper inside at the same time. He struggled to breathe and in between catching air he smothered himself in her juices. He grabbed her by both hips to force more of her into him. He could tell Geri was getting close to having an orgasm, so he wrapped one arm around her back to control her movement. He took the other fingers and slid them back in her, but this time he bit her stem.

Geri was reaching orgasm if he kept tasting and touching her this way. The energy in her stomach moved up her spine and she could feel the vibration traveling her body.

"You're gonna make me," her words stuck in her throat but Benelle finished her sentence as he took his fourth finger and traced it against her other hole while maintaining everything else.

"Explode all over my mouth and face Geri, you deserve it. All over my lips and tongue, I wanna taste it," he said reaching back up to her breasts with his other hand as his fingers moved inside her in unison.

"Do it baby, your wetness is so sweet, so tasteful even now." he said as Geri began to let go.

Her body convulsed as she screamed in pleasure.

"Eat it and make me, eat it and make me, all over your face. I'm creaming all over your..." but Geri couldn't speak as she exploded. She grabbed Benelle by the back of his head until she became too sensitive.

"I could eat all of that every day," Benelle said as they both tried catching their breath.

"I just might let you, damn, damn I can't stop shaking," she smiled and giggled uncontrollably.

Benelle stood up and kissed her. "That's how sweet you are Geri," he said before lifting her up to straddle him. Slowly sliding his manhood halfway into her she could feel that sensation again.

"Whew, you're so tight, so fucking wet. Damn you are so perfect, wait, hold on, hold on," he said before sliding himself back out before placing her back onto her feet. "Your heaven is so good, you were gonna make me bust with your sexiness and I been wanting this too long. Now a brother just feels like a teenager again."

"Don't worry we have all night and, I'll take care of it," Geri said before turning around to face the wall. She stuck her hips out and pulled him closer. She reached back to stroke his hardness.

"Put it inside of me," she said guiding it back into her, but this time it was the curve of his shaft thrusting upward, creating the pleasure pain, adding more moisture, and she knew she was going to reach another height again that quickly taking him into her like this.

Benelle began moaning loudly as his member thickened inside her. He met her eyes as she turned to look at him. He couldn't hide his passion. He leaned forward to kiss her neck and shoulder. "I've wanted you since the first time I saw you walk in my bar, the first time you smiled at me."

Geri put her arms in front of her to gain balance while turning her head towards him. Her sweet secret tightened around his shaft causing her to hold her breath and bite her lip. Her eyes met his again. It excited her to feel the power of his body, to feel herself being pulled back into him deeply where pleasure and pain alternated. She wanted to climax with him, so Geri thrust her hips back in rhythm.

"You're filling me up, you're filling all of my pus.... Ohhhhhhh God!" Geri let out. Benelle had penetrated her deeply, hitting her inside wall and at the angle he thrust she could feel him pushing through her tender spot.

Benelle grabbed Geri by the hips to pull her back into him as he increased his motion. Her back arched and the muscles ripped through her shoulders. It excited him to see her body shake and jiggle. The small diamond in the small of her back deepened each time he pulled Geri into him. He ran his hands over her back before he slapped her ass.

Geri jerked as his hand slap stung her skin with the water splashing backwards onto him. She pushed back against the wall because she could feel the pulsing in his shaft.

"It's so good, so good," his hands slipped back to her waist as he knew it wouldn't be long for his first orgasm.

"I feel you tightening on me every time I," he penetrated her deeply again causing her body to shake. The goosebumps on her skin pulled him closer to his explosion.

"Your face and eyes are perfect; your body and this ass is perfect. You wanted this Geri!" he rotated his hips still pushing all the way inside her in perfect rhythm.

"Oh yes, God yes I wanted it, I feel you deep inside me, you're filling me up." Geri finished letting out a loud moan as her hips thrust backward. Geri felt a huge buildup of energy in the pit of her stomach increasing down the inside of her legs. She reached back and pulled his body into her, feeling his hips slamming into her ass creating the perfect rhythm to reach another height.

Benelle couldn't stop himself this time. Geri had turned him on in a way he hadn't been in a long time, and now he couldn't control his breathing.

"So, fucking sexy, just so damn sexy. You're perfect Geri so fuckin," Benelle attempted to say, as Geri interjected.

"I'm going to, again, all over you… keep…don't stop, please don't stop." She said as she moaned and forced herself to take his manhood.

"I'm cummin, I'm cummin all over your big black…."

but she couldn't get the last word out. His engorged shaft was being gripped by her walls with each thrust.

"You are making me," he said as he pulled out and exploded on her ass. Geri was covered in goosebumps. Benelle held onto her, kissed her neck and ear before turning her around to face him.

"That was intense," tapping her softly on each of her bottom cheeks before tasting her mouth again. They both struggled to catch their breath as Benelle retrieved the wash cloth to begin washing her again.

"You are refreshingly good," her eyes followed him stepping out of the shower to retrieve towels.

He dried Geri off and led her back to the living room, before sitting her on his sofa that he covered with a blanket after turning the heat up on the thermostat.

"More than I ever imagined Geri," he retrieved two bottled waters from the kitchen.

"Geri with a G, how are you feeling baby?" He wanted to make sure, she was still comfortable. This was their first experience together becoming familiar and he knew how awkward some first sexual encounters could be.

“Benny I am more than good, like you said that was intense in the best way,” she answered taking a sip of water.

“Do you need anything else beautiful?” He knelt slowly, kissing her knees before moving up her leg. He kissed her pelvis lightly and her body began shaking.

“Mmmm, no I’m good with that right there,” she whispered.

He stood and led her to his bedroom before disappearing and returning with her cowboy boots.

“I’m ready for round two,” he said as he took her bottled water and placed it on the nightstand. He slipped her boots onto her feet kissing her toes in the process.

“You said something about being outlaws tonight,” he said with a smile on his face laying her back before sliding his body back on top of hers.

The night came and went quickly. Benelle has been more than Geri expected, he was the perfect lover. Gentle and tender in the shower, imaginative and then forceful in his bedroom. She smelled the coffee brewing and knew she had to return to the grind of pushing her business. She pulled her cellphone from her purse and saw three text messages. Two were from Cindy wondering why she wasn't home yet. Cindy included that she opened a bottle of wine and spent the night at her house when she returned her Kitchen Aid.

Geri was laughing when Benelle returned with coffee. "Black with sugar if I remember correctly," he extended the mug to her. He leaned forward and kissed her passionately.

"You are correct Sir," she answered.

"I have to get out of here, not that I couldn't go another round, but I've got business at the office and my sister stayed at my place, so I think she needs to talk about something," Geri said standing naked from the bed.

"Let me throw some sweats and sneakers on and I'll drop you at your car. I need to place liquor orders anyways," Benelle paused walking into his closet.

"You are amaaaazing Geri, maybe we should go on an actual date when things slow down," he finished.

"You mean since all of the tension is gone after last night," she headed into his walk-in closet behind him. She kissed him and agreed, but advised Benelle it could be a few weeks before she would have another free moment.

"That's all good Geri with a G. I am a patient man," he

twirled her around before slapping her ass.

"Shit!" Geri exclaimed.

"No not because of your love tap. I've got a podcast this morning from the office and Cynthia is on it. The last time," but she was interrupted by Benelle.

"Oh, I heard the last time she was on it, she was constructively critical of your guests who called you a," Benelle paused this time because he didn't want to offend Geri.

"A poser who uses your magazine to exploit issues," he finished.

"Yup, those were the exact words before she let them have it. I love that woman even though the hate mail we got after was unbelievable," she dressed and realized how comfortable she was with him.

"I call it as I see it and they deserved every bit of her tirade. That's the one thing people were saying, at least those who were glad she wasn't going to let anyone bully her or you because of gender and race," Benelle added.

"She knows me better than anyone, well you know," she hesitated in reference to her other two friends who shared the same bond. "I wasn't in a position to respond because at that point anything I followed with as a response could've been taken out of context, I can't lie I know she can be forthright, but I almost choked on water when she called them racists."

The last podcast Cindy had been invited to, was a conversation on race attended by both black activists and police officers.

"Oh, she let the police have it, but when the activist's lightweight called you out your name, when she called them racists and went in with facts, it was over," Benelle said as he looked for his car keys.

"Well today is an empowering women podcast, so what could really go wrong? It's been almost four months, so we should be good," Geri thought back about last night. She wanted more of Benelle, but work was calling. Another text came through this time from her assistant.

"Shit, shit, shit. I have an interview in Grandview I completely forgot about. Let me coordinate really quick," she excused herself to his balcony. She called her assistant and told him about the meeting in Chicago, that she would make the interview in Grandview and when she explained what happened on her Chicago trip, she became agitated.

She wasn't sure but blowing up over the phone wasn't her style, it took a lot to set her emotions free.

"I'm ready if you are," Benelle said as she returned in from the balcony.

Geri shook her head in agreement taking another sip of java.

Benelle walked second through the door, locking it behind him. Geri smacked him on his backside unexpectedly and he spit coffee from his mouth.

"Don't get me started Geri with a G," he reached for her hand as they walked towards the elevator.

"That's how outlaws say thank you," she said smiling as the elevator door opened.

CHAPTER 5

JPS

Cindy made phone calls from home after leaving Geri's. She had waited up until the witching hours for her return from Chicago before falling fast asleep on her friend's sofa. When Geri's alarm clock went off, it startled Cindy and after turning it off she knew her day had started. She drove home.

Hot coffee was a prerequisite in the morning. She walked onto her deck overlooking the O'Shaughnessy Dam, watching her dogs off in the distant. She had worked hard to achieve all that she had, but her ambition was still driving her towards success. Her gazebo was being covered in leaves that spiraled away from the branches they once congregated. Fall was approaching but with Ohio weather fluctuating, Cindy knew there would be more days of sunshine to follow.

Her neighbor's property was separated by a small tree line, but as the back portion sloped downward towards the boat docks each side was visible. Cindy appreciated the peacefulness, she had yet to fully renovate everything she planned, but over the past three years the majority had been completed.

She stretched and did a quick workout. Cindy wanted to train with Geri and Mattie but needed to be more in shape to even get started. She never had been close to anyone, not even the girl members of her singing group, but when she met Mattie, she found someone she could trust and who could accept her completely as she was.

Cindy finished with three rounds of planks before showering and changing. Her walk-in closet was nearly twelve feet long and ten feet wide. Part of her renovation was to revamp the previous closet space, and now she had mirrors stationed in between four areas separating her clothes by season, and her shoes were spread out on platforms built to hold them.

She took pride in her appearance, so as she coordinated her blouse and shoes, she felt certain empowerment knowing she could be taken seriously especially when expressing her sexuality with her attire. In an industry dominated by men and companies run by men she had to maintain a high level of professionalism, but it didn't prevent her from being stylish in the process. Cindy would bite her tongue on occasion, but she never lost her voice, and this was one of the reasons Geri loved having her as a guest on the podcast. However, after her last guest appearance Geri had to keep her friend as far away from airtime as possible.

It had been almost five months since Geri felt safe to have Cindy back on air. Strangely enough, the listening audience had grown by nearly forty percent since she had been there to express her views as a Real Estate Agent, talking about disparities when applicants with similar demographics were excluded or given higher mortgage rates because of varying factors. Unfortunately, the other guests chose the wrong person to direct their anger towards, and Cindy aggressively challenged their position with facts. When the podcast ended the two other guests vowed to never come back, especially with her as a panelist.

Stepping out of the stairwell Cindy couldn't figure what

exactly had changed until she noticed that Geri had taken her advice and painted the hallway leading to her office. Geri owned the building and had leased office spaces but still had one third availability. What stood out along with the new paint and additional light fixtures, the entrance to the Magazine's office had been changed into an all glass pane creating better ergonomics and spatial difference.

Cindy saw an unfamiliar face at the desk. A young woman she surmised was an intern. Geri was an advocate for employing college students and even better at second chances for those who deserved it, but once she was done with you; it was final.

"Rochelle," Cindy thought forming the previous receptionist's name that rubbed her wrong every time she greeted her. Rochelle lacked many of the qualifying skills that a receptionist should possess. She failed to write down important business messages for the senior staff. She had an attitude whenever an employee asked for her assistance, and failed to greet guests properly when they arrived at the publication. The last time Cindy saw her she told her to be kind to people or she would snatch her "Medusa braids out her hair," the college girl complained and quit.

Cindy approached the desk and waited for the

receptionist to end the call she was on. She marveled at the way Geri expressed her personality of being open. When she designed the office space, she wanted everything transparent with no boundaries, so energy could flow easily, and employees could interact.

The open space was bordered with four offices enclosed in glass. These designations were for editors and heads of each department. Alongside photo and video pre and post production for their recent online content. The largest of the offices were broadcasting a live podcast where no topic was taboo. Former guests of the podcast included law enforcement and activists sharing the same platform. Move America Forward Again, a grass roots organization attempting to counter the divisive effect of the elected President. Unlike the Democratic Party who failed to acknowledge the positive impact that The President had made on the economy and job growth, MAFA was quick to recognize achievements made under the administration but they made clear their stance against him, and anyone who put foreign interest above the United States of America. They were intent on making sure the special counsel would see "the collusion" investigation through until the end, while calling out elected officials who shifted their stance repeatedly.

The “Mueller Investigation” was an explosive topic as members of the GOP, The DNC and MAFA deliberated why the public deserved to see the entire report. In the end MAFA, was viewed as a bridge for common citizens across political parties to stand united. The midterm elections had passed and with the House of Representatives controlled by the Democrats, more inspiring conversations were to be had.

Geri’s popularity had grown in recent years not only because of her magazine, but from the platform she used to help public schools receive better computers with up to date programming.

She spearheaded a grass roots movement to help find single parents additional help. Geri had been recognized as one of the ten influential people during a city event held by the Mayor’s office attended by the Lieutenant Governor.

“Good morning, I am so sorry for your wait. I appreciate your patience,” the younger woman said adjusting her glasses with a smile on her face.

“Hi, I’m Cynthia and I am here for the podcast today,” Cindy responded after realizing it was the strawberry blondes first day so she would be polite, after all she wasn’t that Resting Bitch Face

Rochelle, who previously held this position.

"I have you here," as her ballpoint pen moved slightly down a piece of paper searching for names.

"Oh, Uhm, Cindy. I am sorry, I mean Ms. Marcom said her sister. I assumed, oh lord, I'm sticking my foot in my mouth right, now aren't I?" She paused as she reached across her desk to shake Cindy's hand before standing up.

"I'll take you up, oh you know your way," she began stuttering.

"It's ok take a deep breath, what's your name?" Cindy wanted to reassure and help calm her.

"Elizabeth, Lizzie, Liz," she was visibly nervous, and Cindy had a good clue as to why.

"Liz, I take it that my reputation proceeds me, and I will admit that I kinda made a scene the last time I was here. But in my defense, I am very defensive of my sister and any type of Nationalist "black or white" who insults her... well you know the rest." Cindy paused extending her hand to Liz's for a proper introduction.

"I'm going to let myself in Liz," as the office phone rang, allowing Liz to answer.

"You'll fit right in, just don't let anyone ever give you any shit," she finished, before walking through the glass doors into the office.

A few smiles were thrown towards Cindy and she saw a group of employees nodding in agreement.

"Cindy you're a beast, a wizard with words and I apologize that I couldn't get you back sooner. If it was up to me girl, shoot, you'd be on at least once per week. But the forces that be, be scared of you girl," a skinny dark-skinned man said, approaching Cindy with elation. He had twists in his hair and well- groomed facial hair. The green studded earrings matched his green polo shirt.

"Sal if I was them, I'd be scared too hunty," Cindy hugged him genuinely. "How is Michael?"

"Michael is off saving the world again. Diplomatic liaison my ass, he just can't get conflict out of his system," Sal hesitated as he took her by both hands.

"Girl you look good as usual and I love that blouse but don't be exposing all of the goodies. Today we have something simple as women's body image and fashions, why or why not. There is no opportunity for a repeat escalation with this. Unless one of these heifers come in here demanding shit."

Cindy's blouse was low cut showing an excessive amount of cleavage, she accompanied it with a jeweled necklace that matched the red stitching in her blouse. Her red two- inch heels completed the outfit. She trailed Sal as he walked into his office.

"I needed to feel sexy and inspiring today Sal," Cindy replied without offense in her voice.

"I ain't saying no names honey but somebody wasn't in the best mood after the Chicago trip," he sat down at his desk, sectioned off from the podcast sound room inside the same space, giving him some privacy.

"I said I wasn't touching this til you came back," leaning back towards a cabinet behind him. As he put his passcode into unlock his safe Cindy saw the pattern. She immediately noticed the gun and two magazines sitting next to the bottle of Pendleton Canadian Whisky she had given to him and Michael along with a bottle of Hennessy.

"Sal you are such a badass," Cindy sat forward as he poured two glasses of the brown liquid. She knew Michael had taught Sal how to shoot and respect guns, with his background in the military and wanted Sal to be protected.

"Michael said I needed it just in case one of these podcasts get out of control. He understands why Geri keeps our conversation open to everyone, but after security was forced to remove those nationalist guests, I got my CCW and my black ass will shoot somebody ya heard me," they toasted to a good show and tilted their glasses back.

"You ready?" Cindy asked as she stood and walked towards the sound booth. It was more like a room with a table in the middle surrounded with five chairs and microphones stationed above each. It resembled a radio station, but it was low budget compared to real ones.

"Good afternoon my lovelies this is a day to rejoice in being alive. We saw the former NBA Champion wear a short suit to the NBA finals last year. He won't be in the playoffs this year with that 'hot mess' of a team out West; but was the outfit hot or not.... hmmmm honey, let me tell you, with or without clothes that man, well maybe let me not say anymore because anyways," Sal paused giggling as his guests laughed with him.

Cindy was good at initially measuring people and today's guests were no exception. Something about Dr. Meider didn't feel authentic.

"On today's show called 'Fly or Bye' as I'm get the hell outta here, I have Robin Drake, fashionista extraordinaire. Labeled as an originator for plus sized women. Her last line included sporty summer wear and swimsuits. You can check some of her stuff out in last months

"Under the Sun" issue. Also sitting at the table with us is Dr. Johanna Meider, a Psychologist with a local college who has recently published a book titled "Witness the Rebirth" about women reclaiming their bodies. We also are sharing this broadcast with Shawna Maryland, fitness instructor whose clients include professional athletes. She also has started a program to teach better eating habits. Last, but not least Cindy," he said flatly.

"Honey you know I'm just playing; my girl Cindy is back for an easy discussion about clothes and fashion," Sal finished and quickly took a sip of drink in a covered mug and dove right in.

A lot of positive conversation was had over the course of the first two hours about the pitfalls that society puts on women and how to overcome the objectification of the female body. They spoke on the differences that women play in society and on the corporate front including some strategies to level the playing field.

Robin spoke about the importance of recognizing how emotions also play a role in self-image.

"For example, a woman cheated on, can often exhibit self-doubt where she had never experienced it before. The whole, am I good enough, or what's wrong with me conversations we have with ourselves, they all have a part in the story of our lives. Especially how we view each other;" she concluded and reached for a second doughnut and her chair bumped into Johanna accidently.

"Do you have enough room?' Johanna asked before sliding the doughnut box towards the fashion designer while rolling her eyes.

Cindy noticed the eye play when Robin had not, and it rubbed her the wrong way, but she would keep the peace and let Sal run the podcast effectively.

There were some disagreements; Robin believed women regardless of body image should be comfortable in their skin. Shawna interjected that women wanting to better themselves mentally and physically should also feel comfortable getting in shape. In the end they both agreed that it was about being comfortable but then Johanna disagreed slightly.

"I believe the rebirth starts with a vision of who you want

to be and not who you are."

"You can't get to somewhere if you don't know where you're starting from," Cindy replied out of instinct when she disagreed.

"How would you have gotten here today if you didn't have a starting point?" Cindy asked.

Dr. Meider thought the question was amusing and replied, "GPS," in a condescending and sarcastic tone.

Cindy had already watched Dr. Meider turn her nose up slightly earlier, when Shawna talked about her plus sized clients who find out the strength they really have with the proper support behind them, and another quick eye roll as Shawna spoke about overcoming her own childhood obesity and negative self-image.

"GPS?" Cindy asked shaking her head in disagreement.

"Today it should be JPS," and chuckled right back.

"JPS?" Sal asked as the other guests tried to figure out the abbreviation.

"Yeah JPS, Johanna please stop. Are you here to promote your book or really talk about empowering women?

You've rolled your eyes and turned your nose up at these ladies who are speaking on a personal level and you're the educator. You are part of the problem," she hesitated and then decided not to blow up another podcast.

Sal smiled and interrupted. "OK ladies now, now, let's keep this dialogue beneficial to our listeners. You all have been so enlightening today and our time is nearly done for this session," Sal said as he read off how to find each guest before Johanna felt the need to get the last word.

"That was witty and just because I disagree with some of their means doesn't undermine either of these people," Johanna said without realizing she had insulted the guests.

"These people, what does that mean, these people. You don't get it, perhaps you've never had negative self-imaging or battled with weight gain. Maybe you don't even understand the true nature of our struggle but when you refer to them or anyone as "these people" you are being demeaning to them."

"That's not what I meant to say," Johanna interjected but Cindy wasn't having it.

"Maybe that's not what you meant to say but clearly it was your intent to say. These women; Shawna and Robin are the true heroes and should be commended because even with their struggle they are helping people. So, Johanna please stop with your "I am above this attitude and apologize to these queens," Cindy paused as she took another doughnut from the box and smacked down on it.

"If you want a doughnut or anything ladies don't let anyone stop you from being your best version, especially the fake ones." Cindy finished.

Johanna left the broadcast room in haste as Sal ended the podcast, thanking everyone as she advised she had a previous engagement.

Sal thanked her for coming but Shawna and Robin were silent.

"Thank you JPS," Cindy said as Johanna walked away.

Cindy saw Geri walking into the office shaking her head.

"You just can't help yourself huh?" Geri asked as she greeted Cindy and Sal. She had just returned from an interview with a Judge seeking re-election. The interview was insightful.

"I can't stand no fake ass bit," Cindy started to say as Geri hugged her.

"Sal, can you send the guests a thank you bouquet and for Johanna send her something extra," Geri said.

Sal agreed and walked toward his office as Geri and Cindy headed up one more flight of stairs to Geri's.

Geri could see the entire office from her floor. When she looked out her window there was a wooded area frequented by deer and other wildlife. It helped her remember her youth growing up in Wisconsin.

"I finished that bottle of Merlot you opened and washed your dishes. How do you leave dishes to do when you get back from a trip?" Cindy paused to look at some of the pictures they had taken over the years. Some from college, but many from the years after graduating, and a couple from the time they vacationed with Mattie in Colombia.

Geri had a newspaper article framed on the wall behind her desk. It was an article about a riot when they attended college. Geri, Mattie and Cindy were on the front page; arrested and shoved into the back of a police cruiser. Mattie and Cindy were yelling out of the window, as Geri had maneuvered her body to be able to kick the back window in such a limited space. That was the beginning of a sisterhood that stood firm through everything.

"I knew you were going to end up doing it with that OCD gene you got." Geri laughed out loud.

"Whatever, whatever. So, what happened in Chicago?" Cindy asked before she plopped down into Geri's desk chair.

"Greed happened in Chicago, now don't get me wrong it was an amaaaazing offer financially but not nearly enough to cancel out my dreams and these 'executives' said there would be a clause prohibiting me from being a principle in any new publication for five years." Geri motioned her friend from her desk.

"That's greed and eliminating their competition in one fell swoop. At least you know they have concern, so maybe we should reevaluate how to gain a larger percent in the Midwest, only makes sense and then have them come to you for better leverage." Cindy replied.

"That's exactly what I was thinking on the flight back, but I got sidetracked last night." Geri toned down her evening.

You got sidetracked last night, girl you for some D last night, I've been trying to figure out who but can't so just tell me," Cindy interjected as Geri smiled.

"Benelle," she replied with smile to match.

"Benny from the bar, like Jenny from the block?" Cindy asked without giving her time to answer. "Damn what got into you? He is kinda sexy, but you just decided last night was theeee night?" She asked hesitating again,

"Don't say another word, we gon need a bottle for the play by play. You gave up some yams last night and LaLa has a date tonight," speaking in reference to their friend Sheila who had not really dated in years.

"What time tonight, you know we need to triple check her gear selection for tonight, or she may end up looking like the good 'church lady' and she has too many assets for all that," Geri emphasized 'ass.' While Cindy shook her head in agreement before responding

"Mattie has it covered, she's picking the kids up from James to stay over night. I'm gonna stop by after my seven o'clock showing, I think it's gonna be pizza night," they were interrupted when Sal knocked on Geri's door.

"Your 12:40 just arrived, I put him and his partner in the conference room along with a folder with the contract," he quickly excused himself.

"If I get time I'll stop over Mattie's after catching up on these last two days. Hopefully these guys will lease the remaining space and I can bank more money," she closed one of the shades above her window to reduce the early afternoon sun glare before she walked towards the door.

"Good luck Geri with a G," Cindy said following behind her.

Cindy waved at Sal and a few others who were giving her a thumbs up from the podcast earlier.

She saw Liz answering the phone as she walked back into the receptionist space.

"It's a great afternoon Under the Sun today how may I direct your call?" Liz asked twirling an ink pen in her hand.

Cindy smiled and took the pen from her and scribbled something on a post it. She folded the note and handed Liz the ink pen back before placing the note on Liz's desk.

The elevator door opened, and a courier had two large bags in each hand. The aroma of the Indian spices triggered her taste buds. Instead of walking the stairs she entered the elevator and watched Liz's face light up as she read the post it. "Don't ever take shit. You'll do great here."

CHAPTER 6
HOW MAY I HELP YOU?

The morning had come too soon, and as soon as Mattie closed her window she thought about her actions from the previous evening. She hoped the young woman had recovered physically, although she could imagine the demon's she would have to contend with realizing how close her life had been to being taken.

Her grandmother was already up and working in the small garden on the backside of the building. Their family ties were deep in Georgia, mixed with blood from Native Americans and slaves. Somewhere in the history of the family, land was willed to them. Over twenty acres that had already paid taxes on the property. Grandma Redd and her remaining sister of four, held ownership over the deed. Throughout decades people and corporations sought to purchase the land but the sisters knew that their history ran along the riverbanks of the streams flowing on their property. They knew the bloodshed spilled in the name of family. Grandma Redd left that life she had known to become Mattie's anchor when her life was drastically altered.

"Granny I'm taking off; do you need anything?" Mattie said when Grandma Redd entered through the patio sliding door. She had a small spade in her hand and was slipping off the green gardening gloves she wore.

"I'm fine baby, I will be snacking on those cinnamon bun rolls all day. Mrs. Charlotte may swing by this afternoon."

Mattie kissed her as she left. She had a few minutes to walk to the bus stop. She slid her sunglasses on, readjusted her gun holster, and pulled her book bag over her shoulder. The early morning chill was beginning to fade as the sun reached higher into the sky.

The bus ride was uneventful except for the conversations about the city not being safe anymore. Silently Mattie agreed, as she looked for any information about the mall incident, but a phone call interrupted her search.

"Good morning sunshine," it was Sheila.

"Good morning Lala. I hope you're not calling me to get out of your date again," Mattie said. Sheila had a habit of cancelling dates on the day it was supposed to happen. Her excuses ranged from overtime work or can't find a sitter, but all three friends knew she had not really gotten over her ex-husband after three years.

"No, I'm just making sure you are coming later to help with stuff. I'm nervous because this guy seems interesting,"

"Of course, I will be there, do you know where he is taking you yet?" Mattie wanted to get an idea what type of outfit they would go for.

"Not sure, but ok I have to go, I'm in the ER finishing my shift, I'll see you tonight," Sheila answered before hanging up. Mattie exited the bus at her stop, walked into the building and onto the elevator. When she sat down at her desk, she was greeted by coworkers who had customers on their line complaining. The first few calls were simple adjustments to accounts but the woman she was on the phone with now was testing her patience.

"I apologize for any inconvenience that has been caused. It is typical though for our company to interrupt services when payment hasn't been received, and I can understand that you have to have your internet on to take online classes; however, the fact remains that your bill, your invoice hasn't been paid in three months. We have verified that your address is correct, and it is also the address you received the disconnect notice," Mattie was explaining to a customer, a self-described upset and irate customer.

Mattie was an escalation specialist for an entertainment company that provided television and internet services. Her clients used cell phones primarily and had no use for traditional land line phone services. Mattie sat back in her chair and shook her head after listening to the customer beginning her tirade again.

"Y'all fucking around with the wrong person today, do you know how hard it is out here in this muthafucking world right now? I ain't get no bill in my fucking mail, if I woulda got a bill for y'all piece of shit service I woulda paid it cause I pay all my bills on time, so don't tell me I ain't paid my shit, you need to turn my internet back on!" the female customer yelled at her again.

Mattie didn't respond, she kept quiet as the woman on the phone started conversing with a man in the background.

"This fucking snotty ass bitch on the phone said the bill ain't been paid in three damn months and my shit is turned off, I got finals this week and an online exam tonight in two hours," she said loud enough making sure Mattie heard her. The man began agreeing with her saying Mattie's company was a monopoly and he would look into a different service provider for her.

"But hold up, didn't you put yo credit card on file for direct payment to dem muthafuckas?" he asked the lady in the background adding gasoline to the fire.

"Hell yeah that's right, are you still on the phone, Hello!" she yelled causing Mattie to lift the ear piece away from her ear.

"Yes, I'm still listening Ma'am," Mattie said in a monotone voice looking at the pictures on her desk with her attention divided. This was nearly an everyday occurrence.

"I've got my credit card on file so it is deducted every month when that muthafucka is due, so tell me how my shit ain't been paid, turn my muthafucking internet and television back on right now dammit I'm tired of going over this stupid shit with y'all people," The customer kept screaming and talking loudly into the phone receiver breathing heavily.

Mattie handled calls like this nearly four hours per day. The calls were often long and drawn out, so in a four-hour period she spoke to only six to eight people daily. Hardly complaining about the calls, because it was the position she accepted. The pay was nice, but since she was responsible for her grandmother, she kept the job for the health benefits, because she had enough money to never work again. Something only her friends knew. Mattie had entertained opening a business of some sort, but she felt it better to invest in her friends' dreams.

"Ms. Thompkins, the credit card that was listed on file is invalid; it has been invalid since May," Mattie responded to the latest out lash without emotion, but she was chuckling inside, she took the opportunity to push back without being overtly offensive.

"Invalid, Invalid what da fuck does that shit mean? I got money in my account, y'all people are fucking ridiculous…invalid…turn my shit back on right fuckin now!" she yelled again. In the background Mattie heard the male speaking again before she could respond.

"Oh, damn shawty, remember that's when you closed your old account," he tried saying in a hushed tone. Mattie took that opportunity to type notes onto the account.

"*Sub had cc on file but changed banks w/o notice to*

company, all charges and deposits are sustained."

"Dammit, shit, that's right, fuck, fuck…fuck," the woman paused. When she started speaking again her whole demeanor had changed.

"I, I'm sorry for going off on you and blaming your company, my bank, I switched banks and forgot. Can I just pay and have my services turned back on please?" she asked a little more politely but still frantic.

Mattie was deciding if she was going to dig her nails into this woman after being called a snotty bitch, so she was choosing her words carefully to have maximum effect, plus she got a percentage on the past due amounts she collected.

"I can take your payment right now with your new credit card. We'd have to take the full balance of course Ms. Thompkins," she wanted to remain as professional as possible.

"That's fine, I just can't believe I didn't call in the new card number, my bad. How much is the total again?" She asked. As politely as Mattie could muster, she answered

"The balance is two hundred sixty-five dollars, and

seventeen cents, Ms.Thompkins," Mattie answered. Ms. Thompkins read off her new credit card number along with the expiration date. Mattie thought about her grandmother and how she was always saying '*kill em with kindness baby.*'

Her grandmother was full of wisdom, but she was ill from respiratory diseases and was on oxygen. The illness didn't stop her from keeping the house clean or crocheting; although on days her arthritis did slow her down when she worked in the garden. With the thought of her grandmother on her mind she decided that she would be a better person and place Ms. Thompkins new order for service, so she wouldn't have to pay a substantial deposit. "Someone will pay me back one day" Mattie thought as she translated the information from the closed account onto the new application. She was, however going to let the customer realize the enormous favor she was doing for her.

"Ms. Thompkins, normally we would ask for a deposit once the services were completely disconnected. The deposits range from one-hundred dollars to three-hundred dollars, I'm gonna bypass the deposit for you and have your television services turned back on today and your internet tomorrow," she finished feeling empowered because she hadn't let this woman push her over the edge.

"Tomorrow, tomorrow one of my finals is today!" Ms. Thompkins began escalating the conversation again, but this time Mattie cut her off before she got started, she got the money that was owed to her company, so she could care less if Ms. Thompkins reopened her account.

"Ms. Thompkins, I've been courteous and kind to you this entire call, I have not interrupted you til now. Your payment was late, regardless of any reason provided, clearly our company was not at fault. We have received your payment for the services rendered already. If you want this order cancelled just advise me you no longer want our services and if, in the future, you do decide to return to us you will be asked to pay a three hundred-dollar deposit. But I will not be disrespected again on this phone call. We want your business, so I've waived the deposit. The television will be back on today and the internet tomorrow because a technician must turn it on from the terminal. Do you want to keep this order you just placed Ms. Thompkins?" Mattie asked firmly, she had had enough of this whiney ass woman on the other end.

"Yes, I'll keep both services Madison," she answered slowly. Mattie was unsure if it was because the customer was shocked at being spoken too in that manner, or if it was something else. It didn't matter so Mattie ended the call as usual.

"Thanks for calling, we appreciate your business," she waited for Ms. Thompkins to hang up before snatching her headset off and tossing it onto her desk.

"They are unbelievable today," one of her coworkers named Grace said as a matter of fact.

"I'm tellin you Ms. Grace, I just had a lady call me a snotty bitch, snotty bitch. I'm usually a dumbass or uppity bitch, hold on," Mattie paused as she skimmed down the list of names she had been called so far. The list was taped on the side of her cubicle.

"There," she said after writing it down.

"That wasn't on the list; Hell no, I woulda thought that made the top thirty at least," Grace said pulling a light weight, blue, spring jacket from the back of her chair.

"I'm about to go to the store, you want something, you know what just come on with me cause I'm the one that need to vent right now anyways," the older woman pulled Mattie by the hand.

Grace was the closest confidant she had at her job. She was a great mother and wife, a reliable co-worker but they were over thirty years separated by age. So, besides an occasional call on the weekend or email, their contact was primarily done at work,

"Ok, ok let me grab my cell phone," Mattie reached into her desk drawer.

"This man jus told me if he ever found out my real name and where I worked, he was gon come down here and kill me, he called me bitch and stupid cunt, just to name a few before I hung up on him, but you should've heard him Mattie talking to the woman in the background. He told her to shut the fuck up and sit in the corner and he'd deal with her when he was done with me, that she had to be broken in. I sent an email to asset protection to contact the police, but this man got me so upset…I need some fresh air and of course coffee," Grace finished.

"Damn Ms. Grace that would have me shook up too, but you know all those people be doing is talking mess over the phone, you gone be ok?" Mattie asked pushing the locked door to their department open gaining them access to the entire floor. On the first level were the two places to get food. One was a small store that carried sodas and snacks;

a place where the lottery could be played; the other was an actual restaurant that made on the spot food entrees.

"These customers fail to realize that we have all their information, I mean their date of birth and social security number. Not to mention their credit card information along with their address, if someone wanted to terrorize them it would not be hard, and they wouldn't even know," why she had this ready to roll so easily off her tongue wasn't as important because it was true. She had imagined shoving Ms. Thompkins credit card down her throat until she choked on it to teach her a lesson.

"Damn I don't know Mattie, but what I do know is the gorillas are looking at you like a banana," the older woman laughed as she looked toward a table of five males turn as they both exited the elevator.

Madison had many attributes that were attractive, she had an athletic body with shoulder length, dark, black hair pulled back in one ponytail. She often wore it this way. At one point she pulled her hair back in two twists, but that was short lived when a male coworker told her those were handling bars, indicating how a man holds onto a woman's hair when having sex doggy style. It wasn't that Mattie didn't enjoy sex, but since her broken engagement she hadn't had an appetite for sex. When she did want it, often she pleasured herself instead of dealing with the aftermath of momentary intimacy. She never allowed her physical appearance to be the reason people respected her.

High cheekbones fit perfectly with the shape of her light greenish eyes. She favored her mother but was a spitting image of her grandmother at the same age. She was five foot seven and weighed one hundred and forty pounds. The daily workout regimen she maintained kept her strong, and studying different martial art forms for over twenty-five years continued what her parents had started. Her major reason for training was to be prepared for the unexpected, and this was the reason she felt comfortable at the mall handling the criminals.

"Ms. Grace those pervs will say anything and everything you can imagine, the one still staring told me that he'd give me his paycheck just to have dinner with him. I laughed and told him my sugar daddy takes care of all my needs," she handed cash to the store attendant for her bag of cheese popcorn, candy bar and Pepsi.

"I don't know how you don't gain no weight eating all that junk food, I know some women who would literally kill for your metabolism," Grace said pausing as Mattie let her walk out the store first.

"And sugar daddy, girl if they only knew. You as close to having a sugar daddy as my momma is, oh damn my momma already got one and she don't think I know. How is she going be over seventy and be fooling around," she adjusted her burgundy purse strap over her shoulder.

"Ooh I'm telling her you said that when I see y'all at church Sunday, but seriously are you going to be ok?" Mattie asked the older coworker in a more serious tone.

Grace took a sip of coffee before answering. "Yeah, I'll be fine, I just don't want no more psychos on the phone, not today at least."

Today's workload was no different than most, other than Ms. Grace being threatened by a customer. However, it was Friday already; the week had passed by quickly. Cindy was driving her Mocha Almond QX80 everywhere and washing it every two days, so she insisted on driving tomorrow to event night.

Tomorrow was 'event night'. A night that Mattie, and her friends chose each month to hangout. It was Geri's turn to choose. She was the artsy type always collecting pieces of art and going to starving artists shows. So, it came as no surprise that Geri had picked an evening of poetry and spoken word. Mattie got various explanations of what the differences between the two were, but remained clueless.

Mattie enjoyed Saul Williams and Ed Mabry, but Geri had a long list of favorites. Maya Angelou and Nikki Giovanni were staples, along with Paul Laurence Dunbar. Geri collected CD's of artists both locally and nationally, and she had books on poetry from those of varying backgrounds. Her last issue of "Under the Sun" featured an upcoming artist named Barbara Fant whose life story was inspiring.

Mattie's phone vibrated and as if on cue a text message came through from Geri that read 'my sisters, tomorrow night we embark on a journey, a voyage of transparent ideas and hidden messages, promptness is required...' The message continued "…and for those of you that don't know what I'm saying, I'll say it this way, y'all bitches better be on time and I have stuff to share."

Mattie chuckled, her day was halfway over but she was still curious about what happened last evening after she left the mall. She rationalized a return visit to buy a new comforter set and new pillows for her grandmother might prove beneficial, but unnecessary. Her grandmother always showed surprise and appreciation, but Mattie knew she was a grounded woman who didn't need all the extra adornments Mattie wanted to give.

Grandma Redd kept Mattie sane in an insane world. She was the daughter of a Cherokee Indian woman and a fair skinned Black man. She was as old school as it got. Mattie cherished her in the true sense of the word.

Mattie missed and respected her mother for standing up to an abuser while protecting her honor. Unfortunately, the legal system showed injustice when sentencing her mother to over twenty years in a state-run facility.

Mattie never trusted the legal system from that point. Alongside car sales people; lawyers were high on the slimiest job list.

"Girl you know Cyn is gonna wanna show up in her new ride for everyone to see, you know how she be trying to shine, just meet me at my place it will be one less stop to make."

She noticed the security guard smiling and watching her pull her badge out her back, jean pocket before swiping the scanner to get back into her department. As she walked down her aisle, a man and a woman were talking with Ms. Grace at her desk.

"Asset protection," Mattie thought. When she heard the woman speaking to Grace it was confirmed.

"We listened to the call and informed local authorities. We're here to make sure you feel safe; can you give a statement. We may have to pursue something later down the road…are you ok to give a statement Mrs. Dunbetter?" The woman asked. Asset Protection served many purposes, and this was just one.

"Grace you ok?" Mattie asked.

Grace shook her head affirmatively before answering the woman.

"Yeah I can give a statement, let me grab my purse and inform the union," She replied bending over to type and send an email to union stewards.

"I'll be back; if you leave before I get back, I will call you tomorrow. Is Lala going tonight?" Grace asked Mattie, standing back up to accompany Asset Protection upstairs to their department.

"Lord yes she's going thank God," she paused pulling

the phone from her pocket as it vibrated.

"Well it's about time she started living again, but don't forget to remind her about excessiveness," the salt and pepper haired woman hugged Mattie. Grace knew Sheila through having a friendship with Sheila's mother at an early age.

"I won't, but call me tomorrow, Ms. Grace."

A follow up text message from Geri came through, as Mattie watched her older work companion escorted to the security offices.

"She ain't no boss, but yeah I'll pick Sheila up from the hospital after her shift and be over about eight, and I'm going to share how my return back from Chicago was that night, you'd be proud of ya sista. Is Grandma good?" Geri's message read.

Mattie couldn't remember a meaningful time in her life after graduating high school that Geri hadn't been present. Mattie always said Geri would be the person most likely to help her stash a body without question.

Geraldine Marcom had become friends with Mattie and Cindy in college. They met at a student rally on campus by chance. The rally was held on behalf of a student harassed and beaten by police. The cops had issued a statement saying the student resisted arrest. The news ran with the official police version of the story for about four days until a video surfaced of the altercation. The video showed a different account. In it, three officers pepper sprayed and beat the student for nearly two minutes after he had passed out from being drunk. The officers hadn't taken that kindly to being various sorts of pigs and rental cops. The first blow shown was right after the black student told an officer his wife and he had sexual relations.

Clearly the drunken students' language and behavior was inciting, but the officers were sworn to protect and serve. Not to be judge and jury while perjuring themselves at the same time. The rally turned into pandemonium and the state police had to be called out to control what had become a riot.

That night Cindy, Geri and Mattie were arrested, and they spent the night in jail. Geri had called the police everything from "overseers to corrupt bigoted officers and various racist bastards," all three women were placed in the same police cruiser. Geri was so riled up that she took her heels and kicked the patrol cars window so hard it cracked.

Cindy and Mattie were shocked to say the least. They thought most white people were self-centered and selfish and couldn't view the world in a real sense. Geri was the catalyst for a shift in their thinking. That night locked up, the three college students shared their life stories and became friends. What the three shared was a camaraderie based on core values.

Geri was taller than Mattie by nearly two inches, and she had cut off her hair to less than a quarter of an inch. Her eyes were piercing blue and with her short blonde hair she had gained entrance into the business of modeling in college. Her body frame was tall and slender, but from working out with Mattie weekly she had muscles in her arms and legs. She was such a stunning woman that people often forgot about her hair. Of course, with such a low cut, she was hit on by both men and women. Something she simply accepted as human behavior. She hadn't modeled since junior year in college because she didn't like the lifestyle, or being around so many people who were considered beautiful who had eating disorders and low self-esteem. Being down to earth helped balance some of her outlandish ideas on life and art.

"Granny is doing good, finishing Lala's baby girl's blanket, I've gotta run by the mall after work, and then two workouts before grabbing the little ones. If you wanna come by tonight I'd say, eight-thirty would be fine," she sent back before sitting down and throwing her phone on top of her desk.

She pulled out her post it and wrote Grace a note 'I left early, call me in a few to tell me how you're doing'. With that done she grabbed her Pepsi and cheese popcorn and tossed it in her backpack. She waved and said goodbye to a couple people on the way out. Heading down the escalator her phone started vibrating again. It was Cindy calling.

"Damn girl I don't know how you do that shit, it's just plain creepy. I'm just now leaving to go to the mall," Mattie asked pushing through the glass turnstile.

"I don't know...whatever," Cindy said and then the phone went dead. Mattie looked down at her phone to see if she had lost signal.

"Mattie, Mattie!" Cindy was yelling as Mattie walked out the building holding onto her cell phone. She was standing by her SUV at a metered parking spot in front of the building. Cindy wore a blue pant suit with a white blouse and blue heels. She met Mattie halfway and gave her a hug.

"I'm calling it quits early today, lunch?" She turned to walk back towards her car.

"Well yeah if you gon be slacking today you can run me to the mall to get Granny's comforter and pillow set, I'll buy lunch," Mattie paused opening the backdoor to Cindy's car placing her book bag on the floor.

"…and a burger and fries Cindy, I ain't paying for you to eat like you have them dudes paying for yo ass," she finished before sitting down adjusting her seat position and rolling down the passenger side window. When Cindy got in the car and closed her door she responded to her best friend.

"Uhm, I don't want no damn burgers and fries, you can at least get me some pasta or something, if I want a burger or fries, I'll eat some of yours cause that's all you gon get anyways," knowing Mattie loved burgers and fries, it's what Mattie ordered the majority of the time. Cindy smiled at a couple of people staring at them as she put her seatbelt on.

"You know I thought you were going to blow up again and be banned from that podcast. I keep telling you that your mouth is gon write a check that ass can't cash," Mattie said pausing.

"Speaking of ass, guess who has a real date tonight?" Mattie asked

"Guess who already knows," Cindy answered and continued.

"Now guess who gave up some yams last night?" Mattie waited for her to continue but Cindy kept talking about Sheila.

"You have to make sure LaLa is not dressing in some respectful mother's shit or one of her her mama Barbara Jeans outfits Mattie, and honestly she needs some sex," she giggled knowing their friend could be very conservative in her appearance.

"So now getting back to you side stepping, who did Geri stay with last night?" Mattie asked.

"How you know it was Geri and not me?" Cindy asked in return.

"Really?" Mattie was always first to know about any of Cindy's relations in the past.

"Whatever, whatever you just make sure LaLa is accenting her curves this evening. I can stop by Ange's and grab pizza and be to the house about eight tonight," Cindy replied.

"Uhm no thanks on you picking up food, Your 8:00 would turn into 10:00 and I can't have our niece and nephew starving. I'm going to get her outfit together and go get the kids from James. We are having movie and game night if you do stop by just be ready, because Grandma asked where you were for Sunday service last week," Mattie said as a courier on bike rode right in front of them and Cindy pressed on her car horn.

"Watch that shit Lance Armstrong!" she yelled out her window.

Mattie shook her head, whether in agreement with her friend's sentiment or responding to Cindy yelling out the window. This quality was one of the things Mattie appreciates about her friend, her ability to speak truth unfiltered. Mattie scanned through the XM Satellite stations and heard the baseline to a song they grew up singing.

"Oh, that's the shit, turn it up some," she told Mattie.

Sade's 'No Ordinary Love' was playing on the radio, a song Cindy's mother use to sing when they were teenagers. As Cindy pulled out into traffic both women began singing with people staring at them while the music played loudly.

"Didn't I give you, all I could give you…baby…this is no ordinary love, no ordinary love."

CHAPTER 7
HONEY

Mattie listened to her friend attempt to make excuses on not meeting her date. This was the main reason she had shown up, to force her out of her comfort zone with gentle nudges and positive reinforcement. Sheila's divorce had been tough, and she found her way through by always staying busy with her children, work or friends. Males were a distraction, and men came few and far in between. Mattie decided to jump into Sheila's seventh reason to cancel her date.

"Lala, you have to let yourself have a good time without us, just watch your liquor," she sat on the bed helping Sheila get dressed for her date. The king-sized bed swallowed Mattie's body and her shadow fell onto the chambray colored walls. Mattie wasn't certain of many things lately, but she had no hesitation pushing her childhood friend towards having an actual date. It had been more than six months since she had her last, and almost a year before that.

The way Sheila looked at it she was making some progress.

"I'm just gonna sip wine tonight so no need to worry. This man is persistent since Geri had us fill out those online dating profiles," Sheila paused,

"Think these jeans will be ok Mattie?" she was wearing the personalized A.P.O jeans Mattie had bought her three friends, when she received the first portion of her father's life insurance policy. Learning how to become a single entity was hard after divorcing, separating emotional baggage even more difficult, and Sheila was still learning.

"The whole outfit is perfect." Sheila was such a naturally beautiful woman, but she failed to recognize it at times.

Sheila accompanied the jeans with a yellow brocade crop top and matching waist length blazer. Sheila's dark skin was highlighted against the yellow and the jeans accented her hips. Mattie knew that Sheila had a difficult time seeing the beautiful woman inside her. Her ex-husband James never complimented her, he was too busy pursuing women and not realizing that everything he wanted he already had. Now Sheila was having a night out with a professional man for dinner, after meeting online over two months ago.

"I heard they have added security at the mall today, you heard about the teenage girl they tried abducting last night. Weird ass story, the cops arrived, and the kidnappers were already handcuffed. I don't know what the hell this city is turning into nowadays. I am taking my mace with me tonight," Sheila finished.

"When Cindy and I got there, the parking lot was on swoll," Mattie paused to change the subject because she didn't want to get into a discussion with Sheila about being careful and all the other things she would hear from her dear friend had Sheila known it was her hand helping in the apprehension.

"You know I've got some crazy messages from that dating site. At first, they were nice and charming, but I never responded and then they got so mean girl, and then,"

"Facts. Downright disrespectful," Sheila interjected staring at herself in the mirror.

"For every decent guy there are five hundred and fifty bum ass posers. I'm going to have to tell Geri tonight, that it's just too much," Mattie finished as she walked to Sheila's closet to pick out the best shoes to match her outfit.

"Facts but Geri ain't trying to hear none of that, she's

been in grind mode since the beginning of the year. She's worked hard and smart to build "Under the Sun" and she's so close to national publication." Sheila said. Geri had gone to Chicago for a meeting with one of the largest syndicated publication companies. Starting with her graduation gift from her parents, fifty thousand-dollars and a half-matching investment from Mattie, Geri had built a regional magazine that zeroed in on middle class and urban areas of influence. It was tedious and time consuming for the first three years. Then she got an interview with a Congress woman, Natalie Starr, who spoke out against police brutality. Not long after the interview her readership grew, but it was an attack by the Congress woman's adversary that threw Geri into the limelight.

Congressman Jack Carpet had researched Geri and brought college footage up of the night Mattie, Geri and Cindy had been arrested for protesting as undergraduates. What Congressman Carpet failed to vet was the reason for being arrested. Congresswoman Starr embraced the video of Geri and used it as a bridge to fight her current crusade. The video went viral and Geri was accepted in greater fashion by urban culture seeing that she had been soldiering in this same injustice they had fought for decades.

Sheila was a bit nervous, she knew the kids would have fun with Titi Mattie, but she was anxious about having a real date after nearly a year. The sting of divorce, the feeling of failing at something so important had dulled. Sheila was nervous that she was not ready for one on one, face to face dialogue or what could follow.

"My palms are sweaty Mattie, this is the first time in a long time that I am doing something for myself, girl's night excluded. This guy seems nice, professional and has been persistent, I just don't know what to expect," she finished.

Mattie decided to be blunt. "Lala, you keep thinking about expectations, and what ifs, but who cares. You're going out on a date, with a man. You're going to have dinner. One, and no more than two glasses of wine."

Mattie paused to stare directly at her friend who responded affirmatively. "With all this body he's going to be stuttering over his words thinking how to impress you. Just have fun girl," Mattie finished.

"I am, I mean I will," Sheila paused.

"Geri will be upset if you changed anything right now," Sheila doubled down on her earlier statement.

"Yeah, yeah I know. I won't," Mattie said as Sheila tried interrupting her,

"Honestly, I won't change anything but to change the subject for now, the lil ragamuffins." Mattie said speaking regarding Sheila's children.

"I am taking them shopping to get them whatever they want, to dinner at Texas de Brazil, and then movie night with me and Grandma at the house. We are having ice cream, popcorn and

pizza for late night snacks. They will not be coming home until tomorrow late afternoon. So, enjoy yourself tonight." Mattie finished giving her friend a well felt reassuring hug. Sheila often failed to recognize just how powerful she was as a mother, a woman and friend.

"Mattie do what you want because you always do," as she nudged her friends' shoulder.

"James will have the kids ready at 6:00, he said 5:30 but knowing him we are giving him that additional half hour," Sheila finished as they both laughed. James was Sheila's ex-husband and he was always thirty minutes behind no matter the task. Something Sheila hated when they dated, and tolerated when they married.

Sheila and Mattie had known each other as children. Their fathers joined the military together and were deployed in the same unit. When they returned, they ran side hustles together to earn money. Her father was murdered less than one year after Mattie had become a foster child. They had lost contact for a few years, but when Mattie could live with her grandmother who moved from Georgia to care for Mattie, they reconnected.

"I'm gonna be late, I need to run to the bank and take some cash out. I've limited my credit card use for special occasions. Cindy knows about finances and credit. My score is way higher now," Sheila put on the Chanel Black Wedged Espadrilles.

"Woman you look amazing," Mattie paused as she opened her backpack.

"Here's some cash give it back to me later. You're not going to be late," she finished.

"What would I do without you?" She reached forward to hug Mattie.

Mattie side stepped and backed away.

"Uhm nope you're not messing that up." referring to

Sheila's makeup that took two attempts to match her eye shadow and lipstick with the final outfit chosen.

Sheila laughed and took one final look at herself in the mirror. She saw a nervous woman, fearful of the unknown, of what the evening would bring, but she saw a woman who was embracing her fear.

"Mattie," Sheila said lowly staring back into the mirror to make eye contact with her closest friend.

Often, she could determine what most of her friend's feelings were especially when they were emotional. When Sheila was angry, she took on the personality of her mother Barbara Jean who spoke her mind firmly. But this energy, coming off Sheila couldn't be determined so Mattie waited.

"I do have a fat ass in these jeans," Sheila finished staring into the mirror before bursting out in laughter as Mattie joined in.

...

Jonathan had made reservations for dinner at a new restaurant that served a variety of southern dishes, along with a few Caribbean foods. Sheila's nervousness had passed after her first glass of wine and appetizers.

Jonathan kept his full attention on Sheila, she noticed his eyes travel the course of her body, but his intent seemed on listening to her story. After the second glass of wine as their dinner entrées were served, he excused himself to take a 'business' call but at first glance Sheila could make out what she believed was a woman's picture as he answered. When he returned, he seemed even more upbeat sharing that his partner had a great first round of meetings. They were in the programming business as he explained.

The conversation at dinner had eased Sheila's nerves, he was attentive and as she finished her third glass of wine, she decided to accept his request for her return to his flat. He lived in a newly renovated apartment on the east side of the city.

Sheila nervousness resurfaced when she walked off the elevator and he used his key to open his apartment door, but after one more glass of wine, she undressed in front of him.

Jonathan hadn't expected to be directed in the way he had. It had thrown him off guard when she undressed and asked him why he was still clothed. She forced him to kiss her breasts and nipples. She wouldn't kiss him although he tried repeatedly, instead she forced him into the bed and climbed on top of him and took control.

"I said don't move," she said rotating her hips to pull more of him inside of her. He was a below average sized man in the groin, and she needed to have control in this position if she was going to feel enough to orgasm. She knew he wasn't going to last long if he started thrusting upward, something she learned from past sexual experiences.

"All that sweet talk at dinner, mmm," she moaned. She closed her eyes, attempting to maximize her pleasure. This was only sex, a function of having needs and as Sheila rode him, she had a flashback to having sex with her ex and it excited her.

"I haven't had sex in a long time and haven't felt," she paused as his hips began to move. She knew he was getting close to having an orgasm. So, she stopped.

"Damn why, why you stop," he asked holding onto her hips staring up at Sheila.

"Because tonight is about me," She answered and turned over, so he was on top before pushing him off and downward to eat her sweetness before he could say a word. She had always been submissive to her husband, something she had been proud of. But this was different, there were no feelings involved just two adults seeking satisfaction, and Sheila didn't give a damn until she was satisfied. She had stopped herself at four glasses of wine fully knowing anymore would be dangerous, but she needed it to push herself when she accepted his offer for a night cap.

He hesitated and looked up at her and smiled. Sheila raised an eyebrow when his lips kissed the inside of her thighs. She was going to enjoy as much as she could with him tonight.

She wondered why he was rotating his body as he licked her sweetness. She felt completely an adult, knowing exactly what she needed. She flinched with both pleasure and pain when he bit her, she gasped, and in that moment, he had reversed his body across hers. She grabbed his manhood and began stroking it. She had never been so bold before and attributed it to the white wine. The more he kissed and licked the wetness of Sheila, the harder he became inside her hand. He tried to pivot his hips towards her mouth, but she didn't allow the transition. Sheila knew it was the alcohol that gave her this freedom to lay with a stranger. She did kiss the tip of his hardness but was not accepting his manhood in her mouth.

The sixty -nine position was increasing her desire. His weight kept her upper body in place, but he was skilled enough not to crush her. Sheila felt turned on being partially constricted and as he slid two fingers inside of her, she gasped and found that more than the tip of his manhood had slid inside her mouth. Feeling the effect of the alcohol and her excitement had caused a momentary lack in judgment as he began moving his fingers at the same speed, he was moving his hips. Her senses were being overwhelmed, but she grabbed him by his shaft and stroked it over the top of her breasts. She felt wetness flowing down her ass, she wasn't sure if he was from his mouth or something else initially but then she felt the explosion from her creamy chasm.

"Oh shit!" She moaned still holding onto him as her cavities were being filled.

Sheila gasped again as she had an orgasm from his mouth and fingers. Realizing his body was stiffening she took her hands and pushed his hips off her because he was beginning to cum and she wasn't drunk enough to have him 'accidentally' orgasm anywhere near her face. Without complaint he moved quickly to her side and came on her breasts.

He tried to kiss her passionately as she tried to catch her breath. Sheila felt a release of pinned up energy. It had been almost two years since she had sex. She gave him a peck on his lips.

As he moved to the edge of the bed, he blew out the candle closest and laid back down to try and wrap his arm around her.

"I need to clean up, wash cloth, towel," Sheila was more firm than intended but she was clearly indicating that she was not gonna stay the night with him.

"Bathroom linen closet," Sheila couldn't help but see the fullness of her body in the mirror as she rolled off the bed. After having two children she became more voluptuous. Minor stretch marks were her badge of honor for bringing life into the world, and as she made her way into his bathroom, she felt weak in her legs.

"You have a phat ass," he mumbled as she turned the bathroom light on.

She found a wash cloth and towel and chose a quick shower instead of washing off. She was out of her comfort zone. She dressed in the bathroom after showering and ordered an Uber. When she opened the bathroom door, he was sprawled out on the bed fast asleep snoring. She blew out the remaining candles gathered her purse and coat. His phone lit up and on the screen was a picture of a woman and her name read "honey".

The phone call was immediately followed by a text message that read:

"Trip was cancelled, I'm heading up. Unlock the door," Sheila laughed and walked back into the bedroom. She stared briefly at him, realizing she would not speak with him again. She pulled her panties off and put them next to his cell phone on the couch on the way out.

"That honey won't be so sweet when she finds these," she thought as the door closed behind her. As she approached the elevator door a woman in sweats, with a scarf wrapped around her hair was getting off as it quickly closed behind her. She saw the genuine smile in her eyes making eye contact.

Sheila thought about the times James had cheated on her, and wondered if the other women had been lied to as she had been lied to over the past two months online.

Subconsciously she slowed her pace. She realized she was about to speak with the woman, but instead nodded her head and smiled. She pressed down on the elevator button and adjusted her shoe.

The woman walked to the door she had just left and walked in.

"Honey," her voice was light hearted as the door closed behind.

Sheila had to wait momentarily for the elevator to return to her floor and as she stepped onto it, her eye brows raised.

The previous light heartedness had been replaced with the sound of a woman scorned.

"Honey is sour now," as the elevator door closed behind her, Sheila remembered the anger of being in Honey's shoes.

CHAPTER 8

WHERE'S GRANDMA?

Mattie woke up when Cindy moved on the couch, and made breakfast for the kids who stayed. Before going shopping they dropped the kids off at their fathers and shopped for clothes to wear that evening. Afterward she had Cindy drop her off at home, before driving to work out with an instructor where she trained in Brazilian Jiu Jitsu. Mattie had earned her black belt and red stripe after her return from Colombia and was often asked to help instruct purple belts and higher. The day had passed quickly, and the orange fading sunrays were barely peaking over the tree line in the park.

Grandma Redd was resting her feet and watching reruns of Sanford and Son. Her grandmother meant everything to her. She reminded Mattie of her own mother in many ways, she couldn't imagine surviving life if she had been without her anchor.

Mattie's other links to a semblance of a healthy life were

the three friends that were truly her sisters in every sense except one. Her life was completely transparent except for a few details of her time spent in Colombia after college graduation. Some things from that time could not be shared because of the nature of the business her adopted family pursued, it kept her sisters out of harm's way.

Her high motor kept her busy; work, training, volunteering to help feed the homeless, and providing care for those she loved was in her everyday makeup. Mattie had been tested when she was younger to measure her IQ. She was recognized as a genius and at one point in time she had been a card- carrying member of Mensa. She read anything she could get her hands on, but Mattie's compulsion related to anatomy, pressure points and various religious practices. Her parents grew up in the church and Mattie was no different, but as she aged she opened herself to learning other religions. She remained Christian but was willing to accept there was a reason God allowed different ways up the mountain to glorify Him.

Mattie took a nap to rejuvenate, woke up and laid her clothes out on her bed, and heard the knock on her door. Thinking it could be one of her tenants she went to answer the door, but out of habit Mattie looked out the window to see if she recognized any vehicle or person out of place. She walked over to the door and opened it after seeing Geri's truck parked on the street.

"Where's Grandma?" Geri and Sheila walked past her as she opened the door.

"Well hi to the two of y'all too and don't think y'all getting off that easy, I want to know some juicy details you whores," she replied laughing loudly as she hugged them both.

Mattie owned a decent sized building, buying it before the city began restructuring the county. She remodeled it herself, putting in new dry wall, windows, and the plumbing throughout. The other side of the building had received upgrades for her to rent it out as two different apartments. In the process of doing all her work she created two additional bedrooms for her side, so now it was a four-bedroom home with three and a half bathrooms.

Wood flooring dominated her home and there were two skylights on her side of the building. One was in the kitchen above the counter, and the other in the master bathroom. The wood flooring in the living room contrasted with the furniture. Khaki green leather sofas and two love seats. Artwork on the walls ranged from pictures of Indigenous people of the Americas, to Goli masks that Geri had bought for her. Her fireplace was wood burning with a large mantle extending the space, above it, a mounted fifty-two-inch-high definition plasma television set.

Mattie had good taste for her window treatments; a company called DW Design designed every window treatment for her. She had invisible blinds in her living room, which gave complete privacy when closed, and a soft sheer appearance when opened. In her office she had them install Photoverts, blinds with a picture scene on them. Her choice of scene was a picture of a young black girl holding a flower and in captions above it, it read 'What God has intended for you goes further beyond anything you can ever imagine'. It was something Oprah Winfrey had said years ago. All the other bedrooms had soft window treatments to make each room reflect a common flow for the entire interior.

"She's in her room right now; y'all can go say hi," Mattie said walking with them "...but hold on let me make sure she dressed."

As they walked down the hall, wide enough for her

elder's wheelchair to navigate, they passed Mattie's room. Sheila threw her bag onto the bedroom floor. "I still gotta do my makeup and I'm doing it in yo bathroom."

"Whatever just make sure you clean my shit up this time," Mattie replied without any hint of anger.

The accessories in the bathroom were Greek Accents and she had two large face basins. Why she had chosen two basins she never could fully rationalize, besides the fact that it was a good deal when she bought the counter.

As they continued down the hallway, Mattie leveled a picture on the wall. She had painted the walls a Merlot color with white crown molding. All the pictures in the hallway were old black and white photos of her family before the tragedy. She loved contrast. She thought it peculiar that her family had always looked happy in the pictures with everything that had happened in her younger life. That was the largest contrast she knew.

Mattie knocked on her grandmother's door.

"Grandma," slipping her head into the room.

"Yes baby," she sat forward in her seat as Mattie entered.

"Geri and Sheila wanted to say hi, are you decent?"

"Yeah, yeah baby, come in," as Mattie pushed the door open, Geri and Sheila walked over to the chair she was sitting in.

"Hi grandma, hey grandma," they both reached down to hug and kiss her on each cheek, being careful not to knock the remains of her dinner off her television tray.

"Hi babies, I don't know why it makes a difference if I was decent or not," she said pausing to catch her breath,

"…we all women folk and I gots the same stuff y'all got," her red toned skin was unblemished, her gray hair was still as lustrous as it had been when it was jet black, and her eyes seemed greyer now than green. Her strong cheekbones and facial features were something Mattie inherited. She favored more Cherokee than black, but she knew from oral history, that there were blacks and red skin indigenous people inhabiting North America long before the history of slavery.

Mattie had already put the comforter set and new pillows on her grandmother's bed. It was a light powder blue comforter with matching pillow cases. The colors matched the light blue sheers and top treatment on her windows along with the border running around the top of the walls.

"Ooh that's nice grandma, real nice," Geri said bending down to touch the comforter.

"Yeah Mattie got it for me baby, it's purty. How y'all been?"

Sheila and Geri started telling Grandma Redd about the ride over. They had stopped at a gas station and two kids were caught trying to steal beer and ice.

In that moment Mattie took the dinner plate off the TV tray to scrape the leftovers into the trash compactor. While she was in the kitchen, she poured a glass of sun tea for her elder family member.

"I'll cut that and start Grannie a plant for her window," she thought looking at one of her three plants soaking in the last bit of sunlight coming in from the skylight in the kitchen.

Mattie loved her grandmother more than anyone or anything. The older matriarch had given her valuable information over the years. She was never one to come right out and say something if she wanted the lesson to be learned. Grandma Redd told Mattie that her ex fiancé was no good at action. 'Words get you to the door baby, but action gets you through it,' a simple phrase, it took Mattie nearly six months after the engagement to understand what her grandmother was trying to tell her earlier. In the end Brian was simply a good talker with big ideas but no follow through. When he asked Mattie to borrow the rest of the money to pay off her engagement ring, she gave him the boot; that was over two years ago.

Mattie took a sip of the tea to make sure she hadn't put too much sugar in it, and headed back down the hallway. She was hoping for an enjoyable evening; the last time Geri took them to listen to poetry she almost fell asleep.

"So, you heard Cindy got a new ride grandma?" Geri was asking when Mattie walked back into the room and placed the tea on the television tray.

"Thank you, sweetie," she used both hands to secure the glass from her granddaughter.

"Yeah baby she done came over to show grandma, Cynthia buys stuff cause she surching for sumthin baby, jus like all y'all youngun's," she paused again to get more oxygen.

"All four of yall turned out ok, all's I can do is pray. I'll see y'all at church this Sunday. Let grandma finish this blanket for yo baby girl Sheila," she sat back in her chair after placing the glass on her television dinner tray.

Sheila said thanks and kissed her on the cheek again. Geri looked like she wanted to say something more, but she just smiled and hugged her before leaving the room.

"Madison, baby," her silvery voice had always brought calm to Mattie.

"Yes ma'am."

"You kno The Lord has blessed you with real good true friends, that's more of a blessing in today's world, I'm proud of you Madison and grandma loves you very much," she finished.

"You're my blessing grandma and I love you too," Mattie understood the wisdom in her grandmother's remarks.

"Do you need anything else though? I am about to hop in the shower and get dressed. It's Geri's night, so we're going to some poetry joint," Mattie kissed her on the forehead before heading towards the door.

"Poetry, that girl is more romantic than the rest of y'all, she jus need the right man, just like you baby, but Grandma is fine y'all have a good time, jus tell me before you leave," she finished as Mattie closed the door slightly behind her.

Sheila was in Mattie's bathroom putting her make up on and Geri was looking out the bedroom window.

"It's eight o'clock now what time you tell that hussy to be here?" Geri asked.

"I told her we needed to be there at eight thirty, so she should be here around nine," Mattie answered while kicking her tennis shoes into her walk-in closet. Geri laughed and walked out the bedroom heading into the living room to watch television.

"Eight thirty Mattie, the show don't start til ten o'clock," she walked away shaking her head.

"I know right," Mattie replied but Geri was out of earshot, so she changed the subject.

"Don't turn the water on while I'm showering Sheila, I'm sooooo serious too, don't turn the water on and mess my shower up. You can clean all that shit up when I'm done," while she adjusted the temperature in the shower. She went into her room to undress and threw her clothes into her dirty clothes hamper before slipping her white robe on.

"Well turn some music on," Sheila said as Mattie took her hair band out.

Mattie shuffled through her book bag and pulled out a CD to put in her Bose sound system. As the introduction of the CD came on, the songs were jumbled, and the beats were completely off rhythm as they were being mixed. After nearly thirty seconds of random beats, a predominant rhythm came through that slowly mixed all the tracks together in a way that the mix sounded perfect.

"Damn who is that?" Sheila asked while brushing away some extra foundation she didn't want on her face.

"Gov White and you ain't heard nothing yet, he's hot, real hot. He's done a few tracks up north but he's blowing up out west in Cali," Mattie said turning the volume up before walking back into the bathroom.

"I am serious Lala don't touch the faucet," Mattie stared at Sheila in the mirror as she walked behind her with one eye brow raised.

Sheila stared at herself in the mirror too, making sure her peach eye shadow was spread evenly and that she hadn't put on too much eyeliner. Sheila was dark with very smooth skin; her smile was intoxicating and brilliant white, just like the whites of her eyes. She was the shortest of the bunch standing at five foot four inches and she weighed about one hundred and fifty pounds. She was short, but a voluptuous built woman. After two children and a divorce, she had never been able to shed the last fifteen pounds after having her second child.

Sheila walked out of the bathroom to ask Geri what color looked better for lipstick with what she was wearing.

"It doesn't matter what color, they ain't gon be looking at your lips tonight Lala with that entire ass on the loose," Geri was flipping through TV channels. She had a glass of tea sitting in front of her on the table.

"The peach color Lala."

Sheila thanked her before walking into the kitchen to see what there was to snack on but decided to wait until she was done with her makeup.

"Damn you been in there almost fifteen minutes already Mattie, I gotta pee," Sheila said walking back into Mattie's bathroom exaggerating about how long Mattie had been showering. She was closing the top to her eyeliner and eye shadow still deciding on what color lipstick to wear. She threw her concealer into her bag and put on the lipstick Geri recommended. "Mattie, I gotta pee."

Mattie turned the water to the shower off and pulled her towel from the towel holder and began drying off before stepping out of the shower.

"I'm done go ahead, you do know you could've used the main bathroom room or half bath," She said as she stepped out.

One of her favorite moments was taking a long hot shower at the end of the day. It helped her wash away the daily bullshit she had to deal with, plus it served as light meditation. Often, she found her mind wondering on what she would do to some of the ignorant people she had a chance encounter with. She had silent talks with herself about what circumstances would have to exist for her to kill someone or violently hurt them. It wasn't all the time, just when she wondered how much of her parents were in her, after all she was their daughter, and their behaviors helped create who she was now in her early thirties.

Mattie walked over to the second face basin to brush her teeth. She wiped away the small amount of steam build up on the mirror. Sheila knew her father. Out of her girlfriends, Sheila and Mattie had real childhood memories they could share together.

"Ju make such a mess." She said to Sheila as she brushed her teeth moving her hair to the side of her face.

"I'm gon clean it up," she flushed the toilet, and after washing her hands, Sheila turned the volume up on the music.

"Damn that sounds bomb, you gotta make me a copy of that. And I'm still waiting for my copy of DJ Rad n Quik, stop slippin' on my shit." Sheila was saying as she put the last of her make up into her cosmetic bag.

"Yeah, yeah," Mattie kept bobbing her head to the music.

These two were grade school friends through seventh grade, until Sheila's dad was murdered while her brother Junie waited in the car. Junie was only six years old, and all he saw was his father running towards the car after leaving a convenient store, being chased by a man who yelled at him, "Be afraid, what's up!"

Sheila's mom took a new employment position in a city an hour and a half away, attempting to lift her children from the unsafe environment. After two years in Cincinnati she got laid off and moved back to Columbus, but Mattie had already moved in with her grandmother. Throughout high school Sheila and Mattie emailed and talked on the phone. Mattie had seldom returned to her old neighborhood, feeling an emotion inside that she still didn't understand after years of counseling. Her mother had shot her father causing him paralysis while defending her honor. His subsequent death through infection was not attributed to his injuries and the insurance company had no choice but to pay off the life insurance policy. Parents were supposed to love and honor each other, but what Mattie learned was that not all families shared the same values as those predominantly displayed on television.

Mattie's father and Sheila's father were hustling partners as much as they were friends, they had trust and respect for each other after being in the Armed Services together.

"You got anything to snack on besides grandma's meatloaf? Sheila walked out the bedroom.

"What the hell are you watching Geri that is disgusting?" Mattie heard Sheila say. Geri watched the History Channel and National Geographic mostly. So, when Sheila yelled 'Oh God!' all Geri did was laugh.

Mattie had finished dressing, but she carried her new

shoes out into the front living room. As she set down both Sheila and Geri had their eyes glued to the television set.

They were watching National Geographic in High Definition. The crispness of the picture and color quality was not what gained Mattie's attention; instead it was the sight of chimpanzees hunting monkeys in the wild. A community of Chimpanzees had cornered three monkeys and there was no retreat for them, just then the realization that this episode was going to end up with the monkey's demise.

"Oh, my gawd, you two are really weird," Mattie sat down on the love seat and put her shoes on the floor next to her. She picked up the bag of tortilla chips that Sheila pulled out the pantry and ate a few before taking a sip of Geri's sun tea.

"Uhm go get yo own," she slid her glass back in front of where she sat on the long sofa. Mattie was now fixed on the television like both other women.

"Damn," Sheila said as one of the monkeys was caught, ripped apart and eaten. "That just ain't right, that's like primate cannibalism." Sheila covered her face with her hand acting like she wasn't watching.

"That's what happens in the wild, nature Lala… nature.

Human behavior is three times as bad," Geri started to say when the program cut to commercial.

"Don't start with all that psychoanalytical shit tonight Geri." Mattie commented as her cell phone began vibrating on the coffee table. "It's Cindy, said she's on the way."

Cindy always blamed a late appointment for her tardiness. If she wasn't one of the top real estate agents in the state it would have never been an accepted excuse. Truth was she was always late.

"What time is it?" Geri asked.

"It's about nine o'clock," Mattie responded before leaning over to take another sip of Geri's tea.

"Let me use the bathroom now," Geri said as she stood up to move around the corner of the kitchen where the formal dining room and half bath sat separately.

"Are y'all done with these chips?" Mattie asked Sheila who was waiting for the program to come back from commercial.

"Yup I am," Sheila said at the same moment she was reaching for another handful of chips out the bag.

"Michelle is going to meet us there, I had to twist Henry's arm the other day," Mattie said.

Mattie had to focus as she put her shoes on. She had to wrap the two black leather straps across her calf. Crisscrossing them until they fell right beneath her toned calf muscle; the three -inch heels highlighted the definition of her legs.

"Those are some bangin ass shoes Mattie," Sheila said as she finished taking a bite out of a chip.

"I know right, I got them at the mall. I wasn't gone buy em but they started calling my name, plus the manager gave me his discount because I was such a nice granddaughter," Mattie paused as Sheila started shaking her head affirmatively.

"And no trick you can't borrow em," she finished.

"Wasn't nobody gon ask you to borrow yo funky shoes, I'd just take em, and you wearing the shit out of those jeans, you bought a top from them too, damn. You've been holding out on me?" Sheila said eating another chip before reaching over to drink the rest of Geri's tea.

"I ordered the outfit through an online company a couple

of weeks ago…you think this is too much?" Mattie asked Sheila as she wrapped a black bandana through her belt loops.

"Nah, that looks good. I need to get a membership to the gym," Sheila said as Geri came back out.

"Lala, if you got a membership, we would only have to get Cindy on board, but I'm gon tell you the first month is a bitch and Mattie don't be playing around," Geri interjected. She looked at her glass of tea and shook her head, it was empty. Mattie took that as a cue to turn off her lights and music in her room.

"Four hundred exercises a day get you these." Geri said patting Mattie's stomach when she walked past her. She complimented Mattie on her strapped blouse as well.

"Not as exhibitionist as you, I'm gonna have to keep an eye on you since you got your girls hanging all out your white hooter shirt." Mattie said walking back to the living room.

"Save the story for everyone." Mattie said to both women.

"What story?" they asked in unison.

"Uhm the story neither one of you have even mentioned since y'all got her," Mattie finished as the doorbell sounded.

"Who is it?" Mattie said pressing the intercom.

"Who else is it gon be picking y'all raggedy asses up?" Cindy's voice came back through the speaker.

Mattie buzzed her in, she was grateful that she had a top-notch security system, but she had to tell her new tenant to not prop the door open, and her grandmother to lock the patio door. She had two rentals now, both on the other half of her building. She split the other half in two and made moderate enhancements to rent it out. Her mortgage for the building was nearly three thousand dollars, but she rented each half for nine hundred- dollars so she only had to pay the difference; a bargain for nearly two thousand square feet. She earned twelve hundred dollars per week before taxes, and still had a substantial amount of money spread out in four different banks, because each lending institution was only insured up to two hundred and fifty-thousand dollars by the Federal Government. She had investments that were growing slowly, but always increasing. Mattie was set for the rest of her life if she didn't make bad investments.

She had learned from Cindy that doubling her mortgage

payments increased her equity as well as her credit.

"Where's Grandma, she in her room?" Cindy asked before greeting her friends.

"Yeah she's in the back," Sheila said as she stood up to give her girl a hug.

"And you probably want to button that top button at least before you go in there though, Geri got her shit all out tonight too, what y'all call each other on the phone and say this is hooter night?" Sheila finished laughing profusely as she pulled away.

"No, we didn't call each other to coordinate our outfits, but hell yeah let me button this cause we ain't got time for no lecture, and I gotta make a quick stop on the way. Y'all had me rushing like a mad woman to get here." She was wearing a Dolce and Gabbana outfit; a Canary yellow blouse with wide collars. Her breasts were pushing through her shirt, but it fit perfectly everywhere else. Her mini skirt was a natural muslin color, but Cindy's shoes brought the outfit together. They were open toed sling backs with leather straps. The heels were nearly three- inches but it was the golden yellow stitching on the leather straps that combined each piece of the outfit perfectly and matched her blouse.

“You better pull that shit down too before you even go back there,” Geri said giving Cindy a hug.

“I barely got this over my ass and hips, I can’t pull it down, I’ll make it quick,” she paused watching Mattie look her up and down.

“…Grandma probably wore stuff like this back in the day, she was a hot Pocahontas.” She said smiling and walking down the hall towards grandma’s room.

“Yo momma is a hot mamacita with her firecracker wig,” Mattie responded shaking her head.

“You do look nice; although that shit is tight…can you even breathe?” Mattie added placing the couple of dishes into the dishwasher while Sheila put the bag of tortilla chips back into the pantry. Geri walked back with Cindy to say goodbye to Mattie’s grandma. When Sheila and Mattie walked to the back to say goodbye, they heard Cindy explaining like she was a young girl again.

“Granny I just gained a couple pounds that’s why it fits a little snugger,” she said trying to pull her jacket together nervously.

“Baby we all gain weight, but that skirt child, you ain’t

get no taller have ya?" Mattie's grandmother asked Cindy.

"No ma'am I…I haven't," she felt the eyes of all three friends watching her as the elder woman spoke to her and each one was smirking.

"Baby you gotta leave a little something for the imagination, and that go for all y'all," she added staring at Geri who forgot to fix her top button again before coming back into the bed room.

"Yes grandma…yes ma'am," they all replied.

"Grandma we have to go, call me if you need anything…I love you," Mattie said kissing her followed by Geri and Sheila. Cindy waited until they were done before hugging and kissing her too.

"Granny, thank you, I love you too," Cindy said while bending over to hug her.

"Y'all have a good time and be careful…leave my door open," she said letting Cindy go before sitting back in her chair.

"Girl I told you, you were just asking for trouble," Sheila said grabbing her purse off the soft leather couch in the living room.

"Yeah, yeah, I am trouble, but we gotta go, I have a stop to make really quick," Cindy said opening the door to leave.

"Hold on, close the door; I gotta set the alarm," Mattie said pausing putting her alarm code into the keypad after Sheila closed the front door.

"Ok, let's kick it bitches," she finished closing the door behind them. Once they were outside, they could see the park across from where Sheila parked, a few people were jogging around the trail and a few guys waited on the side for their game to play basketball. One of the safer parks in the city because of night lights the nearby residents maintained and a neighborhood block watch. The mayor was using this neighborhood as a model to build throughout the city, so more patrol cars frequented the area giving it the illusion of being much safer than it was.

"Ooh girl yo whip is sparkling," Geri said opening the backdoor behind the driver's seat. As Sheila closed her door she asked if they could stop by the liquor store to get a bottle of something to drink

"As long as yo ass ain't driving later tonight, then hell yeah we can get a bottle of Patron?" Geri said looking through her small purse for a mirror to check her lipstick.

"And Lala you are not gon be smoking all my shit either like you did last time," Cindy said starting the car. Although Sheila was a nurse, she was privy to any drug testing timelines at work and event night was the only night she partook.

Mattie was already skimming through the discs Cindy had programmed in her audio system and found Rad n Quik to play.

"Mattie, I need a copy by Sunday," she hesitated before sitting up and extending her hand between Cindy and Mattie in the front seat.

"...and I got my own shit to smoke if you ain't sharing," Sheila told Cindy waving a huge joint of weed in her face.

"If any of y'all burn holes in my leather I swear," Cindy said like she was serious shaking her head up and down.

"We aint paying a dime for anything that's for all those flunkies you got," Mattie said turning the volume up when Cindy tried to say something back.

"Just drive before we late," Geri said watching Sheila light her joint hoping that it was some decent marijuana.

"Ok damn but y'all aint gon be bossing nobody

around tonight," Cindy said hesitating while looking through her side mirror as she pulled out into traffic with the music amplified.

"…and let me hit that ladies," she finished.

Chapter 9

The Price of Freedom

The line had already started to form when the women pulled up to the spot. It was a club, but the owner was marketing it as a place to hold special events on nights it wasn't spinning records for party goers. Geri knew the owner through an employee at work; she was the owner in a growing regional magazine, along with being an editor she came across a lot of different people with varying backgrounds in her day to day job. As they were finding a place to park Geri texted the owner to meet her at the door, so they wouldn't have to wait in a line.

Cindy couldn't find a close parking spot, so they had to park towards the back of the establishment away from the brighter street lights on the backside of the building. Other vehicles were following them, and by the looks of it many people must've heard about opening night and decided to give it a try. As they got out and made their way to the front, they walked past thirty or more people standing in line at the entrance frowning as they walked past, the security guard standing at the front waved Geri and her friends forward.

Michelle was walking towards them in the opposite direction waving them down.

"Ladies, I thought I'd never get out. The babysitter was late, and you all know my husband," she said as she hugged each of them.

"Excuse me, Geri?" The doorman asked the group of friends before telling people waiting in line to slow down.

"Geri?" he asked making sure he had identified the right set of ladies to let in.

"Yeah yeah, you got it, I'm Geri."

"You ladies can go right in," he finished standing in the way of the next person in line, allowing Geri and the four women entry inside. The usual grumbling could be heard in the line from both men and women who had been waiting already for nearly fifteen minutes.

As they entered music was being played by a live band coming through the surround sound speakers throughout the club. Drake's 'In My Feelings' was complimenting the atmosphere of the front room. To the right of the entrance, about thirty feet away, a bar was situated with two bartenders dressed in all black filling orders for liquor and appetizers. Nearly fifty bar stools sat around it, and every seat was occupied with a few people leaning through those sitting down trying to get the attention of one of the two servers.

"Geri Marcom," a tall, dark, bald man greeted her as she walked past the bar followed by her friends. He wore a crisply groomed beard on his face and one diamond stud earring in his left ear. Cindy was responding to someone texting on her phone, Mattie and Sheila were whispering to Michelle at Geri's side.

"What's good Max, you remember my sisters, right?" she asked leaning forward to give him a friendly hug. Max was dressed in dark blue jeans with a serious crease and a peach colored button -down shirt. He wore a light weight camel jacket with peanut butter wingtip shoes.

"Of course, how could I have forgotten the

symposium?" He answered waving and smiling at a few people walking by who were trying not to be so obvious in getting his attention.

"Listen your table is reserved; I gotta make sure that the sound technician has the wireless microphones hooked up tonight, so everything flows smoothly. Reserved tables have a complimentary bottle of champagne, and if you're performing tonight then drinks will be half off for your table. You gon brave the stage, because I've got your name on the short list? We're gonna be filming the performances and putting them on our website and making copies for DVD," he said, with his attention divided between people he knew and his employees. He was waving at the sound tech pointing at the surround sound speakers in the front of the club. The sound tech gave him a thumbs up to indicate everything was already set.

"What if Geri don't do it, but one of us does, we still get half off drinks?" Cindy asked putting her phone back in her small matching purse walking to stand on the other side of Geri with her eyebrows raised.

Max smiled and shook his head, slightly amused. Cindy had called one of Max's friends gay at a symposium because he told Max he looked handsome, so Max knew he needed to tread lightly because there was no telling what could come out of her mouth. Cindy didn't have an issue if he did enjoy same sex relations, only that he should be out in the open and sharing that information with his partners. The way she saw it said it was as a matter of fact.

"Tonight we only have a few artists we are allowing for open mic, so tonight is Ms. Marcoms' opportunity to share her words, but we will have at least one night of spoken word every month moving forward, so feel free to come out and join us then," he paused as the sound tech had come over to whisper something in his ear.

"I have your table reserved in the back, remember half off drinks Geri, ladies," he finished before excusing himself.

Sheila nudged Geri on her arm. "He ain't so bad girl, didn't you say he owns Club Mojito too and now this one? He's doing alright from the looks of it."

"He's alright, he might've had a chance if he wasn't such a player, but he's a real cool dude to hang out with, but it ain't no telling who he done had relations with up in this joint, and I ain't never been a number," Geri paused to say hi to a couple she had met at a poetry slam in Chicago, "And anyways Grannie said keep all this until someone is qualified to take care of it." She finished by rubbing her hips. Mattie laughed, and Sheila rolled her eyes playfully. They walked towards the back where the performances were going to be held. The two sections of the club were separated by one large wall. On their way to the back they came across tables with merchandise on display; one painting stood out among others.

A few tables were set up with canvas paintings and high-quality photos. Other tables displayed books and CD's, both music and poetry. A painting of a ship on an easel is what caught Sheila's attention where the vendors had set up their stations. Sheila took a closer look at the painting entitled "A Price of Freedom". A large ship was carrying African Slaves. The uniqueness of the painting, however, was the dark figures jumping off the ship into the ocean. Sheila saw the female artist speaking to someone giving them change for a smaller copy. When she looked at the price tag hanging from the bottom of the original canvas painting, six hundred dollars, she shook her head and walked back to her friends.

A few people had congregated in small groups throughout the front portion of the club. This was the type of function Geri appreciated. She went to traditional clubs with her friends for 'event night' to dance, but she would rather be somewhere that people didn't argue or act ignorant because they got liquor in their system and began exercising their ego's.

"I'll be back there in a second," Cindy said walking away as she noticed one of her male associates sitting at the bar. He was a decent looking, brown skin guy with curly black hair who followed Cindy as she approached him with a seat waiting for her.

Mattie had separated from her girlfriends too. She was taking in the moment and walking past a couple of the vendor's tables. She took her time at a table that had books on display like 'The Isis Papers' by Frances Cress Welsing and 'Stolen Legacy' by George J.M. James, but she had read most of the titles already. When Mattie came to the next vendor who was selling oils and incense, she stopped to see what he had. She only wore oils because her skin was sensitive, and most perfumes gave her a rash, plus oils lasted longer.

"You have Ed Hardy for women or Gucci Bloom?" She finally asked after picking through his selection. He had a slender build and long limbs. He had a baritone voice with an east coast accent.

"For you my queen I do have those," he handed a small bottle of oil to Mattie.

"I've also got some new scents, Tiffany & Co. and Tom Ford for women. Any three for ten dollars," he paused waving his hands across his whole ensemble of items.

"I've got incense too; tell you what if you buy three oils for ten bucks, I'll throw in a few sticks of incense too," he finished by smiling at Mattie looking her up and down. He had not taken his eyes of Mattie. He kept trying not to be so blatant, but he had figured he had nothing to lose he tried a different dialogue.

"Those are some really nice shoes," he said attempting to engage in more conversation. Mattie said thanks and kept looking for another bottle of oil. She held onto the Ed Hardy and Gucci oils searching for something else. She didn't want to have an awkward moment and she wasn't here trying to find any new friends.

"What's that?" She pointed to a bottle that didn't have a label. It was in a darker bottle that the rest, so it intrigued Mattie.

"Oh…that's Paris Hilton," he said twisting the cap off the top of it smelling it just to make sure.

"No, I don't want that mess; I'd smell like my sister. Let me get the Michael Kors along with these two and you can give me that whole bag of incense too, you gotta a whole bunch of it anyways."

The vendor looked at Mattie. He wasn't sure if she meant to buy or as a gift with her purchase, he decided no need to argue about the bag of incense since he was already making a profit. With Mattie at his station more people were now paying attention to his table.

"Do you think your girls want anything?" He asked pointing in Geri and Sheila's direction. Evidently, he had been checking her entourage out earlier, because Sheila and Geri hadn't been around Mattie when she was going from table to table.

"I don't know…Lala…Geri," Mattie called out a couple of times to get their attention before they turned to see what she wanted. They both shook their head 'no' as Mattie held up her bag of merchandise.

"No, we're all good. Good looking my brother," as it rolled off her tongue he smiled and winked at her.

"Oh gawd," she thought. It wasn't that he didn't possess a certain attraction or physical attributes, but Mattie had standards and he didn't meet them. Unkept hair and dirty nails were huge turnoffs, and his dreadlocks were scraggly and his nails needed help. Mattie then noticed his black oversized t-shirt was covering a hole in his back pocket. The front of his shirt had a 'peace' symbol on it and she found herself remembering all the times she struggled earlier in life and spoke to him for a few minutes about how he made his oils and incense, but she was certain to make sure she didn't lead him on because in the end personal hygiene was a must for her.

Taking a closer look around the front space, Mattie saw that mirrors extended along both sides of the room, which gave the front area a larger appearance and helped it look more crowded, although it was getting packed. Where the vendors were set up, the mirror extended to a set of stairs that was roped off with a sign hanging from it; 'VIP is closed for tonight's venue'. As she made her way through the crowd to find out if her friends were ready to go to the table, she felt people staring at her. She kept her chin high and glanced around at the same time without making eye contact with anyone.

"This spot is alright Geri, you picked something decent for a change," Mattie said smiling as Geri took her bag to see what Mattie had bought.

"Whateva hooker, what else they got over there?" Mattie told her about the incense and Paris Hilton oil, something she knew Geri would want. Geri excused herself and bought two bottles of her favorite fragrance and another fragrance, she got a bag of incense for free too.

Geri approached the booth as Michelle was speaking with the artist about purchasing an original piece as Mattie and Sheila looked on. "I'll pay for it now and get it on the way out, I can do that?" The artist assured her she would be around after the show.

"I gotta go to the bathroom," Sheila said walking away towards the restrooms where a small line had formed.

"Ok I'm coming too, Geri can you ask Max to put her painting somewhere safe that way we don't even have to worry about it later?" Mattie asked before following behind Sheila navigating the same quick openings of people standing around socializing.

Geri found Max who took the painting into his office and guaranteed its safety.

Michelle saw someone she knew and excused herself,

Geri told her once they regrouped, they could head into the main showroom.

"I'm gon head back in a minute," Geri weaved her way around groups of people to the bar where Cindy and her associate were sitting having drinks and a conversation. She waited the last few steps as a group of three finished taking pictures on their cell phones.

"Hey girl this is Juan, Juan this is one of my sisters Geri," Cindy made the introduction. Juan looked Dominican with curly, dark black hair, his skin looked rich and tanned. He had two rings on his right hand, and a Movado Watch on his left wrist.

"Where are the ladies?" Cindy asked before taking a sip of her Chocolate Martini.

"Bathroom…I'm gonna head to the back, we get that bottle of champagne, do you want us to order you something else?" Geri asked, feeling Juan stare her up and down a few times already. Both women noticed how his eyes wandered. It wasn't unfamiliar territory to have men checking them out, but it was tacky to do it so blatantly and rudely when he was doing it to her friend.

"No, I'm good, Juan is about to buy me another drink,

you want something too?" Cindy asked. She was a little peeved that Juan was disrespectful and decided she would get one farewell shot on him, and after tonight he would never get another call or response from her. Somehow men always thought the grass was greener on the other side Cindy use to say, and now Juan was proving her right.

"I'll take a quick shot or two if y'all take one," Geri answered. Both women were on the same page, 'spend this fool's money. Over fourteen years of being friends and going through serious life crisis they knew what each other were thinking.

"You gon take a shot too, right?" Cindy asked Juan.

"Of course, I can't let y'all without me, now can I?" the cockiness in his voice could be heard as he waved the bartender down.

"Listen my man; let me get three shots of Patron for my people and put it on my tab," he finished ordering before glancing at Geri's cleavage again. Geri shot him an evil look and he began fumbling with his cell phone before drinking down the rest of his beer. Juan was trying to be discreet looking around at other women through the mirrors, but he didn't do a good job concealing it. As the bartender brought the three shots back, Juan had no idea that any chance of pursuing Cindy was lost.

"We need a couple of limes," Geri added to the bartender who shook his head affirmatively. The shots were supposed to be single shots, but they appeared to be doubles.

"That's a helluva shot," Juan said raising his glass to make a toast, but Geri interrupted him.

"To keepin it real," Cindy smiled and shook her head back and forth before joining in the toast.

"To keepin it real…thanks Juan," she added, and Geri also said thanks slamming her glass on the bar top reaching for a lime while Cindy took her shot.

"Alright I gotta get our table, are you coming?" Geri asked Cindy, giving her the option of leaving without being overtly rude to Juan. He wasn't that different than most men and his behavior wasn't that unusual, but respect was a huge criterion and he didn't have theirs.

"Yeah I'm coming."

"Yo, can I sit up there with y'all?" Juan asked, interrupting Cindy who was still dealing with the after burn from the shot. But it didn't stop her from answering him.

"There's only room for five, but I'll try to get at you before we leave or sumthin," Cindy said excusing herself.

"Will you take this to the table please I gotta go?" She handed Geri her Martini. Juan also stood up as if he were going to give Cindy a hug, but she turned and walked away without making eye contact with him. Geri grabbed her drink and followed, leaving Juan in a moment of bewilderment before he set back down and ordered another beer.

Mattie and Sheila were walking out as Cindy pushed the women's bathroom door open.

"Somebody got the nerve to be blowing it up in there," Sheila said when Cindy passed her heading into the restroom. There was a sitting area for women with two large red cushions with gold stitching. Each cushion could seat four people comfortably, but only two girls were sitting down waiting when Cindy walked in.

"I don't give a fuck cause I gotta pee." She acknowledged Sheila's statement, but ignored it at the same time.

"We'll be at the table," Geri said louder than she had intended. The tequila had moved through her body and she was feeling warm. Carrying her bag of oils in one hand and

Cindy's Martini in the other, she navigated her way through the crowd followed by Mattie and Sheila. As they approached the doors to the performance area, Michelle had caught up to them. A large stocky man with a clipboard in his hand was standing directing people.

"This area is reserved ladies," he said with a deep low voice, it appeared that he was trying not to look intimidating to them, but the size of his arms and neck, made that feat impossible. The scar under his right chin didn't help either.

"Geri Marcom, party of five."

He scanned down the list until he found her name.

"Yeah, I got you. Your table number is five, enjoy yourselves tonight," he stepped to the side opening the double door.

"Thanks," Sheila said following behind Ger and Michelle. Mattie slowed as she approached the door.

"Our fifth is gonna be coming in a minute, her name is Cindy and she's gone have on a two -piece skirt outfit with a yellow shirt," she thought he had to have been over six feet five inches, and damn near three hundred pounds. His shirt was pure irony, it had a smiley face on it with a caption;

'don't start no sh..'

"Hey, your girl is going to be performing, huh?" He asked with his eyebrows raised.

"Who, Geri?" Mattie asked slightly confused.

"Who knows she ain't done poetry since college," Mattie answered him and began walking through the door wondering if Geri was going to perform again.

"Mattie, hold up," Cindy said maneuvering through the people beginning to form a line to get in.

"Ok…cool," The bouncer stepped back to let Cindy pass. He couldn't help to watch both walk away, they were looking spectacular tonight. It wasn't until they were almost to their seats that he turned around.

"Come on dawg," a male's voice came through from somewhere in the stagnant line waiting for entry. As the bouncer turned around, he addressed them all.

"This area is reserved; if you don't have reserved tables go down that way to the other doors!" he yelled using the clipboard to point them in the right direction to the door about forty feet away.

More than half in the line were now separating themselves and mumbling how it was bullshit that they had to go get in somewhere else.

As Mattie and Cindy sat down at their table, Cindy reached for her Chocolate Martini and took a sip.

"Mattie you're driving home tonight, it's your turn," Sheila said.

"No, it ain't, I drove when we went to Second Saturday last month and this is the second event night since then, so I ain't up for rotation yet, don't even try it. I don't know whose turn it is but it ain't mine, I'm getting my drink on," Mattie said picking up her empty Champagne glass.

"Nope remember Geri drove twice back to back cause you had that migraine and was getting all sick and shit in the truck," Cindy chimed in after putting her nearly empty martini, glass down on the table.

"What…that was, was…damn!" Mattie said realizing they were right. She shook her head and pressed her lips together.

"If we get our champagne early enough you can have that and a beer or something, you still buzzing from that blunt right?" Geri hesitated as she waved at a couple of the members, she knew that were playing in the band.

"I'd drive but I've already had a double shot of Patron, plus I'll have to drink a little more if I'm going to get up on that stage," she finished.

"So, you are doing something, you' getting yo ass up on stage like in college?" Cindy asked leaning forward picking up the flyers for upcoming events and the itinerary for tonight's event that was sprawled out on the table.

"Yeah, I'm gonna do the open mic, I wrote something about The Creator and Grandma. I was gon tell her before we left but I got nervous about the whole damn thing. But yeah, I think I'm gonna do a lil sumthin sumthin," she was nervous.

"You might not want drink a whole bunch then," Sheila interjected.

"Naw I'm gon get another shot before we get the Moet," Geri replied looking around for one of the three servers assigned to the reserved area. Their table was the fourth table from the entrance. Twelve tables were set up and people were filing in finding theirs. Luckily Geri's table was in the front row, nearly center to the stage. They had great seats.

The band was set up behind the stage on an elevated platform. This was the second weekend the establishment was open and from the fantastic reviews of opening night in the city's newspaper, the word was out that this was the place to be this weekend.

Tonight, was a special night. It was going to be hosted by Kwame Hill, a published author with more than just poetry books on his resume. He was National Poetry Slam Champion two years running, he had played small roles in a few films, and had his most recent book now on the Bestsellers list. His energy and wording would make the night enjoyable. The open microphone allowed people to share their poems, but tonight only a few were selected because of the two headliners. The second featured artist, K'ella, was an outstanding poet and a fantastic singer. She had a song making its way up the Rhythm and Blues Charts.

"Sorry to keep you ladies waiting. I'm Kendal and I'll be serving you all this evening," he said as he showed them the bottle of champagne he carried behind his back. He had a server's apron around his waist.

"This is your complimentary bottle ladies," he paused as he popped the cork. He poured each champagne glass halfway before sitting the bottle onto the table in a container of ice.

"May I bring you ladies anything else, something from the kitchen maybe?" he asked.

"Five shots of Silver Patron and a Corona light," Mattie answered.

"And bring a basket of chips n salsa, actually bring all that and an appetizer sampler too." Sheila said.

"Do you want to run a tab?" he asked.

Cindy smiled at Geri and nodded towards the bottle. It was a bottle of 'Dom Perignon'; a much higher quality of champagne than Moet.

"Here you go," Sheila said handing him her credit card.

"Thank you, I'll put the order in for appetizers and get your drinks to you," he excused himself. He was six feet tall with broad shoulders. His waist was tapered but his legs looked strong. Just a shade darker than Mattie, the contrast of his light hazel eyes with his dark hair gave the impression that he was mixed.

Nearly all the reserved tables were full, and the standard tables towards the back of the room were taken. The capacity of the building was three hundred and forty -five people but with VIP closed people were finding a spot anywhere they could.

The band was now engaged, playing J. Cole's song 'Middle Child' and a few couples were dancing throughout the room. Cindy leaned forward to make sure she was heard above the music.

"Damn Geri that ain't no damn Moet that Max sent over, Dom P," she said turning the bottle, so everyone could see the label.

"Damn," Mattie said taking a sip.

"Don Pa right on" she finished as they all started laughing.

"He still ain't gettin no yum yum from me," Geri said. It was a nice gesture by Max, but she had read somewhere that "presents aren't promises', so even as she accepted it and they drank down the bottle, she didn't take the position that she owed him anything.

"Somebody got some yum yum while I got some dumb one," Sheila said as Geri laughed with her.

"Let's get some drinks in us before we start hearing all

the nasty things our parents never told us about," Cindy interjected. Mattie didn't let the point be overshadowed with the joking.

"Make sure you thank him at least," she reiterated as the lights begin to dim on the stage.

A man walked on stage casually and just began talking.

"Alcohol and liquor, weed and bud," he said loudly tapping his fingers on the microphone.

"Alcohol and liquor…weed and bud…!" he repeated a second time, but louder than the first. The background conversations began dwindling as their attention focused to the stage. The band was now playing softer but still carrying a rhythm.

"Alcohol and liquor…weed and bud!" He said so loud that everyone stared at the stage.

"I thought that would get y'all attention, and if any of you law abiding citizens here in Columbus got any of the later, please meet me outside on the patio," he said as the crowd laughed.

"Tonight, we have the perfect event of spoken word, poetry and a live performance by one of my faves, K'ella, she is in the building with some blazin word and song. I wish I could sing or play an instrument like them back there getting down, in fact give it up to the band, these muthafucka's been playing some good shit all night, so give it up to em," he paused as most people applauded.

"For those of you, who may not be familiar with me, I'm Kwame Hill and I'll be your host tonight. Throughout the night we'll have an open mic session, so if you had wanted to do a piece tonight and you haven't submitted your name hold your hand up," he said pointing his index finger like he was counting.

"Ok, so that's nine people, well you nine are Johnny Come Lately, what's y'all excuse, y'all all ride together or sumthin," he said stepping away from the mic like he was laughing at his own joke.

"Nah I'm just bullshittin, tonight's open mic portion is a little different than the usual venues. Tonight, with the help of a few people, we've narrowed the open mic down to five people, and each one of the five poets has been notified. They'll have five minutes to showcase their work, so our main features can bless you with their talents. The sandman ain't in the building, but I promise you if any of the open mic participants get long winded, I got it under control," he pointed at the sound man who turned his mic off and then back on.

"So, any of y'all who think you gon be," he kept talking as the sound technician kept turning the mic on and off.

"I'll pull your cord," he finally said waving at the sound man to leave the microphones channel open. People were laughing with him in the audience.

"We're gonna get started in a little bit so get all your drinks and grub so you won't be interrupting the performances, like Erika Badu said 'we artists and we sensitive about our shit', and tip y'all servers tonight, they gon be working like crazy slaves to make sure you have a great time so take care of them…and Max you've done a wonderful job making this event happen. So, give it up to Max and the servers and one more time for the band, and fuck it give it up to yourselves cause you coulda been anywhere else other than here!" he finished clapping and pointing all directions across the room before walking off the stage. The band started playing again and more people moved towards the bar area.

"He seems like he'll be a good host," Cindy said sitting back in her chair to bob her head with the beat of the music as Kendal returned with the five shots of tequila and the beer for Mattie.

"He's been featured on Def Poetry twice and travels across the country. National media just came out with the twenty most influential artists of last year, and he was the only poet on it," Geri said reaching out for her shot glass.

"Damn I ain't never heard of him," Mattie said leaning forward with her shot of Patron extending it to the center of the table to make a toast. She had to drink early and cut herself off in less than an hour.

"Well to five bad ass women and to Geri's hook up," Mattie said raising her glass.

"And to Geri slaying em tonight," Cindy added and then the five women tilted their glasses back.

Geri hadn't performed any of her work since senior year in college. She had suddenly stopped performing about the same time she stopped modeling, the only reason she had ever given was that she was a better writer than performer. Neither Mattie nor Cindy ever really understood because she was excellent at both. Whatever the catalyst for tonight, Mattie didn't care. She was grateful that Geri was going to share her gift again.

"Ladies, here's your chips and salsa, appetizer sampler," Kendal said as he returned placing the chips and salsa closest to Mattie. He put the sampler platter in the center of the table. "Give me a second and I'll bring some plates, would anyone like water?"

"Yes, five waters and a bunch of napkins," Sheila answered staring at him for a second longer than before.

"Ok, I'll be right back," he turned and walked away.

"I'm glad he's got his nails clean," Michelle said taking a bite of her lime again.

"Hell yeah, I woulda tol his ass too, I woulda been like damn you need to go wash yo shit," Cindy said. Mattie and Sheila laughed leaning into each other.

Michelle thanked the ladies for making sure she got out again and spoke about how Henry had been under pressure from a triple homicide case that sparked an eruption of city-wide violence.

Geri seemed to be saying something under her breath, but no one could hear what she was saying

"What the hell are you mumbling about?" Sheila asked.

"Just going over my piece in my head, I'm nervous as fuck, you have no idea; these are world class poets, world class." Geri said nervously taking a sip of champagne.

"You're world class," Mattie interjected.

"At least that's what ole boy told you in college, you got world class pussy," Mattie started cracking up at her own joke.

"She is world class," Cindy said slurring her words slightly as she leaned forward.

"Don't even think about it, you've gon over it a million times already bein the perfectionist that you are, fo real girl," Cindy finished just as Kendal returned with the small plates, water and napkins.

"Plates and extra napkins, I grabbed some wet naps from the back in case y'all get a little bit under y'all nails," he smiled and pulled out straws from his serving apron.

"Anything else you need for right now ladies?" he asked taking a quick look around the table to end up on Mattie.

"Nope we're good," Michelle said tossing her lime onto the saucer.

"Well I'll keep checking back on you, oh, and I may be performing tonight if I'm lucky. If so, we already worked it out to have someone take care of your needs if I'm unavailable," he shook his hands once again as if asking 'anything else' before walking to another table he was responsible for.

"World class poets? he serving us and he's world class. Geri you better get up there and do yo thang… slay em!" Cindy was getting excited and had been louder than previous. She took a couple of chicken wings and onion rings off the sampler platter.

"I don't know about putting all that on your stomach beforehand though." Mattie said watching Geri slam on a few mozzarella sticks.

"I know, I know, I'll just drink a beer with you because I am already buzzing. I probably shouldn't have smoked and drank, I don't want to be slurring like Msh. Champsion," she said, and they all started smiling at Cindy.

Cindy gave them the middle finger while dipping her wing into the ranch dressing.

"I got the damn munchies," before licking her fingers. The lights began to dim, while the band decreased the sound of their playing, and the spotlight focused on the microphone stand. Some sort of African drum, maybe a Congo, was being played overshadowing the band but it was on beat with the music. Kwame walked back on stage with his arms raised above his head.

> *"Who has experienced a more traumatic ordeal than our ancestors? It's been nearly five hundred years of enslavement in a foreign land of digression, learned to be slaves by suppressors who ripped us from the first land that The Creator made fruitful and although the exact numbers we may never know, I am sure that the long tow across the Middle Passage of an evil destitute system, is a timeless testament to The Creators' true soulful rhythm. They said that one third survived, so that must mean two thirds died and if twenty million were captured, then nearly six point three million survived and heard the song of an unpleasant rapture,"*

Kwame's words flowed effortlessly with the sound of the drum. He spoke of the Middle Passage and how dead African bodies were covered under insurance, and how Africans were traded for rum and molasses or other commodities. But it was the ending line of the poem that made people think

"*And honestly I'm not bitter in this hour, because some hands of Africans also played a part, which makes the taste more than plain sour it makes it insipid and somewhat bittersweet,*" when he finished, he had painted a visual picture for everyone to follow with each word he had spoken.

"I wrote that in response to hearing about the Holocaust repeatedly, repeatedly, and how Jewish people say never again. For you people that think it was all made up, the Holocaust was real, but so were our ancestors' trials. In any sense both acts were extremely in-humane and we need to remember where we've been," he paused as if he was contemplating something.

"Okay, now that I got my angry black man piece over with. What's up Co, we gon start this off tonight with open mic. To the late stragglers as I stated earlier, the open mic will be different. The chosen poets have been told and they're ready to do their thing. Please give em your attention and be courteous. Our first poet to the stage is from Dayton, Ohio," he hesitated again like he was figuring something out,

"…ain't that an hour away from here?" he asked.

After receiving a few responses from the audience, a

woman called out 'naw it's about an hour and a half away.'

"What's one and a half hours away Alex?" Kwame said repeating it and smiling. As more people caught on that he was referring to Jeopardy, the more people began laughing.

"So, from one hour and thirty minutes away we have Jessimen, so give it up for Jessimen," he finished by clapping his hands and wishing her good luck as they passed on stage.

Jessimen took the stage saying she was grateful to have the opportunity to share the stage with so many talented artists. And she hoped the audience would enjoy her piece. She advised them that it had been inspired by President Barack Obama during his first campaign compared to the current holder of The Oval Office. She had the guitar player strum a melody as she spoke. Her content was good, but her deliverance was off slightly. Overall, she gave a solid performance.

Kwame introduced the next two poets who performed before a brief intermission.

"When we come back, we'll have our last two artists share with you, and please don't forget to tip your servers. They bustin they ass to make sure you have an enjoyable night, so don't be skimping out on the tip, if you ain't got enough to tip then have one less drink…and who out there gon get yo boy a drink? I'm just bullshittin my drinks are on the house. But before we take a break, I'm gonna leave you with something to think about, so hold onto your purses and close yo eyes," he paused laughing

"I'm serious close your eyes. Y'all know at some point in Earth's history all the continents, the land masses were connected. They said Atlantis was a great nation with hidden secrets. Although nothing has been found to support the claims, Atlantis remains part of a variety of myths across the planet. The past always leaves a trail, a path to follow, thus I have entitled this The Path Remains Out There," and before starting his poem, he told the band this would be done acapella.

"The water fell beyond both valleys and the sand it gave way to shore. It was a secret rendezvous outstretching Mali near the heart of Atlantis and under its pounding core. Black maidens danced feverishly to drips of rhythmic vibes and the nomads waded tediously in order to survive. The wisdom of the Elders followed the path of those yet to come, nocturnal dreams of knowledge where swallowed while rivers joined the sound of shallow drums…"

The poem went on for a while and when Kwame was finished people began clapping.

"Thank you, good people, after a brief intermission we'll have two more poets before our features, and yes I am one of the features…ye ah, so get your drinks and grub, cause once we get started again we gon ride this muthafucka out." he said before walking off the stage imitating how children play 'choo choo train' and nodding at the band to start playing again.

CHAPTER 10
SPOKEN WORD AND POETRY

"Those first three poets were pretty good, but Kwame had some verbal skills. His delivery is perfect, and his flow is smooth. I bet he has a mouthpiece on him that work like a machine," Cindy said following him with her eyes to the bar where he and Max were talking.

"Yeah, I can see how polished he is; I bet that more than half of these people up in here had they eyes closed…that was slick as hell," Sheila added taking Mattie's champagne glass from her to drink down the rest. Sheila wasn't an alcoholic, but she loved alcohol, and once she got started, she would mix drinks.

“Shit it was more than half,” Mattie said as a matter of fact while she looked around for Kendal. She was hoping to order another beer but thought against it since she was the designated driver and she still had a buzz. Mattie didn’t mind Sheila taking her drink, truth was champagne made her feel sick in her chest.

“You think you gon be next?” Michelle asked Geri who was back to mumbling with her lips.

“Probably so and I got butterflies in my stomach. I need another drink,” she answered taking hold of the champagne bottle.

“No Geri, you don’t, you can have the rest when you’re done, and I’ll buy you another shot but ya can’t have it right now,” Mattie said wrestling the Dom Perignon out of her grasp.

“That’s fine you’re right. I don’t know what could have possibly possessed me to agree to do this tonight,” Geri said sitting upright in her seat crossing her legs. Her hands were sweating but they felt cold.

“Just get it together and represent,” Sheila said touching

her on the shoulder as she stood up.

"Bathroom?" Michelle asked waiting for a response from someone.

"Yeah I'm coming with you," Cindy said as Sheila also joined them walking away with Michelle, leaving Geri and Mattie at the table.

"Breathe and relax, you gon do fine, you were the shit in college…jus like riding a bike," Mattie told her watching people swarm the bar area. People were engaged in conversation talking about the performances and how nice the place was set up. Some others seated in the reserved area were talking about the host and the three performers already done.

"He real nice and I kinda liked the first and third person. That second poet was just yelling, he probably shouldn't have been yelling so damn much," a woman's voice said but Mattie couldn't make out who said it.

"Either that or not drank as much as he did, don't y'all think he was drunk?" A man's voice was heard next.

Mattie saw it was an older man wearing a light weight black fedora talking at the table behind her. A woman chewing on onion rings was sitting next to him and two other men were standing at their table.

"Y'all think he was drunk?" The woman asked with her mouth wide open full of food.

"Hell to the yeah, he was gone," the man said who was sitting down. Mattie looked closer and saw the wedding band on his hand and figured it was nice to see older married couples still getting out on dates.

Mattie let that conversation slide away from her attention and found Kendal was taking off his apron walking to the bar. He looked over and saw Mattie staring at him, so he smiled. She smiled back. He then gave his apron to one of the bartenders who placed it under the cash register. When he turned back around, he noticed Mattie still looking his way, so he walked back to her table.

"Is there anything else I can get you all? I think I'm next, but I can get an order right now and send it in beforehand, I think I've got time," he asked both women but clearly his focus was on Mattie.

"No, we're good for now," Geri answered looking up at him taking a break from rehearsing her piece. She caught the tail end of a little eye play and silent dialogue between the two.

Kendal wiped the bottom of his lip, indicating to Mattie that she had something to wipe off hers.

“Thanks Kendal.”

“No problem,” he replied but he hesitated as if was choosing what to say next.

“I'll be back to finish serving you, I mean your table ladies,” he said slightly blushing as he walked away.

“Damn you got him falling over his words,” Geri told Mattie while she took a sip of Sheila's champagne.

“One little sip ain't gon kill me,” She acknowledged Mattie who was shaking her head before replying.

“I think he's more nervous than you are,” Mattie stated, attempting not to watch him walk away, but he was a handsome guy and seemed somewhat different.

“Ooh Mattie, you were checking that ass out,” Geri said turning to see where Kendal had gone. Mattie didn't respond to her statement, instead she changed the subject.

“Max has got a good idea of what this city needs, this event is on point. Next time we go somewhere I'm getting an entire bottle of something to myself too," she said scooting Cindy's chair under the table as two servers carried trays of food to the table where the married couple were sitting. For the next ten minutes Mattie let Geri silently recite her poem in her head and wondered why Kendal had her attention. He was courteous and handsome, but it was something else she couldn't pinpoint.

Sheila and Cindy were walking back to their table talking loudly with each other, as Michelle spoke with a group of people she knew before returning to their table.

"Oh, my gawd, some chick is in the bathroom damn near passed out in the stall with vomit all over the place and her punk ass dude was on the outside yelling at her for embarrassing him. If he was any type of man, he woulda been in there helping her, instead of having other people take care of his broad," Sheila said sitting back down at the table.

"What?" Mattie asked making sure she understood.

"Some woman was on her hands and knees, leaning against the stall in the bathroom all sick and vomiting. She was throwing up in the toilet, on the toilet, on the floor. They closed it down after pulling her out to clean it up. We had to use the dude's bathroom," Cindy said pausing shaking her head.

"I don't know what her dude's problem was yelling at her and shit. Max had security carry her outside and her sorry ass boyfriend is at the bar, tacky ass fucka," Cindy said.

"Max just put her out like that?" Geri asked with her eyebrows squinted because she didn't think he was cold hearted like that.

"He called her a cab but she ass out on the curb," Sheila answered before sipping on her warm champagne.

"Where's our waiter Kanye East, I need some OJ or something, this shit is all warm now, was gon make a Mimosa," Cindy was saying as Geri interrupted her

"Oh, you mean Kendal, Mattie's new eye candy?" Geri said snickering.

"Huh…yeah Kendal, where is he?" Sheila asked again looking around searching for him.

"He's by the bar but I think he's actually performing next," Sheila pointed towards where he was standing speaking with Kwame. From the looks of it, Kendal and Kwame were friends or had known each other as Kendal laughed and punched him playfully in the shoulder.

"Damn, I honestly thought he was fucking with us, he was serious about it. I hope his shit is better than that second clown, that dude needed to call it quits," Cindy said reaching for a napkin to wipe off the water on the table from the ice evaporating out the glass.

"You're talking about the first dude, second poet, right? Hell yeah that fool was on some shit, what the fuck was he even talking about, the black hole of sector eight and some shit," Sheila said laughing as the lights began dimming again.

"Alright we gon keep it moving. This next brotha I've known for about four years, he's a talented artist who has placed in regional poetry slams on the west coast…and if he got a couple of his new CD's with him make sure you cop one. I'm telling you he may be the next Paul Laurence Dunbar or Khalil Gibran. I have no idea what he's gon be doing but whateva it is, please welcome Kendal to the stage," Kwame stepped back from the mic and gave Kendal dap before stepping off the stage. "Thanks, thanks, well I hope you all enjoy this. I'm gonna do something a little bit different tonight. Kwame always says get out your comfort zone and dare to be bold, so tonight I'm gonna freestyle a piece. With so many beautiful people in here, they say there's someone for everyone. So, I've been inspired you know by the most stunning woman I've seen.

> *"Standing in this moment right before my thoughts hit the air, I was caught by surprise by a quick silent stare. You see right here in this moment, I've watched you...eat...drink...smile and speak with others and even now I simply want to know what you think. So I paid closer attention to the thoughts your eyes made and what your posture portrayed. I watched the magnificence of you travel from your hair to your legs. Then I had to help take the money, you know, laugh tell jokes to those coming in...I even said something funny although my attention was divided. The words of wisdom were being spoken and the background talk from the tables was subsiding. Through the poet's conversation you traversed away to face and hear the presentation, in a few mere moments my ideas traveled faster than the speed of life because you were already demonstrating, that by your presence I had been affected, without dialect or even digestion...yet does a goddess have to speak to truly be infectious. So, I sat without a word from lips, my eyes would slowly shift from the poet on stage to the next verse in your page. Fantasy or fiction I'm*

reading and writing. Vying my time until I can hear you say hi my name is Hauset or Isis. My crisis is my patience in being impatient because I see that the quality of your soul and the essence of who you are…are not separate.

I've noticed you because you're noticeable but for the past couple hours all these cats keep walking back and forth trying to decide if you're approachable. But like I said I've peeped yo style and saw why all those other dudes quit, cause they came at you like you were common and saw yo shine they didn't know how to adjust they spit. I recognize the queen in you the goddess that The Creator made, the Anaksanamun from way back in brother Imhoteps days. The energy of your essence in infinite and from the longing in your eyes…mentally…spiritually…physically no one has yet to penetrate who you are really way deep down inside. So now I see your dilemma, like tonight is this the place you really should've came, cause every question posed so far has probably been… hey baby can I get yo name? When no games allowed, I already know is your motto, cause I've seen all the balla's and hustla's approach you with the Dom P and Cristal bottles. So, before your answer is given on whether or not you should leave and dip...take one mo shot for the road and pull out the keys to yo whip. Relax my queen I only want to know a part of who you are and if we share the dialogue of gods' I'll get your name as I walk you to your car. Who am I, I'm the substance of obsidian and the black seed of humanity. People may talk bad about us behind our backs, but we won't hate because after all we're all family. Would that get me a grin, am I breaking through your smile prohibition, well while you're open to thought let me tell you I'm diggin every last idea of all the thoughts we have yet to mention. I come straight at you because crooked lines don't fit and I was made to be vertical. Everybody keep speculating about what's the deal but I have heard of you. Finer than Halle Berry, Lupita Nyng'o and Jada Pinkett too and I pray as we enjoy conversation that you are as deep as Queen Maya Angelou. There are different levels and different planes. I don't have tactics or play childish games. I only have one purpose therefore a simple plan to be the alpha male that I am and a God -fearing man. So tell me should I come back to your table or head straight back to the bar. Perhaps I'll just introduce myself to you personally first...I'm Kendal ...and you are?"

When he finished, he received a standing ovation. The applause was so grand that it drowned out the band who was playing full bore. Kendal attempted to walk off the stage, but Kwame grabbed him by the shoulder and pulled him back.

"Give it up for Kendal, man that was fire. So, who's the lucky woman?" Kwame asked putting Kendal on the spot joking with him.

"Naw I'm playing but whoever might have his attention keep it real cause he's a real good dude and loyal cat..., seriously give it up for Kendal again," he said acting as if he was pushing him out the way.

"Alright I told you we gon keep taking it higher with every piece...let's see who we got next on the mic...Geri, we got Geri coming to the stage," he said.

Geri had already left the reserved tables when Kendal was being introduced. As she walked on stage the silence returned, until a male's voice broke through it.

"Damn, that's a bad ass white girl!" He shouted.

"Hell yeah," Kwame said as he introduced her again.

"Geri," he said walking off the stage backwards like he was still checking her out shaking his head in disbelief.

"Wow," she said shaking her hands at her side to loosen up.

"As y'all can probably tell ya girl is nervous up here, especially after following Kendal, that was so…so original," she said adjusting the microphone down slightly.

"I wrote this poem primarily for The Creator, but a large portion is meant for 'our' grandmother," she paused to point in the direction of the reserved table where her friends were sitting. She took a step back away from the microphone to tell the band to wait before playing. Turning back to the mic she stated the name of the poem was entitled 'Impossible…Impossible."

"How can I escape when you have yet to confine me...In the eyes of my mind you have bound me without restraint for I am willingly committing to sand less dunes and water less dams and only the shadows of your forest. Should I await the sounds of your approval or simply commit to find the submission in which the subtleness of

the control you have over me resides. Incredibly you are proving my ego forgivable while providing the path of remarkable circumstance by pulling forth my full potential out of what was once a half empty glass. Opportunity is now here, once it was nowhere, yet in the steps of love you freed me of what I had once believed were inconsequential actions and decisions, now each step is weighed and measured but not out of fear of being free yet from the expectation of being loved freely. Like each leaf of a branch and each branch of the trees lives because the trees roots are pulling from the soil, so have you been my soil and my sun, beneath and above and in between I was. A mere shadow of The Greatest Silhouette that each soul seeks silently; openly...hoping that the answer is as valid as the question asked, praying that it's received before another self- imprisonment where mediocrity distances the connection and weakens the power struggling to find its' path. Do I love you, as much as a flake of snow gaining its freedom through descending or a blade of grass welcoming its first drop of rain. It is my purpose, therefore it is also my choice and thus you have become a part of me as equivalent to my first thought of my last thought. I breathe you and exhale us only to take in another portion of sustenance...of nourishment to maintain my existence. Without you I am like water without a source; impossible to exist, impossible to flow through a universal pattern between Mars and Venus or a collage of planets rotating without their sun."

Geri said the poem passionately and confidently. Her voice carried clearly through the speakers, but she wasn't yelling like the second performer had. She was living each word. Her physicality was what had drawn the crowd's attention at first, but she spoke so beautifully, and the poem was crafted with meaningful metaphors that brought the audience in.

She hadn't realized that she had her eyes closed until she opened them; she had also forgotten that she was on stage in a room full of people. The band hadn't struck up one single note to accompany her.

"Thank you," she concluded and began walking off the stage. It wasn't until she turned that the applause came. It was overwhelming; an appreciation of her performance and words. Next to Kendal the audience seemed to appreciate her work.

"Damn Co, y'all got some talent in this city. Geri bring that ass, I mean yo self, back over here." Kwame said reaching out for her hand grinning.

"This woman has helped raise consciousness against the injustice against people of color. She is the Founder of "Under The Sun" she's one of the good human beings please keep supporting her. Queens and Kings give it up for Geri one mo time," he finished letting go of her hand.

"Damn she fine, ain't y'all glad y'all came out tonight? Honestly, after Kendal's joint, I was like damn somebody gotta follow that, I'm glad I ain't next…but Geri good job, good job," he said looking out into the crowd like he was searching for someone.

"Hey, where's Kendal…Kendal where he at?" he asked asking for crowd participation to find his buddy.

"Yo, Kendal is that who got you wide open? Because after that piece you might have to fight a couple dudes and women off," he paused hearing someone let out a loud gasp.

"Oh, damn I ain't in San Fran am I …I'm just playing up here, don't be getting all crazy and shit on me Columbus,

Ohio," he laughed again loudly through the mic.

"Ok so now we're gonna get to the meat and potatoes portion of the show. Let me tell you a little bit about our second feature first though. She's not only a world class poet, but a songstress. I'm sure y'all don heard her joint on the radio…she's gone be giving a little set after her poems or maybe she just wanna sing tonight…in any event I'll be doing a few pieces. Now don't get it twisted, I've been told I'm long winded. So, don't be over there hitting the mute button and shit," He smiled pointing in the direction of the sound booth.

"But seriously, must I perform with the strength of a quiet storm, a silent storm...born to spread thoughts through this human's chaotic form, or will I be torn between histories rung of tempting tongues only to yell backwards at the mystery hung…"

Chapter 11

Intoxicating

Geri was being congratulated on the way back to the reserved table from some of the other patrons.

A couple of guys were trying to holler at her, but she kept moving back towards the reserved area without making eye contact to anyone. Geri was wearing one of her classic black pants and white blouse outfits with her hips and breasts standing out showcasing her curves. She heard the same man's voice as earlier saying.

"Shit fuck dem Kardashian broads," he said loudly in a joking manner.

"Damn that was really good, granny is gone love that, we recorded yours and Kendal's," Mattie stood to give her a hug and props as she neared the table.

"Hell yeah girl that was way, way better than I… I thought it would be…that was bomb," Sheila said before Cindy congratulated her too trying to form one sentence out of what she was attempting to say.

"It was ok, I wasn't slurring my words or anything like this hooker right here?" Geri asked taking the rest of Cindy's drink.

"Hell yea, yea you was good, you was fan…fantabulous," Cindy smiled.

"Damn, I wanted sum OJ, where's his ass at anyway, he doing his thang up there, but til he gits his big break dat dude need to be doin his ji zob." She finished slightly sarcastic, letting out one big exhale.

"You should've told him you wanted OJ when you ordered the fourth round of shots, plus y'all keep mixing all that shit y'all gon be sick as hell." Mattie responded evenly staring at the stage listening to Kwame, who had just finished with his first piece and was getting the band ready for his second poem.

"Fourth round…y'all had two more shots?" Geri asked.

"Hell yeah, they yours…and you did real good Geri," Cindy said pointing in the direction of two shot glasses with tequila in them. Geri took one shot and set back in her chair to listen to Kwame perform his second and third poems flawlessly. He had clarity of words and perfect delivery.

He was seasoned as a veteran story teller and his voice didn't falter like three of the open mic poets. The content of his words was full of meaning and symbolism. Although he only had intended to do three pieces, he ended up doing four and each poem led into the theme of the one following it. It was more of a staged dialogue, like a one person play that he performed. It took him a little over thirty minutes to finish, but when he did, he received a standing ovation. Kwame had just painted a visual picture with his words that had texture and depth to his content.

"Thank you, CO," he hesitated looking down at Max who was waving at him. Once they had each other's attention, Max began tapping his watch and showing both of his hands to indicate to Kwame to take a brief intermission. Whether it was because he wanted to maximize his profit at the bar or because K'ella wasn't prepared yet, he didn't know.

"So, we're coming up on the grand finale, y'all doing ok?" he asked pausing to let them answer.

"Good, good…y'all been an excellent crowd and it's been cool to share with y'all tonight but we're gon take a quick, and I do mean quick ten-minute break before we bring K'ella up to do her thing," he said before excusing himself.

"What time is it?" Sheila asked pulling her cell phone from her purse. She ended up answering her own question though.

"Damn it's close to one o'clock," she said putting the phone away.

Is it after midnight fo real, time been flying." Geri commented after downing her second shot of Patron left on the table.

"Ladies I apologize for the delay," Kendal said as he approached their table with a female waitress standing with him.

"This is Char, she's gonna finish up taking care of your needs, I wanted to introduce her, and I also wanted to know if anyone wanted a CD of some of my work?" He asked taking a disc out from his slim black leather attaché bag strapped across his back.

"Who does that?" Cindy asked out of the blue.

"Who leaves in the middle of work? I don't know what type of tip you expect to get now when you ain't even done serving us, you was at fifty-percent," Cindy added tapping her empty shot glass on the table. She was still slurring so it wasn't clear if she was trying to be sarcastic or funny, but in her drunken stupor she couldn't fathom why he was leaving before the night was over.

"Oh no, I just came in to help Max out, as far as the tip if you don't mind, just give it to Char. I don't work for Max. Oh lord I don't think I could take it," he paused laughing. "...I was just lending a hand because three of his workers he hired this week didn't show up."

"Well anyways I don't want to interrupt you all, I just wanted to introduce Char...oh and Geri that piece was so intimate, you did awesome," Kendal said complimenting her.

"Thanks man, but what you did, off the top of your head like that, it was fluid, romantic with content and history mixed all together...nice," Geri paid the compliment back feeling the effects of the last shot of Patron.

"You know I'll take one of your CD's, how much are they?" Geri asked reaching into her purse to pull out some money.

"For performing artists, I give em a copy for free," extending her the disc.

"Now don't be making all types of copies for everybody" He chuckled while Cindy carried a sidebar conversation with Char, ordering more drinks.

"Hold on…Geri you want another shot?" Cindy asked.

"No, I just want a Corona," she answered. Char walked away to get the order filled, but the women weren't done with Kendal.

"So, Kendal, out of curiosity who was you talkin about up there? All intimate and personal and shit, we ain't gon tell nobody," Sheila asked him slowly, attempting not to slur her words like her friend. Kendal simply shook his head like he wasn't giving up that information.

"Oh no…no, you're not getting that until I have a title for it, plus I have no idea what I was really saying. I was just caught up in the moment," he paused appearing to be changing topics.

"I've been serving your table drinks all night, but you barely drank anything," he said talking to Mattie directly. She was paying attention to the entire dialogue but hadn't joined in because she didn't have anything to say until now.

"I'm the designated driver tonight."

"Oh, that's real, I wish more people took it as serious as you all do. What's your name?" he followed up.

"I'm Madison," she answered looking at him. His eyes were light hazel with a mixture of green and he had perfect kissing lips. His demeanor would've placed him around forty years old, but he looked like he was in his early thirties.

"Madison, like Madison Square Garden or James Madison, it's a beautiful name. It fits you perfectly. Would you mind if I named that poem after you?" he asked, and in that moment, he was tuned completely into her and her response. It was out in the open now. Sheila had the answer to her question.

Mattie was shocked, she had no idea that he was talking about her on stage. She had captivated him to do something different, something vulnerable that had taken him out of his comfort zone, and he had succeeded. The silent strength in his question, along with the hidden suggestion of more dialogue between the two would also be answered with her response.

"Did you really just make that up or were you acting to draw us into you?" Mattie asked him because she wondered if he was trying to play her.

"Madison, that was new I just made it up, it wasn't an act, I wasn't thinking about how everyone would take it," he responded smoothly.

"Then yeah that's fine, you can name it after me," she finally answered him while reaching out to shake his extended hand.

"Thank you, if you don't mind, I'd like to give you a gift in exchange for your generosity," he paused reaching into his black bag. He pulled out a small paperback book.

"This is more of my work, I mean, stuff I've already published. I only have three of them left in print, but this one is yours Madison…hold on let me sign it," he said pulling a silver and black Cross Ink Pen from the inside of the bag.

"My email and other contact information are written in there. Anytime…feel free anytime to call or email…text," he said laughing out loud.

"Honestly your presence is intoxicating; I hope you enjoy, Madison…ladies," he finished and walked away with his bag hanging over his shoulder.

Mattie held the book in her hands, but she was stuck watching him walk away again. His legs were firm, and his back and shoulders looked strong, and he was a pleasantly handsome man.

"Damn don't burn a hole in his ass Mattie," Michelle said

"So you's intox…intoxicating…dat was smoove as hell," Sheila said. She had consumed Patron like it was water.

"Hell yeah that was smooth and he's fine Mattie," Geri added sucking on a lime.

Mattie didn't say a word. She wasn't going to be answering questions right now to add to anything they were saying. They were drunk, and she was sober. She didn't want to be the brunt of the conversation now, or on the ride home. Char, the waitress approached the table with the tequila and beer.

"Right on time." Mattie thought silently

"Here you are." Char was down to only serving their table; the other tables Kendal had been serving were being waited on by the other waitresses.

"I didn't know if you wanted to drink out the bottle or if you needed a glass." Char told Geri handing her the Corona and a frosted glass to go with it.

"I've got fresh limes for you," but Sheila and Cindy had already tilted their glasses back. Char put the cup on the table anyways.

"I'll put em right here just in case," she said, taking a step away from the table.

"Char…let me get a Ciroc and Cranberry juice too," Sheila added as the lights dimmed once more on the stage.

"Damn, you ain't gon be throwin up in my whip mixing all that shit," Cindy said.

Kwame was introducing K'ella to the audience and Mattie took that as an opportunity to finally look at the front of Kendal's book. 'Normal Chaos' was the title. She slid the book into her bag with the oils and incense before sitting back to listen to K'ella begin performing. The night was going perfectly…until…

CHAPTER 12

AMBULANCE REQUIRED

"Mat…tie you can smoke tha res of dat blunt if you wan…na," Cindy was trying to say evenly but she was really drunk and so was Sheila. Geri had a huge buzz, but she wasn't quite as inebriated as her two friends. It had turned out to be one of the best 'event nights' in over two years.

"Nah I'm cool, I'll save it for tomorrow," Mattie responded, taking the car keys out of Cindy's hand while walking out the door of the club. It was still favorably warm outside as they walked down the short alley to the back parking lot. Mattie was complaining about how the straps on her new shoes were uncomfortable and digging into the back of her calves.

"I'm taking these hoes off as soon as we get in the car, they're tearing me up," she finished. They would've left twenty minutes earlier, but Max was congratulating Geri, while making moves on her at the same time, figuring she was more vulnerable to his game because she was drunk.

K'ella had performed two poems and then broke out into song. She could sing live, a talent many artists had lost over the years being only studio singers. K'ella was still on stage with the crowd dancing to her songs but Sheila wasn't feeling well so Mattie decided it was time to go.

"Max was basically…basically eating yo pus…pussy." Sheila bumped into Geri for support. She couldn't find the right combination of movements to walk by herself, especially in her heels right now, so she needed assistance for balance.

The back of the building had flood lights on each corner of it, but the city's light poles were dark. The city had not done maintenance or put in new lamps so as they turned the corner, they were simply four shadows walking in the night. Budget cuts were said to be the reason, which many didn't understand with the renovations going on in other parts of the city.

The parking hadn't been filled with new tar for the potholes remaining, so when Cindy started fussing that she almost twisted her foot it was warranted. Mattie hit the alarm on Cindy's keyless remote and watched the lights blink on and off and the horn blow once. That's when she noticed a figure leaning up against the back wall of the building.

It was a male wearing a dark hooded sweatshirt, smoking a cigarette or something that Mattie couldn't make out because his head was hanging. He was leaning with one leg on the wall, but he remained fixed in one spot. His jeans were baggy and sagging. His posture wasn't casual, although he was standing like he was relaxed.

"Tha shits was so freshus, da ho mutha, mutha-fuckin night. Geri…I loves you, your so talen…talented." Cindy tried to bend down to adjust the strap to her sling back shoes without splitting her skirt.

"I think, maybe I love you too," Geri said slurring her words slightly. She was holding Sheila up so she wouldn't tumble and trying to maintain her balance, so she wouldn't fall or trip into a parked car.

Mattie was still paying attention to the hooded male who was now moving slowly in the direction of Cindy's new car.

"This shit better not be happening to us right now," Mattie thought silently as she lifted her purse reaching inside for something.

"Damnit, I left the pepper spray in my other purse…fuck…fuck…fuck," she said to herself silently reevaluating her options. She had a permit to carry a concealed weapon, but she didn't all the time—especially when she was surrounded by her friends.

"Maybe he ain't gon try to do nothing," she kept thinking inside her head. She went from maybe he's an employee taking a break to the probability that it was exactly what she was hoping against; a robbery for their belongings or Cindy's ride.

She thought about saying something to her friends, but they were drunk, and didn't want them acting out if she was wrong creating a scene, plus she didn't want to take her eyes off the man, but maybe that's exactly what they needed some type of commotion. She was thinking faster than she was coming up with answers.

"But he keeps moving with us," she thought. As she

moved to the driver's side door, he had turned down their aisle and let his cigarette fall to the ground.

Cindy and Geri were walking behind the car to the passenger side, while Sheila was leaned against the rear door of the driver's side. That's when Sheila noticed the male and tried to say something. The words stuck in her throat because the alcohol had slowed her reaction.

Then it happened. The hood fell from his head as he reached into his waistband to pull a handgun out.

"Give me yo," he started to say stepping forward. His voice was aggressive like his motion when he closed the distance between himself and the women.

Mattie reacted without thinking. She let her bag and Cindy's keys fall to the ground, and in the next movement she took her right hand and grabbed the male by the wrist of his gun hand to control his motion. With her next movement she turned his wrist outward to get a better striking point to help release the weapon. She struck right above his wrist and the gun dropped to the ground followed by a loud 'pop'. It wasn't the gun being discharged; it was the sound of bone breaking.

"Aagh!" The man yelled, trying to wrestle his arm away,

but the way his shoulder sagged, and his arm was hanging Mattie had damaged it badly.

Cindy and Geri were slow to react because they were still talking about how much fun they had when Mattie was making her next motion. Mattie still held onto the arm of the mugger and shifted her weight, so it would push him into the car. He tried to push back but Mattie kicked him in the back of his knee to help move him off center, breaking her shoe heel in the process. She had to use more position than strength, something she learned from Jiu Jitsu. As he bounced off the car, she was already making another move by holding his arm above her head and then stepping into his side with a viscous elbow right beneath his arm pit.

The screaming from the assailant rang loud into the night. He was scrambling on one hand and his knees trying to get away, but Mattie kept kicking him and stepping back before he could grab her.

Geri had run to the driver's side passing Sheila, who was still leaning against the car trying to stand upright but she was having a hard time. She was, however, screaming now at the top of her lungs for help.

Cindy had fumbled through her purse and was on the

phone with 911.

Geri saw the gun on the ground. She picked it up and pointed it at the man.

"Mattie...Mattie...Madison!" snapping Mattie's focus off the man who she was still kicking on the ground. Mattie stepped back away from him and Geri handed her the gun.

"You better not fucking move muthafucka or I'll blow yo fuckin head off!" Mattie stated as a matter of fact keeping the pistol pointed on him. Her adrenaline was raging through her body and she wasn't feeling fear, she had known this feeling before in Colombia and it was intoxicating. Mattie felt powerful. She had disarmed and subdued him. 'Once you got em down, there's no need to let em up', she thought feeling the grip of the gun in her hand.

Geri stood next to her telling Sheila to stop yelling and calm down. Sheila was still panicking trying to stand upright without help, but Geri wrapped her arms around her so she couldn't move. She didn't want Sheila getting any closer to Mattie while she held onto the gun.

Cindy was on the phone still slurring her words as she explained to 911, they were being robbed. She was raising her voice because the 911 operator was making her repeat herself.

"Where? We're in da fucking parking lot at Da Island, the new club on Fifth…Fifth Ave," she yelled into her cell phone trying to sober up, but she had had too much to drink.

"Don't fuckin tell me to calm down, he tried to rob, send the fuhkin police. He had a gun!" She yelled again at the dispatcher on the other end who had irritated her.

Other people who had filtered out of the club saw what was happening and ran towards Mattie and her friends. Some were already on their cell phones calling 911, and others had run back into the building to get help.

"Damn he look fucked up, y'all whooped his ass," a big boned, light skinned women wearing dark dress slacks and a green blouse said, as the backdoors to the club opened with Max and two of his security guards at his side.

"What the fuck, are y'all ok…any of y'all hurt?" Max said running past the small crowd as police sirens were heard in the back ground coming closer. He hadn't noticed Mattie bearing down on the injured man on the ground until he got closer to the car and heard the man cursing at Mattie.

"You fuck, fucking bitch. I'm gon kill, kill you…you

broke my arm, and my knee," the man said moving gingerly around on the ground. The way he was grunting Mattie may have done more damage than just that.

She was still holding onto the gun pointing it at him. She was tempted to squeeze the trigger. She was mad, upset and angry when she should've been frightened. She was in control. All the times she had wondered what it would feel like to serve justice; not like the kind her mother got, was flashing in her mind holding this criminal's life in the power of her hand. She understood what was keeping her from tightening her finger, but she didn't know why she felt the need to do it.

"Mattie, Mattie you wanna hand me the gun? The police are pulling up and they may think you're," Max was attempting to say when Mattie responded firmly

"No," without emotion keeping the thirty -eight caliber pistol centered on the man on the ground. She wanted to see what a bullet looked like piercing him in the stomach and perhaps the shoulder to watch him bleed out. Mattie could have aimed it at his left hand holding his arm rendering him completely helpless.

Geri stood next to her holding Sheila with one arm and

didn't say a word; she was nervous; speechless and emotional right now. Her thoughts were frantically moving in her head as she watched Mattie keep the gun on the assailant. Her friends had seen Mattie with guns and rifles before. They had even gone to the shooting range with her and she was the best shot of anyone at the range at any time they went. They knew she owned at least two handguns; one was a revolver like the one she held now, but Mattie also had a small stockade of weapons in a storage facility.

Mattie had her finger on the trigger and her eyes fixed on him;

"Eight pounds of pressure and 671 feet per second," the numbers flashed in her mind thinking of the force to squeeze the trigger and how fast the bullet would travel. With a small amount of force and at this range, it would be instant death. She had taken lives before, and this would be no different, except she would be breaking a promise she made to God during her departure from Colombia. A promise given at a time of extreme duress as enemies of her Colombian family attempted to murder all the women of the family during a baby shower. In the end, Mattie rescued David's mother and his niece in the process. The three men sent to murder them however found death at her hands. Mattie understood she could not cross that line in this moment, but she was fighting the urge.

Sheila and Cindy stood behind Max and Geri, but they all looked on as police cruisers pulled up with their sirens blaring into the night until they parked just leaving their lights flashing.

"Mattie, will you at least put the gun down on the car? You know how they are," Max said again pleading with her. It was true, recently the police were shooting first and asking questions second with the deaths of two city police officers in a drug raid over a month ago. Criminals said they had to protect themselves, and the police said they were enforcing the law.

As the first patrol car pulled into the parking lot it was followed by a second. The doors to the first car swung open and both officers had drawn their weapons, already pointing them at Mattie. They positioned themselves behind the doors to their cruisers.

"Ma'am put the weapon down, we're here to help you, but put the gun down," the first cop said driving the car.

"Put the gun down!" his partner yelled out, raising the

tension. One cop was Asian and the other one black. The small crowd gathered started yelling at the police officers escalating the situation. They didn't want an incident in which people had to apologize after the fact like they did when they shot an innocent bystander at the beginning of the year.

The second patrol car had taken a position next to the other one, blocking any exit. The driver got out with his weapon drawn, but the passenger opened his door and slowly started walking towards Mattie and her friends pushing through the small crowd. An ambulance pulled behind the police cruisers.

"They was being robbed, she ain't the suspect," the large, light skinned woman who had commented earlier said pointing towards the man on the ground.

"It's him, him on the ground," other people started yelling at the cops. The assailant was still moaning, he was in more pain than he was angry.

As the officer approached the back of Cindy's car, Max stepped aside to let him pass. Geri looked at him, but she still had one arm wrapped around Sheila, who was now standing somewhat against the car looking on.

"Madison, it's ok, we can take it from here," Henry said standing next to her keeping one eye on the suspect. He turned around and motioned for the officers to lower their weapons still pointed on Mattie.

"Mattie, I need you to hand me the gun slowly. Madison let me do my job," he said again while she turned to look at him.

Henry was there to drive Michelle home and was bumming a ride from his old partner when he wore a uniform. He wasn't always a good guy. Some of his friend's gang banged. He was an athlete growing up in the old neighborhood. Now he was in law enforcement, sometimes arresting his childhood friends when he couldn't look the other way.

"Here," she said as she handed him the gun, he then motioned for the officers to apprehend the suspect who was still grunting and cussing on the ground. Paramedics had walked close to the suspect when they were told it was ok to check his vitals.

"Oh God, oh my God he don't need no damn ambulance send his ass straight to jail!" Cindy started saying loudly, as the ambulance was now rolling equipment towards the criminal.

He did need medical attention; he would be sent to the emergency room for a diagnosis and released into the custody of the officers. Handcuffed to the gurney, he looked more feeble than dangerous.

Officers were now taking statements from Geri and Cindy. Henry was just finishing writing down Mattie's account of what happened while Sheila was over by a trash dumpster throwing up. "Well we have your statements if we need anything is this the best contact number? I mean do you want us calling your cell phone?"

Mattie was still pondering had she known Ronald Jackson's identity before the cops showed up would she have shot him. From early childhood to now she had been taught to respect life, but she learned that some things required justice. It would have been just to kill him for the offenses against humanity.

Mattie could hear the questions being asked all around her as she flashbacked to the first time she issued justice, when she came face to face with bullies. In fourth grade a group of five friends bullied the playground on recess. She had avoided their direct wrath, but one day the two ring leaders pushed her in the lunch line and said they were going to beat her and her friend up after school. Mattie was more upset that they threatened her friend than her. She waited on them to come out, allowed them to talk as they walked towards her, and as the two ringleaders began taking their book bags off, Mattie kicked one in the ribs and choked the other one out banging her head onto the pavement. Three teachers had to pull Mattie off them. The two girls never messed with her again.

"Yeah you can reach me at that number Henry, I don't want them worrying Grandma," she answered him watching her friends standing about twenty feet away from her. Everyone had been separated, a tactic law enforcement used to make sure their stories matched.

"Mattie I'm sure you realize how lucky you all are. You think you all will be alright to drive home, you guys can load up with Michelle and me, are you sure you are ok?" he asked with genuine concern. When she didn't answer he continued with what he had begun to say initially.

"I don't recommend confronting someone with a weapon. Luckily it worked out for you this time." He finished by giving her a hug and walking her towards Cindy.

"No, he's lucky y'all got here when y'all did because I would've beat him with his own gun, pistol whipped him and then shot him without killing him," but she kept it as a thought that pushed back and forth in her mind. She had a rush being in the fight or flight mode again. She felt alive.

"Hank, thank God it was you who showed up," Michelle said, as she and Geri approached.

"Hell yeah, thank God you showed up because Hawaii Five O was escalating shit, can we go!" Cindy said as the two officers arriving first on the scene were walking away from her.

"Yeah you all can get out of here…oh and Mattie, please do me a favor, don't light that cigar until you're away from here. I'll see all of you Sunday at church, all of you," Henry said walking away emphasizing 'all'.

Mattie shook her head acknowledging the favor he had given her. Almost being robbed or carjacked at gun point would make most people want to get somewhere safe and calm down; instead Mattie was wired right now. She walked over to Sheila who was still throwing up by the dumpster. The large security guard who let them into the reserved area was standing near with his back turned to her shielding her from people looking.

"Lala…you ok, we can get outta here," Mattie said navigating through the chunks of wings, salsa and anything else that Sheila had threw up sprayed across the ground.

"Yea…yeah, tell him that I'm ok, I don't need no, no body guard babysit," Sheila tried saying but she started dry heaving.

"I've got her from here, and thanks," she understood that Sheila didn't want him seeing her like this. Sheila liked big dudes and had commented earlier at the table about him, but this wasn't the time.

"Yeah that's cool, you whooped that dude's ass," he said with his deep voice.

"You know what, I ain't even trying to be grimy," he paused again. "Will you give her this when she's better?" he finished by handing Mattie a card before walking away towards the rear entrance of the club where the music had still been playing.

"You ok…ok, Mattie?" Sheila finally got out as she slowly stood up from leaning on her legs with her elbows. She was wobbly but trying to gain her composure.

"I'm cool, just ready to get the fuck out of here, come on girl…can you walk?" Mattie asked letting Sheila lean against her for support making their way back to the car. Mostly everyone was gone except for the big boned woman and her two friends. She said they stayed to be witnesses in case the 'po lice' acted up.

Only one cruiser remained behind, while the other vehicle accompanied the ambulance with the suspect. An officer rode in the ambulance for extra security. The two remaining officers sat with their interior vehicle lights on filling out paper work.

When Mattie walked by the car pulling Sheila, she heard one of the officers speaking to someone on their car radio.

"That woman put a hurting on the guy, his fibula is broken in two places, his shoulder is separated and a few of his ribs are broken…hold on," the female voice said pausing

"You wanna know who she whooped up on…Ronald Jackson…over," the voice finished in a serious tone.

"Yeah we know, she's lucky…over."

"She may end up getting a reward after prosecution, we're gonna be moving him to county after medical determination…over," the female voice was gone now. Mattie nodded at the officers as she passed.

"Thank you…thank you," Sheila said leaning on the rear driver side car door balancing her emotions while being sick and drunk. Geri walked over to help support Sheila, she had taken her shoes off and carried them in her hands.

"I got her, just open the door," Geri said holding onto Sheila. Mattie grabbed the keys from the hood of the car along with her bag of oils and book from Kendal. She hit the remote to unlock the doors, but they were already open. Cindy was on the other side opening the rear passenger door to help slide Sheila in the back seat.

"I'll sit back with…here with her…til us…until we get back to da house." Cindy pushed out verbally before sliding Sheila's seatbelt on before strapping herself in. Geri was still standing outside the car next to Mattie holding her shoes in her hands and shaking her head.

"Mattie, damn you whooped his ass and saved ours." She closed Sheila's door before reaching out to hug Mattie.

"It happened so quickly, I wasn't even thinking," Mattie tried saying but Geri started crying which in turn had her crying too. Both women were emotional as they embraced.

But it was Geri shedding more tears, probably because she was still buzzing.

"Thank you, I'm so glad we're ok, I love you girl. I don't know what I'd do without you…without any of y'all," Geri started saying emphatically squeezing on her friend.

"I love you too but both of us crying right now, all out in public, ain't helping they ass," Mattie pulled away as she pointed to the back seat.

"Yeah, yeah ok you're right. Let's get out of here," she said walking around the car to the front passenger door to get in.

"Damn, can we git this muthafucka moving, y'all crying…she hurlin, and I don't know which one is gon come for me first, can we go?" Cindy asked leaning up against the inside back door. Mattie put the key into the ignition and started the car.

"Oh hell naw!" Mattie said pressing the control to decrease the volume on the radio which was blaring. She turned the CD changer off and put the radio on to a local jazz station. She was just beginning to slowly calm down, her heart rate had lowered. She took one final look through the rear-view mirror and both Cindy and Sheila looked passed out already.

"You want me to light that for you?" Geri asked pulling the lighter from the center console.

"Yeah but hold on, let me hit the expressway first. Henry took my statement and saw that shit in the ashtray. He asked me to hold off til we were away," Mattie answered her. She made an illegal u turn instead of driving down one more block to turn around. When she had just straightened out, another police car was driving in the opposite direction.

"Damn," she thought hoping her luck was still holding. The cruiser kept going.

"No one's driving home tonight. You and Sheila can take the spare room; I'll let Cindy sleep in my bed. I'll cook something in the morning," she said watching different lights speeding up on her tail end suddenly.

"I know they're not coming back for me," Mattie said as the vehicle started blowing the horn to let them pass. As it got closer, she saw that it was a truck. Mattie started to switch lanes, but the lights were moving too fast and the Sport Utility Vehicle was switching into the left lane to pass her, and then sped up before getting back into the far- right lane to get onto the highway.

Mattie had to veer into the other lane as the SUV screeched onto the ramp. It almost flipped over after taking the second curve of the entry ramp doing roughly sixty-five miles per hour.

"Damn, what the fuck!" Cindy said as her head bobbled in the back seat.

"Muthafucka…muthafucka, can we catch a break already?" Geri said holding onto the dashboard and door.

"I'm stopping to get some coffee, you want something?" Mattie asked clearly tensed again as she drove a half mile down the road to a McDonald's restaurant that stayed open twenty-four hours.

"No…I'm good. Stupid assholes are out tonight," she added before lighting the blunt left from earlier. She took a big pull and handed it to Mattie.

"You can kill that, I'm done…if you need me to drive, just let me know," Geri finished slouching down into her seat.

"Nah, I got it," Mattie pulled into the drive thru taking a hit off the blunt as she rolled her window down to order. Right now, she was grateful everyone was safe and quietly resting. She had a twenty five-minute drive. After pulling back onto the road she began playing everything over about the altercation in her mind. "We are so lucky."

As Mattie turned left onto the ramp to the highway, she thought about one of Grandma Redd's favorite sayings,

"The Creator has a purpose for everything and everyone."

Flashing lights were up ahead on the side of the road, the police had pulled someone over. Mattie could make out the truck that had passed her just a few minutes ago parked on the berm and coming up in her rear-view mirror another set of flashing lights. She rolled her window up as she got closer, after passing, she pulled the blunt out of the ashtray again. After one big hit on it, she started coughing.

"You cool?" Geri asked opening her eyes.

"Yeah girl I'm good," She was thinking it strange that after everything tonight, the two close calls that could've turned out way differently than what happened and changed their lives dramatically, Kendal was still in her thoughts.

"Fuck it," she thought as she pushed the power recline of her driver's seat back and put the car on cruise control for the rest of the ride home.

CHAPTER 13

"RUN AND TELL THAT"

It was hot inside the church, and people were waving their small cardboard fans back and forth, but even in the extreme heat the Word the Pastor was preaching had the congregation energized.

"Praise the Lord for the time He carried your burden, when you were unable to. He knows before you do. When the mountain seems too high to climb or too wide to pass…He created the mountain. He created you, so what's a mountain compared to He, who made it. With God leading the way nothing can stand against you, no economic or global recession. When you're right with The Lord you are spiritually wealthy, and that's the one possession that recession can't touch and through the Son and the Spirit all things are possible, so ain't no such thing as a recession with Gods' Children…" he paused taking a step back from the pulpit to spin around with his hand held high on the red carpet.

"I'm gon say it again, ain't no such thing as a recession with Gods' Children," he hesitated again as the congregation let out a few 'preach the word, and yes lords,'

"We've got some saints in here today. I hear y'all and I feel the Spirit of The Lord moving up in here, adding strength and character to these walls…increasing the level of praise reinforces the substance in this hall. He ain't done building His church. Just like The Lord ain't done with us. He ain't done with you, and He sure ain't done with me. He still strengthening me…molding me," he said taking his hands and rolling them together like he was forming something with clay.

"He still strengthening me, molding me…adding pressure where it's needed so I'm not fragile, that's how The Lord loves me, that's how He loves you. Like the pressure needed to make a diamond, what's pressure when you've submitted to the Will of God? Y'all know we got people up in here who going through hard times. Getting they hours cut at work or just flat out losing their job, having them sent overseas…their livelihood, what human being wouldn't feel the pressure from that? Maybe there's somebody in here today getting they car repossessed and their house foreclosed on, tell me what human being wouldn't feel the pressure from that? I've got friends, other Pastors throughout the nation fretting over the doors to their church closing and I've shared tears with them because they are my brothers, so Pastors get emotional too," he hesitated as he took his handkerchief out of his lapel pocket to wipe his forehead.

"They ask me, they say to me…what am I gonna do…what are my members gonna do? I tell em, Praise the Lord…Praise The Almighty for allowing his blessings to come in strange and mysterious ways, we worried about things, and not blessings. We worried about stuff and not purpose. But just like that diamond needed pressure to be formed and, time to make sure that… all the carbon and oxygen interacting between each other was creating that jewel, so is pressure being placed on us to make sure we gon turn out to be the jewels that God intended us to be. Sister Parks is here today, Praising the Lord. Glory be to God. Now Sister Parks you don't mind if I tell them a little bit about your weekend now do you?" he paused waving his handkerchief to signal to the audience.

Mattie hadn't been paying that much attention to Pastor Morris. She was looking at the back of Sister Roger's hair. She was two rows up waving her fan back and forth across her face. Sister Rogers forgot to tuck the price tag of the wig under the lining and now it was dangling down the back of her neck. When her name was called though, Mattie's attention was on the pulpit and she was waving her head yes to his question without fully understanding it.

"Sister Parks and her friends went out on Saturday night," he raised his eyebrows,

"and ain't nothing wrong with congregating respectfully, respectfully" he laughed.

"But Sister Parks didn't know Saturday night she was gon need a blanket of protection. Our city has been plagued recently with crime…house break ins, car-jackings. Well one of the criminals preying on good people, you know on hard working people, tried to rob Sister Parks and her friends, but that criminal didn't know that Sister Parks is a Child of God and she is protected…she protected by the power of The Most High, there is no power higher than that of God, Amen, now needless to say that powerful blanket of protection surrounded Sister Parks and defended her friends. Ronald Jackson will no longer be victimizing any one in our city. As much as law enforcement patrol, they can't cover everywhere all the time, but God's power is everywhere, all the time, so trust in The Lord my brothers and sisters who are feeling the pressure, exhale and let all the nonsense out and God in. Wear your blanket of protection like Sister Parks and her friends," he paused taking a step closer to the three stairs leading down to the left side of the floor out into the congregation.

"And for my fellow clergy members worried about the doors to their churches closing, I've been there. I've had the doors closed on one of my churches before. Saturday night we were scrambling to get all of what we believed to be important out while they put a chain on the front and back door. Sunday morning, we were congregating in the parking lot having service. What I found out that Sunday morning is that it wasn't nothing important in 'my' church, everything that was needed was sitting and standing on the pavement listening to a sermon, and the biggest lesson I learned that Sunday morning," he said, pausing to walk over to the right side of the stage to stand on the second step.

"What I 've learned, and this is for my clergy, is that was never *my* church…it's His Church. "AND I SAY TO YOU, YOU ARE PETER AND UPON THIS ROCK I WILL BUILD MY CHURCH AND THE GATES OF HELL WILL NOT PREVAIL," it's not our church, but His Church. So, no pressure is too great, and no blessing is idly given, so wear your blanket and Praise The Lord. Remain faithful and you don't have to worry about what you losing, instead, think about the powerful blessings that you are going to receive as a Child of God, stop worrying about stuff you can't control. Things that's out of yo hands," the organ player started playing and the choir stood up.

"We worried about a house, and we still got homeless people. We are complaining about not having steak and potatoes when we got people starving. Praise The Lord, run and tell yo friends that you have a blanket of protection, run and tell yo family that He's always there when no one else is. Run and tell em that ain't no power higher than God's, run and tell em." He finished by walking swiftly out into the congregation as the first note to "Run and Tell That" was sung.

Every seat of the church was filled on both the bottom level and the top. Mattie sat with Grandma Redd in a row with Cindy sitting next to her, while Geri sat one row behind them with Sheila and her two kids.

"I thought you said you weren't going to tell anyone," Geri leaned forward over the back pew before standing up. Sheila's kids, Samantha and Darion, were pulling her up to sing with them.

"I didn't tell anyone, the news probably. I got a couple of voicemails from them but I'm not returning their calls," Mattie answered, standing up to join in the song. She was realizing just how lucky they really were because Ronald Jackson was every bit of a violent criminal as there was, he could have shot and killed any one of her sisters.

She was grateful to have been protected and to be able to exercise restraint. Mattie's resolution was that it was God equipping her with what she needed throughout each step of her life.

All the training her father put her through and all the hard work over the years, the life and death situations was God's will. So, Mattie was standing up and singing loudly with her hands raised in the air joining in the Sunday celebration.

Geri was rocking back and forth with Samantha holding

her right hand and Darion her left, singing with everyone else.

Grandma Redd sat at the end of the pew with her wheel chair right next to her in the aisle. She tugged on Mattie's dress to get her attention. "Help Granny up."

She was slow to rise because she had been sitting over an hour and her joints were stiff. Grandma Redd had been in disbelief when she was told about the altercation. Like Mattie promised, she made a nice early breakfast on Sunday morning. Before her grandmother had made her way into the dining room, Mattie told everyone not to mention anything about them getting into that situation after the event. Unfortunately, Grandma Redd had been watching the news and saw a local reporter broadcasting live in the alley behind Da Island about where Ronald Jackson had been apprehended after a night of poetry. Naturally Grandma Redd asked about it at the breakfast table.

Mattie had no choice but to tell her the truth, she never lied to her grandmother, although sometimes she didn't give all the details. Mattie told her it was no big deal, but grandma Redd listed all the crimes Ronald Jackson had been already convicted of; armed robbery, breaking and entering, assault with a deadly weapon. He had been on the run for nearly two months, after allegedly killing a convenience store worker in a robbery. Later, after everyone had gone to get ready for church service, Mattie saw the report again and the newscaster put his spin on what happened; 'Ronald Jackson was apprehended last night…no he was beaten up and given a broken arm and ribs by a woman he allegedly attempted to rob. He was taken to the hospital and later released into police custody…some justice can be ironic.'

As Mattie stood up next to Grandma Redd at church, she felt the wetness on her cheeks. She was crying. Her grandmother reached for Mattie's hand. Mattie felt lonely at times from missing her parents. Regardless of how terrible things had been in the past, she missed them both in her own way. She wondered how things would be different if…

Cindy stood up, she was still queasy from Saturday night. She put her arm around Mattie who now had tears streaming down her face.

"God will protect you; He keeps his faithful servants in His fold." Pastor Morris elevated his voice above the choir who were now humming the song as the band continued playing.

"No weapon forged against you will prosper; God and one man, God and one woman make a majority," he said jumping up and down from the stage to run up the aisle.

"Sista Parks is proof positive this morning that God takes care of his servants," he said touching Grandma Redd and Mattie's hand before running to other members of the congregation.

"So, don't be worrying about no material things or possessions that you can't control, like a house, or a car or a SUV, a house ain't a home anyways, a job ain't a career. So, Praise the Lord for a home…Praise the Lord for a purpose so you will have a career that can't be taken away," he walked back to the pulpit. The choir began singing again, while many members in the congregation were yelling and screaming in agreement. Some church goers were running up and down the aisle screaming hallelujah.

Mattie wasn't crying anymore, she was now singing loudly along with everyone else. Cindy had been singing lowly but something inside her had been moved and she was now 'speaking in tongues,' Grandma Redd was clapping her hands and saying, 'Oh dear God, yes Jesus,' but she was getting a little overwhelmed and needed to sit down to catch her breath.

Pastor Morris was back on the pulpit, two stepping, clapping his hands and singing with the choir. He was filled with spirit; the entire building was filled with spirit, so instead of sticking to the itinerary Pastor Morris made the last forty-minutes a "praise and worship" session. When service was being let out people walked by Mattie hugging her and telling her that "God loves you…and praise God you are safe". Mattie thanked them before wheeling Grandma Redd up the long aisle and outside into the warm mid-day weather.

More people spoke to Mattie as she waited on Sheila to come out. A few older members came to speak with Grandma Redd, complimenting her on her white and gold dress and matching hat. Henry and Michelle were walking towards them with their son following. Grandma Redd took Henry by the hand to thank him. He bent down to give her a hug before responding.

"Grandma, we were just doing our job, and like I told Michelle, Ronald Jackson ran out of favor last night. Your granddaughter not only put a whooping on him, but she helped apprehended a criminal we had been tracking down for over six weeks," he paused as a short older usher asked for his wife's assistance back inside.

"You can leave Jay with me honey," she bent down and hugged Grandma Redd before walking back into the church.

"My daddy said you beat up the bad guy auntie?" Jay said in a questioning tone like he couldn't believe a woman had beat up a man. He was leaning on his father's hip staring up at Mattie.

"Jay," Henry started to say in a disproving tone.

"No, no it's ok Henry. The good guys gotta stand up to bad guys, right?" Mattie asked bending down to the six-year old.

"Yes ma'am, and God don't like when people are bad, that's why my daddy find the bad guys and put em in jail," Jay gripped his father's hand.

"Auntie Mattie, I'm glad you beat up the bad guy," Jay continued as Mattie reached out to give him a hug.

"Oh Hank, you are raising a good boy," Grandma Redd said as she waved at an older couple walking by.

"Thanks ma'am, we're going to get out of here. If Michelle comes back out before I'm back will you tell her I ran to get the car?" He asked rubbing Jay on the top of his head.

"Oh Mattie, we'll need to talk this week sometime, they're putting him on trial and depending on whether he takes a plea, we're not sure about you taking the stand, the good news is, once he's convicted, the twenty thousand-dollar reward is yours," Henry said, before walking across the street to the parking lot holding his son's hand.

Mattie looked around for Sheila but couldn't see her. Cindy was probably home by now, and Geri was still inside talking to a couple of board members, along with Michelle, about surprising Pastor Morris for his birthday with either a night of bowling or a church picnic after service in two weeks.

"Mattie," Sheila approached the group holding Samantha with one hand and Darian with the other.

"Tweetle dee and tweetle dum had to use the bathroom," Sheila pulled her kids into her.

"Mom, that's not funny," Darian said putting his hands into his black trousers trying to be more mature for his mother since the divorce.

"Auntie, how come you were crying today, are you sad?" Samantha asked, pulling away from her mom to walk to Mattie's side to hug her as if she was consoling her.

"Oh no, baby girl, I'm not sad…not at all. I was just crying because God loves us, and I love you," reaching down to tickle Samantha.

"No auntie, auntie," Samantha yelled as she started laughing.

"Madison cut that out, that girl got on her church clothes," Grandma Redd interjected while holding onto her oxygen tank.

"Yes ma'am," Mattie answered respectfully.

"So, Grandma did you enjoy service today?" Sheila asked changing the subject and the attention off Mattie and Samantha.

"Oh Lord yes, Grandma ain't been moved like that in a long time, I'm a lil tired though," the elder woman reached into her purse for a tissue.

Mattie took that as a cue that it was time to leave.

"Let me get out of here, you ready grandma?" Mattie asked giving Samantha a hug and telling Darian come give his auntie a hug.

"Are you coming over today auntie?" he asked looking

up with his eyebrows raised. Mattie was teaching him a few Jiu Jitsu holds and moves so he wanted to get some more lessons.

"Yeah, I'll be over later, are you cooking still today Lala?" she asked.

"I'm gon put some burgers and dogs on the grill and make some potato salad or something," but when Sheila said she was cooking it was typically a full spread. She came from a large family and Sheila was the oldest, so she would cook for her brothers and sisters when her mom worked late.

"Then I will see you later young prince and princess, but I have to go home and clean off my bathroom counter since somebody smeared makeup on my sink," pointing at Sheila for the kids to see.

"Oh alright, I got you, tell grandma and auntie goodbye," Sheila told the kids before they crossed the street to get into their Silver Chevrolet Minivan.

Mattie wheeled Grandma Redd around the back of the building where she parked. Mattie owned a 2017 535ix BMW it was black on black with only eight thousand miles on the odometer. She hardly ever drove it since she lived on the city's bus line route.

"Baby when we get home, you make grandma some tea?"

"Yes ma'am, are you hungry, we can stop for a quick bite while we're out?" Mattie asked pulling out into the street. Geri was just coming out of the building as she passed the glass doors of the church, so Mattie blew her horn as Geri waved.

"No baby, I'm a lil tired, I'm gon lay down and get some rest, and remind me to give you Sheila's blanket before you leave," she answered leaning back in her seat closing her eyes.

Mattie put the gospel station on her satellite radio. "I won't complain" was playing. Mattie felt emotional again, so she reached out and held onto her grandmother's hand.

The drive wasn't long, usually on a weekday, traffic would be backed up due to rush hour or people shopping at the outlet mall, but it was just a little after noon on Sunday. In an hour the street would be jammed with people trying to find bargains.

Mattie poured Grandma Redd some iced tea, and then opened all the windows in the house after they got home to let some fresh air in. She had taken out the trash bag liner before church but forgot to put a new bag in. She did an extreme core workout and did an extra one hundred burpees.

Mattie checked on grandma Redd who was watching her usual Sunday local gospel program. Once it was over, she would watch old reruns of 'Sanford and Son' and 'I Love Lucy' on TV Land. Mattie went to her bedroom and changed into some sweats and a wife beater. She slid on her slippers and went into her office.

Her desk was handcrafted from Sapeli Pommeli wood from Africa. It had a dark cherry finish to it, and the sides of the desk extended three feet in each direction from the center keyboard drawer. A plastic mat sat under the desk so that the cherry colored leather computer chair could move and swivel from one end of the desk to the next.

The office was longer than it was wide. She had two reclining cloth chairs in the room with reading lamps on opposite sides of them, and the window was covered with traditional cream-colored sheers with a sand colored swag top treatment. Apart from the desk, this room was a lightly colored room.

She walked to the recliner and picked Kendal's book up

and read the introduction again before opening it to the first poem. On the opposite page of the poem was an abstract drawing that looked like two people having sex. The poem was entitled “Inside”. The content was adult oriented, but it wasn’t blatantly forthcoming until the last eight lines. Mattie could picture Kendal writing it with his Cross ink pen he had scribbled his information with. His writings had passion and purpose, she wondered what inspired him.

Why she hadn’t exchanged cell phone numbers that night she had no idea.

“He did leave it up to me to choose…well I’ll just email him something before I head over to Sheila’s,” she thought walking back over to her desk to turn her computer on. She sat down in her chair and leaned back staring at the wall in front of her.

She had two book cases on the opposite side of where she sat, and in between each book case were three high quality framed pictures on the wall. The matching book cases were in the same color as her desk, but not made from the same wood. They were six feet tall and two feet wide with multiple shelves. The picture closest to the left book shelf was from the Million Man March. It was Maya Angelou speaking at the podium. On the wall next to the right book case was a picture of Halle Berry winning her Oscar for Monster's Ball. Mattie had always been torn about it because of the type of role Halle had to play to earn the award, but she loved Halle's drive and resiliency after a few bad set-backs.

However, Mattie's favorite picture was centered directly in between all the others. It was a split picture of Denzel Washington playing Malcolm X and then an actual picture of Malcolm X. Mattie loved Denzel, but it was her understanding of Malcolm Little to Malcolm X that empowered her to think beyond what she thought to what she knew.

She typed in her password to open her system and clicked on the internet explorer icon on her desktop. She logged into her email account and opened her mail. This was the email account that her friends and closest associates had. Sheila had forwarded an online story to Mattie about what happened two nights before. After reading it, she opened the book to type in Kendal's email address and laughed. 'tokendal@yahoo.com', it was so simple it was genius. Mattie hesitated before putting her fingers back onto the keypad.

"What am I going to say?" she asked herself silently,

thinking about how not to sound too forward or too interested.

"Ok I got it," she began laughing at herself because she was making this more difficult than necessary.

"It's an email," she thought clearing her nerves before she typed it up.

"I read a little of your book. Pretty nice, I'm looking forward to reading more. You have my email now, take a moment and say hi, Mattie," she sighed and erased it all.

"Damn that was corny as hell," before she typed something again.

"Kendal, I hope all is well, thanks for the book. I haven't finished it yet. If you're performing locally let me know where. Thanks again for the book," she finished and read her second attempt at the email. This time she only erased part of it and added something else.

"Better," she thought as she read the final draft.

"Kendal, I hope all is well, thanks for the book. No one has ever named anything after me…lol. Let us know if you'll be performing soon. Madison," she pressed send because if she waited any longer, she was going to drive herself crazy.

She was tired, physically drained from the early workout and lack of sleep Saturday night, so Mattie decided to take a quick cat nap before heading to Sheila's.

She woke up with her cell phone buzzing on her night stand. Judging by the way the sun was shining in her room she had taken more than a cat nap, and by the missed calls and text messages it had been more than three hours.

She was still tired, but she rolled onto the side of the bed and text back,

"I'm on the way," she then walked into her bathroom to wash her face and brush her teeth. After using the toilet and washing her hands. She threw on a light weight Ohio State sweatshirt and her red and white Nike tennis shoes.

Grandma Redd was sleeping so Mattie didn't disturb her before she left. She set the house alarm before leaving to spend a little time with Sheila and her family.

Chapter 14

Pretty Fly Chick

The day had passed, and the early hours of the night were coming in as the sun faded into the west. Mattie arrived a few hours after Sheila's cookout began, people were still playing Texas Hold 'Em and Bones on two separate tables for money while the rap music; labeled "hot garbage" was blaring on the portable Bose speaker. Sheila was always first to tell her younger brother's friends that she couldn't understand a word that rappers said, however with a little liquor in her Sheila could move her body to any beat and pick up on any dance.

When Mattie arrived nearly all the food was gone, but

she knew Sheila had saved her a plate. Sheila's younger brother Junie had brought a few friends over without Sheila's permission, so they were given the third degree in front of everyone before being told to eat one plate of food only. Sheila always cooked more than what was necessary; something she had gotten accustomed doing for her siblings when her mother worked late growing up.

Darian was barely six, but he looked up to his uncle with respect. Junie had separated from his wife, but was very active in his triplet's life even with a strained relationship with their mother. He didn't divorce due to financial reasons. He owned a few body and collision repair shops, and his wife several salons throughout the city. On the outside he was a regular guy building a business. Only Mattie and the three distributors who worked for him knew that he supplied a large portion of cocaine in the city.

Darian ran from Junie as soon as Mattie walked into the backyard. He had been promised twenty minutes of her time to show him again how to hold someone in an arm bar.

Darian overheard one of Junie's friends say that he could get out of her arm bar because he had taken martial arts. Mattie laughed and shrugged it off, but after bets had been taken totaling close to $200 and Junie's friends calling her just a 'pretty fly chick' she took his money. By the time he tapped out she knew she had strained some of his ligaments. She spoke with Geri and Cindy before helping Sheila clean up.

Sheila's other brothers, Shawn and Shane, started a higher stake poker game, and Mattie played for about an hour with them before leaving with an extra four hundred dollars in her pocket. Mattie always felt love around her sisters. Cindy had left before the game began and Geri had left with Mattie telling her to be at the gym on time.

Mattie didn't eat at Sheila's, she took her plate home to eat with a little extra in case Grandma wanted any. Running low on gas she stopped at the station to fill up and ended up buying a two liter of Pepsi. Two men were standing near the air machine with their trunk open trying to solicit business for bootleg CD's and DVD's, after telling them that she didn't need anything, she decided to get a workout in at the BJJ studio. When she finished, she got a quick drink with the trainer and headed home.

Walking in the front door she put the plate and Pepsi on her island and walked to the back. Grandma Redd was still sleeping with the blanket Mattie had forgotten at the base of her bed folded up. Mattie took a shower before doing anything else; after she put on pink cotton bottom pajamas and a t-shirt she headed back into the kitchen and heated up her plate. Sheila made barbecue chicken, greens, rice and butter beans, potato salad and baked beans like it was the Fourth of July.

Mattie sat at the island and ate while watching a rerun of Law and Order: Criminal Intent. Vincent D'onofrio played an excellent part. His character was a genius, but he was troubled by mental challenges, as was his mother on the show diagnosed with schizophrenia. His character had knowledge stored in his mind that superseded others. Mattie got into the habit of reading about any subject discussed on the show that she had been unfamiliar with just to challenge herself.

She was tired, physically drained. Ready to call it a night, something prompted her to check her email account, but beforehand, she put some ice in a glass and poured a little bit of water over it. She then poured the water out into the sink leaving the ice in the glass. She twisted the cap to the Pepsi and poured it in. It was something about the pop and ice fizzing that flustered her, so she had figured out a way to minimize it.

Sitting in her leather computer chair, she typed her password onto the log on screen. There were two emails from Kendal. Opening the first one she saw it was a reply to what she had sent.

"Thanks for taking a chance, I know it can be a challenge trying to figure out what to say (honestly I'm an aspiring writer and this is my third attempt at replying) I hope you appreciate my work, and I perform the last two Wednesdays of the month at Café Coffee Bean. It starts around seven o'clock, I would love to see you again Madison," it read.

The second email was to a Messenger link with a request to add Kendal as a friend.

Mattie hadn't used instant messaging consistently in over two years. That had been her and Brian's mode of communicating, toward the end she barely called Brian because Instant Messaging was less personal. 'Accept' she clicked on the optional radio button. She went back to read Kendal's email again to try and decipher any hidden meanings, hoping it would tell her more about him.

"Café Coffee Bean," Mattie thought, trying to figure out if she had heard of it before, she hadn't.

"And I haven't read it yet," she said out loud rereading

the email again when she heard the chime coming through her speakers.

"How are you queen?" it was from Kendal.

"I'm doing well," she sat back and waited.

"Are you stalking me, lmao?" Kendal responded. Mattie laughed out loud before typing back.

"Ain't it the other way around?" She asked as she sat forward in her chair attentively.

"Well yeah but you didn't ask the question first, now did ya?" He responded with another smiley face.

"So not only are you a poet and a writer, you're also a comedian?" she smiled looking at the screen, excited that he was quick on his feet.

"Among other things too, I overheard heard about the incident Saturday night. I pray you are safe, it gets crazy out here sometimes," Mattie smiled at his concern, for her it felt genuine not like most dudes that wanted to sweet talk her to get her into bed.

"Tell me about it; it still hasn't really sunk in yet. It seemed like it happened in slow motion, Sheila, the one who asked you about the title was yelling 'help' at the top of her lungs, but she could barely stand. Cindy, the sometimes sarcastic one was cussing the 911 operator out," Mattie typed back so far he seemed easy to communicate with.

"And you were whooping up on a hardened criminal, a beautiful woman that can break bones, lol…seriously I am grateful that you have been kept safe Madison." Kendal typed back.

"You can call me Mattie, so you were helping Max out, you must be a good friend of his." She responded in casual conversation, but she was trying to get more information from him about his personality. Max was a player and if it was up to Cindy he was also on the 'downlow' with his friend.

"No, I just met Max that night, Kwame asked if I could help out since I used to be in the food business." Mattie read what he responded. She took a sip of her Pepsi and sat it back down on the coaster before she replied.

"That was nice of you, a lot of people would've said no, especially when they don't get paid for it either…we gave Char your tip…a fat tip too. Sheila was drunk when she put it on her card," Mattie was more curious now about him, what he did for a living, if he even worked at all. He seemed straight forward and honest so far.

"Yeah I feel you. I didn't get paid monetarily, but payments aren't always dollars and cents. Sometimes it's the opportunity of performing or a priceless chance encounter," Kendal typed back catching Mattie off guard.

"Priceless?" Mattie asked, she heard that term priceless from one of those credit card commercials on TV, or when describing jewelry, her mother used to call her that, but it had been a long time coming.

"Yes queen, priceless. You already know that your worth isn't determined by outside forces, hold on for a sec."

Mattie was grateful he said, 'hold on' because she was still thinking about what he said…your worth isn't determined by outside forces' and she didn't know how to respond immediately.

"Are you still there?" he sent a message through after about three minutes.

"Yeah," she was still glued to her computer, although she had taken a moment to check her social media accounts.

"I had to make some Ramen noodles, they were calling

my name," he replied adding a smiley face right after.

"Ramen noodles haven't called my name since college. I would microwave some before track practice; I just ate about an hour ago. Sheila had a small cookout after church, and I brought my plate home," she sent the message, but she was following up with a quick question

"So, Kendal, are you from Columbus or did you migrate here like most people?" Mattie was curious about his story, where he came from, what type of family he had. Mattie wanted a better understanding of him, she was very intrigued. He was the first man that had her attention in such a long while, and she needed more information to make sure she was exercising good judgment.

"Wow, well ok…how about tonight I'll give you an over view of my story and tomorrow you will share yours with me, that sound like a fair deal to you?" he asked typing back.

Mattie appreciated his style, he wanted to control what he could and leave the rest up to her, she liked a man who took charge and led. What she didn't like, were egocentric males who thought the world revolved around them, thus making every decision for their own selfish agenda. Kendal was assuming they'd have more contact in the future, but he wasn't being pushy…just confident.

"So, you'll give me a little background info tonight, if I do the same for you tomorrow huh, well that's a deal," Mattie replied. She felt comfortable with his dialogue, and she was anxious to hear more about him.

"My family is originally from the south, but I was born in Ohio. My mother was born in North Carolina and my dad in Alabama. They moved to Ohio when my mother was pregnant with my older brother. I was born in East Cleveland, in a galaxy far, far away," he paused longer than Mattie had expected.

"Sorry I almost knocked my noodles over, but I've got one older brother that I mentioned and a younger sister, you ever been up north to Cleveland?" Kendal asked.

"We used to go to the flats in Cleveland to dance and listen to 'reggae mon,' she had great times in the Flats, but she was much younger then.

"Oh, I remember that spot, it was small and cramped but it was the best music and dancing joint. I can think back to most of those night spots before they closed the east bank of the Flats down, you haven't been back since?" Kendal asked.

"No, I've thought about it, but when we do weekend trips we get out of the state, maybe drive to Chicago or Indy, but last trip we had was to New York. We went for a Broadway Show and to get the hook up on some shopping from some college girlfriends," she drank down the last sip of Pepsi. She ran to the kitchen to refill her glass and came back in to read what Kendal had just sent.

"I went home a couple of months ago to watch a Cavaliers playoff game with my Pops. We go to at least ten games a year together. He's been a season ticket holder for The Cavs and The Browns for the last twenty-five to thirty years. He's been a diehard Cleveland sports fan even before I was born. Jim Brown is the greatest running back in the history of the game if you let him tell it. After Lebron James got us a 'chip', according to my dad, he is better than MJ. I liked the Bulls in college, but I've always been a Cleveland fan, I gotta represent my city. Plus, now that we got OBJ, to go with Baker and the rest of that offense, The Browns are ballin' across the board."

"Were you a Bulls fan or a MJ fan?" Mattie had heard all the arguments before about who was better but she loved Michael Jordan when he played for the Bulls.

"Well, if you're asking like that, I was a MJ fan, but

probably not for the reasons most people were, did you know that after every game, the next morning MJ was up bright and early working out, pushing himself relentlessly, he didn't care so much about the money he got from basketball, he cared about the game and perfecting his craft without excuses, that's why I've been an MJ fan. He never simply thought himself the best; he put in all the hard work, sacrifice and was dedicated. He raised the bar for everyone after him," Mattie read what he had typed again before responding. Kendal was right that most people enjoyed MJ's spectacular dunks and his flair for the game…not the blood, hard work and sweat.

"Ok, so I know that you're from Cleveland with roots down south, and that you're Michael Jordan's spokesperson, lmao, what did you do after high school, you mentioned college," she typed wanting him to disclose even more. She leaned back in her chair and waited for a response.

"Slow down, I agreed to tell you about me and then you can ask follow up questions Nancy Grace, are you an attorney cause I object, nah, I'm just kidding but I attended public schools until ninth grade and my dad sent me to the same all male Catholic High School that my older brother attended. I guess he figured I'd be the same type of athlete and earn a full scholarship too, which I did to play football at a mid-major school, but I also earned a partial track scholarship and partial academic scholarship to the University of Tennessee. I love running so I took the track and academic scholarship. Later on I went to Culinary School where I met my wife, and after graduation I opened a restaurant which fared well enough that I was able to open a few more, but it wasn't my passion, I did it because people said I'd fail at it, that I should do something with my background in my degree, it's not that I wanted to prove them wrong, but instead prove myself right. I sold both restaurants for a very good profit over three years ago and I've been focused on writing and publishing ever since. I mentor and tutor four days out of the week right now to give back, I'll fill in the gaps now if you like, just ask," he finished.

Mattie only read bits and pieces of his response after he said he 'met his wife'.

"What the fuck does he think I am, I ain't second to no one and he trying to be all sincere and shit, was he wearing a ring?" she was thinking feeling herself getting upset. She thought that she had finally met a decent good man and all he was doing was running game on her.

"So how long have you been married???" Mattie typed back with additional question marks. She erased the exclamation point she started to use, because she had to get a little more information before blowing up at him.

"I was married six years, but she passed. I've dated here and there since, but nothing serious and nothing or no one currently, oh shit…you thought I was still married, lol, you have my word I would never disrespect you…you must've thought I was full of shit huh?" he answered what Mattie had sent through.

"Yes, that is correct, if you were married, I wouldn't have thought you were a piece of shit, it would've been confirmed," Mattie responded.

"I said full of shit, lmao…I'm glad you have standards," Kendal typed back.

What woman shouldn't have standards and if hers were higher than most she could live with that because she was unwillingly to settle for less than what she wanted a second time.

"I just think people who make a commitment like marriage should stay committed and work through things until its' completion," her response was straight forward.

“So, what type of restaurants did you have?” She asked quickly changing the subject, she got what she needed; he wasn't married and wasn't seeing anyone.

“When you went up to Cleveland back in the day, did you ever stop at one of the barbecue joints, ya know real soul food spots?” he asked.

“What, you mean like polish boys and ribs; Cleveland's dirty ass city got some of the best barbecue,” she wrote thinking back to those old ‘hole in the wall’ small places.

“Slow down little moccasin, that's still my city. It might be old and a little unclean, but I still love it, but yeah ribs and polish boys, chicken all that. Now don't be tripping on me because I went to Culinary school…but I opened up Sweet Honey's Barbecue.”

“I'm not tripping; sounds like it took a bit of courage Mr. Sweet Honey,” Mattie responded with a smiley face.

“Who's the comedian now? One of the things that made my restaurant different was that I also made a few Caribbean foods like Jerk and Curry dishes, and I had tables to dine in. My first two years were rough, but once people got the word of mouth out, we got a write up in the local paper and everything took off.”

"So, you're an entrepreneur too? I've never been married, close once but as you said that's history," she sent to him feeling comfortable sharing bits of herself with him

"Tomorrow you can tell me all about it, tonight is your turn to ask me what you want to know about me, trust me, I'm gonna be your professor tomorrow night, quid pro quo Clarice," he sent back.

"Okay, then tell me about your mom and dad, your brother and sister, are you all still in Ohio? I know you mentioned mom and dad are still in Cleveland," Mattie asked

Kendal went on to tell her that his sister lived in Cincinnati and taught at Xavier, while his brother lived in Charlotte with his own Insurance Agency. He opened it with money he had saved from his signing bonus in the NFL. He played briefly before his body gave out on him.

"He went hard on the field every time but he's doing pretty good down there," Kendal typed.

"Sounds like your parents did a great job with all of you, you get a chance to get to Cincy or Charlotte often?" Mattie asked. His family sounded decent, like good old fashion families that her grandmother used to tell her about.

"Oh yeah, I'm in Charlotte once or twice every three months. I've got a niece and a nephew in Cincy, and a nephew coming up on his thirteenth birthday in North Carolina next month. So, I'll be driving down there, and it's really not a bad drive just a whole bunch of hills and curves," he sent back through.

"You ever been to Charlotte?" he asked

"No, well yeah, but not exactly, we've driven through Charlotte going to Myrtle Beach and visiting some of Sheila's relatives in Fair Bluff, N.C and Dillon, S.C, we got stuck in traffic in Charlotte during rush hour for over two hours in a hot ass car." Mattie typed back reliving the ordeal.

"Myrtle Beach is pretty cool; did you all ever make it to the sand?" Kendal asked Mattie

"Yeah we made it, eventually."

"Well maybe you can get down there again one day, I love the water. I'm kinda adventurous."

Mattie saw a double meaning behind his statement. She liked his conversation, it was fluid and he had the potential to get a first date. He was the first man that intrigued her in such a long time. It was refreshing but she slow played her response to him, like Cindy said earlier, 'she wasn't no damn spring chicken.'

"Yeah, maybe," she sent back.

"What else do you want to know about me Mattie?" He asked. Mattie thought about what she needed to know because what she *wanted* to know she was still unsure of.

"So, you're telling me that you don't have any one significant taking your time right now, no crazy ex-girlfriends that you can't shake?" she asked him making light of the question, but it was a serious question that required an answer. If she was going to spend more time having any type of conversation with him, she needed a hundred percent clarity on that part.

"No crazy ex's or anything like that, I'm pretty straight forward with any friends I may have. But, to answer your question I have no significant or remotely close to being intimate relationships with anyone, no women in my house."

'Good,' Mattie thought because a significant other meant divided attention, any flunkies she would get rid of or put in their place. Mattie realized that she liked him, because she was making clear she needed clarity.

"Do you have Messenger on your phone?" he followed up.

"Yeah I have it."

"Well, I am logged on to that on my phone all the time, my kids may not have cell phones but they're always on the computer. Tomorrow if you want you can message me and if I see you logged in, I'll say hi, but don't be stalking me…lmao," he wrote back to her before finishing.

"I don't know if you realize how late it is, I'm gonna let you get some rest. I've got to be downtown early for a meeting. But don't hesitate to reach out when you want, I look forward to tomorrow night, good night Clarice."

"Good night Dr. Lecter," she sat back in her chair and stretched her arms before looking at the time on her computer.

"One-thirty damn," she shook her head while she shutting her computer down. In less than three hours she had to be up to workout with Geri and then do a full day of work. Making sure all the doors and windows were locked and the alarm was set, she crawled into bed for a few hours of sleep but before long she was hitting the snooze button on her alarm clock.

CHAPTER 15

HUMANS LIKE YOU

The carpet was multicolored with various tones of blue, red and pink. The United States Flag positioned itself on one side of the Deputy Mayors office, and the State of Ohio Flag on the other. From what Kendal could ascertain there was a strange energy in the air. He wasn't nervous about asking the city for money to help build a partnership with his community center. This administration had vowed to become a participant in the lives of the next generation. Kendal's business plan proved successful, but more importantly it was duplicatable. He believed this meeting with the Deputy Mayor could be a cornerstone to help so many disadvantaged.

He noticed the pictures hanging on the wall. Pictures of The Horse Shoe where he had played in the High School Division I Championship game as a Junior and Senior, was situated between portraits of the city thirty years ago compared to the present. He noticed the cameras positioned throughout the room, and a sign indicating that Video and Audio were being recorded.

Kendal laughed and decided he should record his presentation, so he could hone it for future uses. He opened the program on his tablet and pressed record, before sliding it back into his small black bag he carried along with his attaché. As he looked up, he saw the blur of a body entering the room. The woman wore a grey suit and white blouse. Her brunette hair fell off her jawline and Kendal saw the ruby charm resting across her neck before he saw her face. She had arched eye brows and piercing green eyes. From her free-spirited entrance, Kendal could tell she felt extremely comfortable as she approached the male secretary. She was excited and nearly tripped over herself.

"They're letting me write The Mayors response to today's event little brother," she punched him on the shoulder.

Kendal saw the resemblance as they shared the same hair

color, but his eyes were dark brown, and he had freckles.

"This could be exactly what I need. I know politics are dirty, but my words can help inspire action. Especially when evil and ignorance presents itself on the steps of this building today," she said.

"Well why are you still standing here?" her brother asked with a smile on his face.

"Right," she hugged him again and turned and realized they weren't alone.

Kendal nodded at her as she made eye contact. She left as quickly as she had arrived.

Kendal wasn't sure what the event was, he had noticed the barricades earlier and a very small crowd. Then he realized that a rally was being held for supporters of white supremacists. He believed in the Constitution and understood they had a right to belief and speech, but he also knew that violence could erupt when opposing views defended their beliefs. Kendal saw the red-light line indicator blinking on the phone before the secretary.

"Yes. Yes ma'am."

"If you will follow me," he said ushering Kendal towards

the Deputy Mayor's office.

"Kendal, so good to finally meet you," the Deputy Mayor said walking towards him with her hand extended. She was an older woman with white streaks mixed in with her sandy blonde hair. She wore navy slacks and light chambray colored shirt. Her jacket was laid across the back of her desk chair.

"Thank you so much for your time, I know how much the city wants to help improve the lives of children. There is a bit of excitement in the air I must say," Kendal replied as he shook her hand.

Kendal had expected to hear something about the rally, but she didn't respond to his statement. Instead she ushered him towards her desk before responding.

"City Hall is finally working for the people," she said motioning for her secretary to pour her coffee.

"Would you like coffee, water?" she asked Kendal as she took the coffee cup from her assistant.

Kendal declined the offer for a beverage. He was visualizing the presentation he would be providing the Deputy Mayor and wanted to make sure he hit all the highlights of the program.

"Thomas you may leave," the Deputy Mayor advised her assistant.

Deputy Mayor Schneider offered Kendall a bottled water a second time before he began his presentation, and after a forty-five-minute discussion including bar graphs and pie charts and other metrics of success, Kendal believed he had shown her that with this program they could better the lives of underprivileged children. He had the backing of positive forecasts from Child Psychologists, Department Heads of Business at separate local colleges, and the support of a couple of city churches

"The success we have made with those at the community center is anything short of amazing. Those who have participated in at least ninety percent of our program have earned higher grades. The older ones who have work permits have shown ninety- five percent accountability. We measured their fitness levels at the beginning of the program, at the inception over two years ago, and each child has seen an increase in better health. We are hoping for a substantial commitment over the course of four years from the city," he finished.

The Deputy Mayor thanked Kendal for being so thorough, and reiterated that she would find out what type of commitment the city would be willing to share when her phone rang.

"Yes, send him in."

Both doors flew open as a large burly man strode in. He had girth in his belly as it stuck out from his blue suit jacket. He had curly black hair that was neatly groomed.

"Debbie, my favorite Deputy Mayor," he said as they embraced in a hug.

"One of my most favorite council persons," she said returning the gesture.

"Johnny, this is Kendal Scott the community director I told you about," she said as Kendal greeted him in return.

"Kendal, can I borrow her for a few moments?" he asked extending his hand to Kendal.

"Well, we are just finishing up, Kendal after I discuss this with the budget committee we will follow up, do you have a copy of the information, so I can share with them?" she asked moving back to her desk.

"Actually, I do," he handed her the usb drive and bid her farewell, thanking her for her time again.

"Thanks Thomas," Kendal said to the secretary as he left the office. He felt good about the presentation and couldn't wait to share it with Frances at the center. Everything he had shown Deputy Mayor Schneider could be duplicated something he knew was vital for successful growth.

When he exited city hall the streets had been blocked off and barricaded in more areas. Then he saw the first swastika and group congregated dressed in black. Kendal understood that each group could be dangerous but those gathered in khaki pants and button- down shirts posed a bigger threat.

He was glad he had taken public transportation to the early meeting because navigating the streets, even on his motorcycle in these conditions would be tedious. He reached for his second bag and forgot he had slid it under the chair he sat in. He made a beeline back up the stairs to retrieve it. The Deputy Mayor had already departed with the councilman, so Thomas retrieved the bag from under the chair in the office.

Kendal retraced his steps on the way out of the building once more and saw more swastikas and white men of various ages congregating, separated by two rows of roped areas from protesters. He had protested so many injustices over the course of his life, today his time needed to be managed as he was running an hour behind his schedule. He had a new class beginning at the center for adults teaching them basic computer skills, and he always wanted to be present on their first day to greet them.

He crossed the street and moved in between the protesters yelling towards the white nationalists. The bus line ran along the street, but he had to walk a few blocks before he could cross back to the other side.

Lack of humanity and empathy is what it came down to for Kendal in the hate and fear he was witnessing. Kendal was slow to call someone a "racist," but he knew the difference between ignorance and willful acceptance. He made eye contact with a few in the group as he passed between protesters on one side yelling that the white nationalists were evil and hateful while their opposition yelled back.

"You will not replace us before it turned into Jews will not replace us. Go back to Africa, save our race.... reverse discrimination," Kendal shook his head as he thought about the insignificance of the humans who believed their skin color made them superior. Factual history had shown people with melanin brought about all the major religions of the world, that the world had lost so much history and information as libraries had been destroyed through millenniums of war and conflict.

Kendal had tuned out the voices and was thinking about how to increase the probability of receiving more financial support when he heard "look at the little monkey boy, you're all animals," being directed at a child not older than six.

Kendal abruptly refocused his attention towards the men laughing as they walked away. He had learned about responsibility of his race and defending those in need at an early age from his parents. He approached the group of white males and zeroed in on the one who had spoken to the young child.

"That was pretty weak and basic addressing a child like that. That is nothing but fear of the power you recognize in him. I have heard it all before and the sad part is that in the end I will believe we are all human beings. But, humans like you and your group always find a way to give alternative facts. Fact, while you're yelling Jews will not replace us, all the while you are wearing a Cross around your neck. You would believe yourself a Christian, but Christ was a Jew, and

Jesus Christ looked more like this young king. If you have something to say don't talk to a child. I'm right here. Address me but not that child," Kendal said it so matter of fact that he hadn't been interrupted by the group.

A patrol of four police officers were approaching as the male wearing the cross stared at Kendal before deciding to move on to join his brothers spreading an ideology of hatred. Kendal readjusted his bags and began walking away before he heard a woman calling in his direction.

"Excuse me, sir excuse me," she said loudly to gain his attention.

Kendal turned and walked towards her as she approached with her son in tow.

"Thank you," the young boy's mother said. She had gratitude and pride showing in her eyes. Her son simply stared at Kendal like he was figuring out a puzzle.

An older interracial couple also complimented Kendal on handling the situation on behalf of all of them. As they shared, they had seen the ugly side of racial discourse over the duration of their marriage. The couple continued in the direction where the main rally was being held to protest the hateful speech, feeling reinvigorated after watching Kendal interact with the group of males earlier.

The young child followed behind Kendal as they walked toward the bus stop, he walked with his eyes fixated on him.

"Mommy he wasn't afraid of those men?" he was trying to figure out the right emotion he was feeling. The mother took his hand and gripped it slightly in a reassuring way as she responded.

"No, he wasn't, not one-bit honey," she said with pride in her voice.

As they all crossed the street to wait at the bus stop Kendal introduced himself and spoke about "teaching our children" the lessons not read about in books. The mother agreed as her son listened attentively. As the bus approached and its doors opened Kendal paid for them, and walked towards the center of the bus to stand, allowing her and her son to sit down in the only remaining seat.

When his stop approached, he complimented her on the good job she was doing as a parent, he reached into his attaché and gave his business card to her. The young boy was staring out the window as it continued its way. Kendal waved and smiled, and for the first time the boy smiled in return.

Cars traveling in each direction prevented him from crossing before he reached the crosswalk, but he had to tread closely to the street as a portion of the sidewalk was being fixed.

The freshly poured concrete was quartered off in yellow tape that had been pulled down and surrounded by four orange cones. Kendal could make out the names scribbled on top of the mold ensuring each name would last if it did.

The smoke from the exhaust billowed out as the bus moved forward. Kendal stood on the corner waiting for the light to change. A father pushing a stroller caught his eye, it made him feel inspired knowing that all the negative myths about black fathers being absent were not entirely accurate.

He crossed the street and saw the sale sign “zero money down” in the window of a store that rented furniture and appliances. He had done that once in college and ended up paying $2000.00 more in interest payments. Kendal had never made that mistake twice.

As he walked down MLK Jr. Boulevard, he heard the music coming from a Silver Chevy Impala. He knew the voice instantly and the song that Jay Z had rapped about how he is accepted on any street named after Martin Luther King

Jr. the irony didn't miss him. He walked past the brick community Mount Vernon Townhomes into the lot of a strip mall next to his community center. There were several businesses huddled together; a wireless store specializing in pre-paid phones. A tax preparation company who had been located there for over twenty years. A boutique for women's accessories was popular, but it was the famous Cajun restaurant that had a line forming outside it with twenty minutes remaining to open.

"Mr. K, good morning sir, is it your treat today?" A young black male said approaching Kendal on a red, white and blue bicycle. His hair was braided, and he wore gray sweat pants and a plain white T-shirt.

"Jameson trick or treating is still months away, but if you're still committed to helping print and put the program together for Friday evening, I can pay you a decent wage," Kendal replied as the two of them bumped fist in greeting.

"I was just joking Mr. K, unless you were gon do it, nah nah I'm just playing. I will be on time tomorrow morning to help with the program for sure," he rode across the parking lot before seeing a group of his friends.

Kendal was still playing back the events of his morning

as he walked into the center. Frances was speaking with a small group of seven adults as they filled out paperwork before their first class began. Another group had formed around the activity room where the video arcade and basketball court were located.

This group consisted solely of students and their guests attempting to coax them into having extra time to enjoy the facilities.

"Mr. Litman it's almost time can we just get in ten minutes early?" Two out of the dozen kids ranging from seven to seventeen years of age were attempting to barter with the older bald man.

"Kejuan if I could I would, but I can't so I ain't," he said laughing jovially. He had heard so many reasons why he should break the rules a little since he joined Kendal's team. His role was to be the steady firm disciplinarian, something he was good at.

The group sighed in unison. Mr. Litman was old school in every sense of the word and that's what Kendal respected about him. He understood the value of work and succeeding through discipline and responsibility. Between Frances and him, Kendal had people he could trust who shared his vision.

"Queens and Kings, if anyone can tell me who said:

'Chance has never yet satisfied the hope of a suffering people' I will try to get Mr. Litman to say you earned early entrance," Kendal asked walking towards the group.

"Mr. K, that's Brother Marcus Garvey," Kejuan answered with a smile on his face.

"Very good Kejuan," Mr. Litman said giving him a high five.

"And what about 'The blessings in which you, this day, rejoice are not joined in common. The rich inheritance of justice, liberty, prosperity and independence. Bequeathed by your fathers, is shared by you, not by me. The sunlight that brought light and healing to you has brought stripes and death to me."

"That was Mr. Frederick Douglas talking about the Fourth of July," one of the three teenaged girls spoke up.

"Toya, that is outstanding," the elder gave her a fist bump.

"But I won't let you in early today, because it's open right now," the older bald man buzzed them into the arcade. The group of kids entered through the doors and separated to different areas to entertain themselves.

"So how did it go?" Mr. Litman asked Kendal after the kids got settled.

Kendal told him about the meeting, and he felt much needed assistance would be coming from the city. He spoke briefly about walking out into the middle of the white nationalist rally, but he didn't speak on the altercation. He checked in on the group in the arcade and spoke to them about not entering the swimming pool until the lifeguard was present, unless they had passed an extensive swimming test. Kendal then dropped his bags off in his office and placed his tablet on its charger before walking to the media center where the adult class was beginning.

"Queens and Kings, I am Kendal and I wanted to thank you for allowing us to share some of the information we have learned and taught. I promise you the hardest challenge was showing up today. Frances is a great facilitator, she's patient but she will coach you firmly," he laughed as the class laughed nervously with him.

Frances has been an educator a great portion of her life, and Principal of a High School in Pennsylvania before seeking additional education at Ohio Dominican College.

"Our number one priority is equipping you all with a familiarity of basic computer skills, and at the end of the course I guarantee you will feel empowered. If you need anything my door is always open, when it's opened," he said before departing, shaking each person's hand. When he walked back towards the front desk, he saw Mr. Litman speaking with Henry, who was one of the first policemen to back his community center initiative.

"So, I've heard your name all over the radio, I worked that event and missed all of the fireworks outside," Kendal said extending his hand.

"If you only knew, I was catching a ride to meet my wife and end up apprehending one of Columbus' Most Wanted."

"Another adult class, brother you are putting your foot forward. It's ok if I bring Jay and Michelle to the awards ceremony?" Henry asked already knowing what Kendal's answer would be, but it was respectful not to fully assume.

"Uhm, yeah. I'm surprised you don't have him with you right now. It's about time I met your wife. Especially after allowing you to reschedule your anniversary dinner to speak at the ceremony, it means a lot," Kendal felt a genuine brotherhood between the two of them.

"Oh, no you don't get off that easy you owe me one or two or," but Henry paused and there was a change in tone.

"So, this visit isn't just a cordial one, a few of my sources are saying that the gangs are escalating against each other and have been actively recruiting. So far, the students have been off limits because the center is backed by the Blue Line, but you should keep your eyes open," Henry finished ensuring his friend understood the dynamics were shifting.

Kendal was fully aware of the influence gangs had on younger children from broken homes. Growing up in East Cleveland, Ohio he was prone to the trappings in inner city life, but his parents made sure to stay on top of him, his older brother and sister.

"Thanks man, we are actually throwing in new working cameras on the perimeter of the building and changing light bulbs, especially before the awards ceremony."

"I can lend a hand right now if you want to get started, I've got my drill in the back of the car," Henry could see the vision Kendal had, but it was the determination to succeed that reeled him in. Henry had an off -book background check performed on Kendal when he came into his department seeking assistance. The background check verified that

Kendal had worked hard to build a restaurant business that he sold the principle in. Now it was a small chain of restaurants and he would receive compensation the rest of his life.

"Your help is accepted."

"Mr. Littman, we're going to get to work, can you check on the kids and make sure they're not taking advantage of each other?" Kendal then asked Henry to meet him outside before walking into his office.

After changing into some khaki shorts and Nike sneakers they were able to install two cameras on the back corners of the center before Henry got called in on a case.

"I'll see you Friday. Michelle will be here, and you can tell her all the good works going on," Henry said before getting into his car and driving away.

Kendal knew that the universe didn't make mistakes, and the moment he had committed to helping disadvantaged youth he was directed to networks and people like Henry who made an impact with the programs at the center becoming successful.

A group of three teenaged boys walked across the

parking lot with bags from the Cajun restaurant.

"Mr. K this is for you," they said offering him a bag with food in it.

"I just worked up an appetite, you guys surprise me. Thank you all for this, Lawrence are you sure you don't need any money?" He knew every little bit of money went a long way for families in the neighborhood who often lived paycheck to paycheck.

"No sir, you deserve it," Lawrence answered as all three of the teenage boys shook their heads in agreement.

"Well I appreciate it, the pool is open right now, but if you're going to eat, wait until the second session and let your food settle," Kendal walked the perimeter of the center to count how many light bulbs needed replaced.

The sound of early fall was alive as car radios could be heard, each one vying to be heard mixed in with background dialogue. Kendal had no misconceptions that the neighborhood had the same rules as the streets he grew up in. Respect went a long way and he had the respect of the shot caller who controlled this area, and with the backing of Henry and his police officer friends the center prospered.

Kendal heard a horn blow at him, but he didn't recognize the driver, still he waved out of courtesy. He picked up a few cigarette butts and discarded them, before changing a few of the light fixtures. He was tired but he needed to give Frances his tablet to download the audio of his presentation to the Deputy Mayor.

The center had expanded into an area that used to house two full sized school buses and now was being turned into a gym comprised with a boxing ring, a few heavy bags. There was an area, thirty by thirty, specifically for wrestling and grappling. There were rows of pull up bars on each wall and five climbing ropes secured in the center of the room. Kendal knew self -defense built confidence, and with positive reinforcement many of the negative images built to destroy these children could be combatted. He had a back ground in boxing, but he had studied Jiu Jitsu for over four years, so he was able to have certified instructors donate their time.

Tonight's class was going to be boxing fundamentals with a trainer who had seen over four decades of leather fisticuffs. White Moses, as he had been called for over fifty years, had trained world champions in the early part of the century now, he traveled throughout the city passing his knowledge on. An older white man who had grown up five streets away from the community center, he still maintained his childhood home although he had moved out to the suburbs.

"Mr. Littman can you check in on Tabitha and make sure they aren't taking advantage of her in the pool?" Kendal asked before finding and giving Frances his tablet. He was dragging physically, only working on five hours of sleep over the past three days his body was giving him a sign.

"Mr. K you can go get some rest, one of the new adult students is an electrician and said he can put bulbs in for us. You won't be any good to anyone if you burn out. The reporter from the Call and Post confirmed and will be here for the ceremony we need your fresh," Frances finished as she handed him the bag of food to usher him out of the building.

"You might be right as usual, the city proposal needed focus and I feel really good about any assistance they can offer. I will be back at 9:00 and I can close tonight. Have we confirmed with the cleaning crew to come tomorrow night?" Kendal asked.

The awards ceremony was to honor his students who had been in the program for the first years and as Kendal had shared earlier in the morning, these kids increased both their grades and in doing so found new self- respect and positive reinforcement. He had invited media outlets to attend so he could share the progress of his students and utilize them to help spread his message that education and knowledge of self were cornerstones for success. The only invite accepted was from the local Call and Post, but he knew something was better than nothing, and historically the reach of this publication was specific to those he wanted to help.

"Mr. K it's been two years now, I have it covered, now go get some rest and don't come back today. Stay home, work on your speech, eat and rest. You have been here every day, for nearly the last two months, we can handle one night," Frances said before turning to walk out of his office.

Kendal had not realized that he was burning the candle at both ends because he was simply getting everything finished. He used some of his own personal money to have the swimming pool back into code and also furnishing the gym for self -defense. The project to build new classrooms and a perimeter fence which would enclose an area large enough to hold nearly two football fields which he intended to use for small community festivals and job fairs. He figured the more positive exposure the community center received the more opportunities he and his staff could share. Kendal got up and said his goodbyes before departing. He smelled the bag of Cajun food the three boys had given him earlier.

"Mattie," the thought came out of thin air as he left the center. He wanted to see her, but his time was limited. He was going to invite her to the ceremony but that was still a few days away. Kendal decided he would fit lunch in with her, if she accepted, and cook something to make it more personal. When he arrived home, he opened all the windows and turned the ceiling fan on before sitting down to use his computer.

As soon as Kendal opened his email, he saw the multitude of messages from a woman he had dated over three years ago. She was coming into town and wanted to share some energy as she put it. Kendal took it for face value, and it had been nearly nine months since he had had sex. He only read the first two emails before sitting back in his loveseat. He would think about the offer because it was sex with a friend, but he was fascinated by another.

"Madison," he thought her name. He was attracted to Madison in the purest sense as a man is to a woman but there was something deeper, he cared to learn about her.

"Lunch," he said out loud reaffirming that he would take her lunch if she accepted. "In fact, I'll cook."

Kendal's phone rang from an extension recognized from the community center.

"Kendal, Kendal, Kendal, do you know what viral means?" Frances asked him with a bit of excitement in her voice.

"Frances are you ok, are you sick?" he answered laughing over the cell phone.

"Mr. K told them dudes, he wasn't playing around with that guy, was he?" a faded voice of a young woman came through.

"Mr. K sure did," Frances answered

"Frances what's going on?" he asked curiously.

"Kendal your interaction with those white nationalists was caught on video, every last word and I mean every, last word. You gave them the business and it seems the video is going viral. You are a superstar Mr. K," Frances finished.

Kendal had forgotten about that part of his morning and now after hearing Frances he was still unimpressed. "Those grown men were trying to dehumanize a child and thought they had strength in numbers, and like I always say, God and one person make a majority," he was anxious to see the video and asked her to forward him the link before they hung up.

She also advised him that his presentation for the Deputy Mayor was nearly completely downloaded.

Kendal self-reflected after watching the video and was amazed that there were nearly forty-thousand views. He read a few of the comments and realized that most of his point was made, but people had chosen sides and were arguing first amendment rights and why he had stopped to even speak with the group of men. Kendal understood that his greatest impact would be on the youth at the center, and not a video that people debated. He stopped because a young child was disrespected, and it wasn't going to happen on his watch.

He got up from the loveseat and placed his laptop onto the coffee table. He walked into his garage and took two packs of chicken wings from his deep freezer to brine if lunch was a go.

Kendal peered into his living room and thought about all the previous times he promised to make it a more suitable living space. His vaulted ceilings had an extended large fan situated in the middle. From traveling when Kwame invited him to perform and putting in time at the center, he had no time to turn this into a home. He walked up the stairs to his bedroom, stripped and took a shower. He was still tired and decided to sleep before going back into his office and triple check the itinerary for his awards ceremony.

When he woke, he dressed and went back downstairs. His phone had charged and when he unlocked it, he saw two missed calls from the center and a text message from Frances telling him to listen to the presentation and to advise her what he would like the next course of action to be.

"Strange," but whatever it was he decided it could wait until he got back to his office. There were other messages from his older brother in Charlotte, NC, evidently the video had made its way down there.

"I'm not going to hear the end of it." he said as he pulled his riding gloves on and grabbed his keys. He put his black half-helmet on and backed his motorcycle out of the garage. His condominium community was expanding with new development. Spacious interiors with different layouts were a big attraction for those buying property, but it also boasted a thirty -person movie theatre, Himalayan Salt room and different athletic courts including two for tennis.

The community was backed up against an undeveloped wooded surrounding with access to a wide stream letting out into a large pond nearly three acres in circumference that provided for an excellent path to walk, run or bicycle.

Kendal waved at a married couple about his age as he approached them. The wife stared at him a little longer than expected, but when the man gave him a proper salute Kendal ascertained they had also seen the morning video.

It was just after nine o'clock when he walked back into the center. Mr. Litman was locking the game room and pool area, and Frances was sitting at the receptionist desk with head phones on shaking her head negatively back and forth.

When she saw Kendal approach, she removed the head phones and dove right in.

"That Deputy Mayor is a pig Kendal do you hear me, and that other asshat is just as bad," Frances said handing Kendal the head phones.

"You should sit down or better yet let's go to your office because you're going to be, to be," Frances was saying as Kendal interrupted her.

"It's ok just press play,"

Kendal listened and heard the end of his presentation but what came after that gave him pause that any financial assistance would be coming. He rewound the recording again and as it played, he was formulating how to maximize the position he now had.

"That dark guy seemed pretty sharp," the councilman's voice came through first. There was a pause before the Deputy Mayor responded.

"Oh, he was very sharp, had verifiable data on proven improvements on participants in his program. Had one of the most solid business plans that I have seen since being in office. He has equity to invest alongside any contributions he has asked the city for. But black people will always fail, its inherent in their culture. There are outliers but his community center is near MLK. Jr. Boulevard. The mayor wants this big revitalization plan and he will get it, but not at the expense of kids who have an actual chance of success in life not little ghetto babies," she finished.

"The Mayor's biggest contributor still controls the gangs via drug flow even if he's so called legitimate now. Use the latest task force numbers on city geography and make the case to the Mayor that it's a wasted cause," he paused to lower his voice.

"Unlike the patriots marching on city hall today," he finished letting out a boisterous laugh.

"I have access to an office so we can see everything. I bet the blacks and gays will be shouting like rabid dogs," the Deputy Mayors voice was heard as the sound of her office door opened and closed behind them.

Kendal removed the headphones and stared at Frances who stood with her coat and purse as she began speaking.

"She's a pig Kendal, an outright witch. There's no way we are getting any funding for anything. We have racist people in city hall controlling money meant for organizations like ours and we never get the money." she finished.

Kendal was upset as expected, but he also knew they were closer now to being fully funded for the community center. He stood up from his sofa and put the headphones on the desk.

"Frances don't worry yourself one bit about any city funds. We are going to be just fine," he said with a smile on his face. He hugged her and asked Mr. Litman to escort Frances to her car before returning to his office. His text message indicator flashing on his phone caught his attention. He had received a flurry of text messages from his brother 'I guess college did payoff,' and 'I did not know Malcolm X lived in Columbus' along with 'my younger brother is a wizard' were a few but it was the last one that caught Kendal off guard 'I am so proud of the human you have become even more so, after Janine. I love you Special K," Kendal sent an I love you back and sat down at his desk. He needed to formulate the plan to get a new ally because he knew "the enemy of my enemy is my friend."

CHAPTER 16
SPICY GARLIC

Mattie took Monday off and lounged around all day. She spent a few hours at the park with Grandma Redd, but her day was uneventful. When she woke Tuesday morning, she pushed herself with an extreme workout with Geri who was already waiting on her. She left the gym feeling drained, but it was Kendal sending a simple message that gave her a full jolt of energy. "Good morning."

"Good morning give me a couple of hours and I'll message you back," she hopped in the shower and headed into work for a routine day.

On Tuesday mornings her department had meetings on the percent to goal they had achieved, and what targets they had for the current week. Mattie was sitting back in her chair with her eyes closed listening to Geno, the manager in charge of her department. He was boring and thought he was the company man, two things that never sat well with Mattie. Geno followed the rules to the full letter of the law. He lied once and had a representative fired, and Mattie knew he lied so she never respected him, and her actions showed her lack of regard for him.

She gave him the nickname ‘Yoda’ from the Star Wars movies, but unlike Yoda, Geno was not to be trusted. He was also envious of Mattie because she was already financially secure and didn’t need this job. So, after listening to him forecast what the end of the year bonuses would be for managers if the representatives had hit their goals, Mattie walked out of the meeting to sit at her desk to snack on some crackers and drink a Pepsi.

“Just got out of our meeting with a manager that looks like ‘Yoda’. Do you know who Yoda is?” Mattie instant messaged Kendal.

“LUKE I AM YOUR FATHER,” Kendal replied using a Bitmoji of Darth Vader then quickly sending another message through.

“How you gon ask me if I know who Yoda is, I own the complete saga of Star Wars and The Matrix Trilogy. You know growing up all the classics Boys in The Hood Menace, Scarface. I even thought Fredo could be redeemed. How are you today Madison, sorry for keeping you up last night. I don't get good conversation all the time," as she read the words she smiled because he felt genuine.

"I slept hard, got up and went to the gym before work. My sister Geri was trying to kill me too. She had mad energy for a change, and I was dragging," Mattie sent back.

"I figured you would've rolled out the bed at the last moment, it's refreshing to know that you have will power and you sound like a go getter, that's special, so what do you do to earn a buck?"

"I work for Galaxy Communication, I take escalated calls from people who don't pay their bills, or have some unresolved issue related to not paying their bill…lol…for the most part it's a decent job…nowhere close to rocket science," she responded as Grace and a few workers came back from the meeting.

"Girl he turned red when you walked out," the older woman said passing behind Mattie's desk to sit down next to her.

"Yeah, he looked like a fire hydrant," a younger woman, about twenty-four, named Kim, that Grace had taken under her wing, added laughing out loud.

Mattie's phone vibrated in her hand.

"I know it sounds kinda forward, I'm gonna be wrapping up at the center in a few, had great meetings, can I bring you lunch, something to eat?"

Mattie was hungry and typically she would decline the offer but not today.

"My lunch isn't until around one o'clock," she responded trying to give herself a little time to figure out what she wanted to eat besides a hamburger.

"That's perfect, tell me Madison, any food that you're allergic too that I should know about or what you don't eat?" he sent back to her. Mattie was trying to listen to Grace and Kim speak with her about her whipping Ronald Jackson, in fact a lot of the conversations were about the same thing. Some people, like Geno, didn't know Mattie could hear them.

"She's in shape, but Ronald Jackson was six feet three inches and over two hundred pounds, she got lucky," she heard Geno say. Mattie was about to address him, but Grace told her to let it go.

"Don't worry about him, he just jealous, what y'all want

for lunch?" Grace asked. They often ordered lunch together because the restaurant gave a twenty percent discount on group orders.

"I've got food coming, I think," Mattie said just now remembering she hadn't text Kendal back.

"I'm so sorry, I'm not allergic to any foods, you can grab me a burger and fries from somewhere," Mattie responded while Grace started in with the questions.

"Well can't we just order something with you, who bringing it Geri or Cindy?" she asked waiting for Mattie to respond but she was reading Kendal's reply

"If you want a burger and fries, I'll gladly pick it up…or can I surprise you?" Mattie read it and smiled at his message.

"Mattie, Grace is talking to you," Kim said in a high-pitched voice leaning over the cubicle. It was the way she talked that irritated her coworkers at first, but after two years in their department people had gotten used to it, and she was the top producer.

"Surprise me," she sent back a message with a huge grin across her face.

"Madison Parks, are you not telling me something?" Grace stood up while moving Kim out of the way to stare at Mattie.

Mattie sat up in her chair and pretended to cover her phone up. "Y'all just some Nosey Parkers," she said jokingly.

"Ooh Mattie," Kim said pausing knowing that it was her time to go. This was a conversation she wasn't going to be a part of.

"Just let me know what we doing for lunch, I gotta log in and get some revenue," she finished walking down the aisle to her workstation.

"So, what's going on Mattie, who is bringing you lunch?" Grace asked propping her butt onto Mattie's desk and staring at her waiting for a response.

"Well if you must know, I met someone Saturday night," Mattie replied as her phone vibrated. It was Kendal.

"Well honey do you want to give me your work address, or should I just send the cat woman signal out?" his message read, Mattie laughed and then smiled.

"Ooh child, he got you smiling that's a real good sign,

laughter is important. What does he do for a living and what's he look like Mattie…tell me?" Grace urged her younger friend on. Mattie asked Grace to hold on as she replied with the address.

"127 Lake Front, and I see you still got jokes…cat woman huh?" she sent back with a smiley face sticking its' tongue out. Mattie looked up and saw Grace still sitting on her desk waiting for her answers, but Mattie stuck her index finger up to motion to Grace to hold on while she took a sip of her Pepsi, having her wait a little bit longer.

"I'm just playing, we met at the poetry thing that night," Mattie started by telling the gray-haired woman about Geri's performance and ended up with almost being run off the road.

"He made a poem up about you, girl he got potential," Grace said as more of a statement as she hugged her. Grace was elated that Mattie had someone sparking her curiosity since Brian and her split.

Mattie was not going to settle for less than what she wanted or needed. A few guys had taken Mattie out over the past few years, but they lacked qualities that Mattie found essential. She needed an honest man, and required him to have a good relationship with his family, he had to have goals that he strode toward until completion; and he had to be self-sufficient. One kid was fine if the other criteria were met, but she had settled once with Brian and that was once too many.

"I figure you're a super hero that purrs…one o'clock is good," he sent back. Mattie felt something tingle in her stomach moving down the inside of her legs.

"One o'clock is good, Kevin Hart."

"Ok, I can't wait to see you again Madison."

Grace had been sitting there the whole-time watching Mattie type and her body expression. Mattie was childlike in some of her mannerisms right now.

"I think you may have met you match sweetie," Grace said pausing

"You know I'm gonna be downstairs right when he comes," the older woman sat down and sat back.

"Ok, but leave Kim up here, I don't want her all up in my business, and we better start taking some calls," Mattie finished noticing that she and Grace were the only ones not on the phone. For the next two hours Mattie took phone calls, but was thinking about Kendal. Was he what he appeared to be, was he as handsome and built as she had remembered, or had the lighting played tricks on her eyes Saturday night?

"What if he doesn't like me?" Mattie thought nervously. As twelve forty-five came, she hadn't heard from him.

"He better not be on his own time schedule or have some flaky ass excuse," Mattie thought thinking about some of the bullshit she used to let Brian get by with. Mattie had accepted a past due payment and deposit from a customer. The customer had an attitude, but Mattie didn't respond. She was looking at her phone for a sign that Kendal had arrived and nothing. Mattie was skeptical that she had been played and started getting hot when her phone vibrated.

"I'm outside at one of the tables, are you coming out or am I coming in?" he asked through instant messaging.

"Give me a second, on my way out." Mattie leaned back in her chair to look around the cubicle to Grace and smiled. Grace hugged her because she was happy.

"Well me and Kim better order something now I guess, have a fantastic lunch sweetie," Grace said releasing Mattie.

"Thank you; but let me go so he just ain't out there

waiting," Mattie said looking into Grace's desk mirror checking her lipstick which was the only make up she wore, and that was only to keep her lips moist.

"You look fine now get yo tail out of here," Grace said pushing Mattie as she sent an email to the restaurant for her order.

Mattie rode the escalator down and she could see Kendal through the large tinted building windows. He was sitting in the middle of all the lunch tables surrounded by people. He had a Mandarin colored, Polo type shirt on, and stone washed blue jeans. As she pushed through the revolving turnstile, he saw her and smiled. He stood as she got closer to the table.

"Hey you."

"Hey comedian," she replied, smiling as they exchanged a quick but firm hug.

"Damn this man is fine," Mattie thought feeling the muscles in his shoulders and back. As she let go, she let her hands slide down his back to his waist to feel firmness in his lower back and hips. In that moment her mind had wondered about his body on hers and as she sat down, she thought he caught her staring at his crotch.

"Oh God!" she thought so she tried to change the subject, "So, what you bring me to eat?" moving her eyes to a white bag sitting atop the black iron wrought table.

He smiled back at her. She wasn't one hundred percent sure if she had been caught looking.

"I cooked for you, I've got two types of wings, and potato salad and baked beans…and here this is for you, but you can't read it until you're back at your desk," he handed her a greeting card.

"And here's a salad for you too, I brought Vinaigrette and Ranch dressing," he pulled two small containers out the bottom of the bag.

"Vinaigrette," she said pausing feeling the eyes on them from people sitting around their table. This was the first time Mattie had anyone bring her lunch at her job, so it was new to a lot of people she had worked with before in other departments and currently.

"A card," he was a gentleman too, which caught her off guard. She got cards for her birthday and invitations to functions, not a personal greeting card.

"Kendal, thanks for lunch, and you didn't have to cook

all this," Mattie said pouring the dressing over the top of her salad. It was a beautiful sunny day; the temperature was in the low eighties with a slight southern breeze. Mattie wore white Capri's and a wife beater with a light weight chambray colored shirt wrapped around her waist. She had on white flip flops with French Pedicure toes matching her finger nails.

"You want some of this cause I'm not going to be able to eat all of it?" Mattie asked Kendal. A couple of Mattie's admirers were staring out the window at them, but Mattie simply ignored them like she had done the people sitting outside.

"No that's all for you and I enjoy cooking; you can tell me if you don't like it, I'm a big boy."

She couldn't help but to think that "yeah it looked nice and thick," her mind needed to get off sex. But with the handsomely built man sitting in front of her she couldn't help but to think of sitting in his lap right now.

"So how did you sleep?" she asked before digging into her salad.

"It was cool, I usually don't sleep much, I'm always thinking I've got something to do and my mind races, so I write or read. I was concerned you would be dragging today, but you were up bright and early getting your sweat on," Kendal said staring at her through his sunglasses. He sat into the sun so she wouldn't have the sun shining in her eyes. Mattie saw that his nails were clean, and his hands looked strong.

"So far so good," she was feeling more comfortable after seeing his light hazel eyes checking her out when he removed his sunglasses when a few clouds blocked the sunlight shining down.

"So, you're done at the center today, you said you tutor kids…how old are they?" Mattie asked as she slid her salad to the side and covered it up. It was really a meal all to itself, but she wanted to taste more of what he had prepared for her.

"My kids range from five to age eighteen; they're real good kids that have been misdirected. The kids that have been with me for the last two years have made vast improvements in all their course work and are leading by example, it's a process. Friday we're having an award ceremony for them, if you're not busy maybe you can come, bring your sisters if you want, I've been reaching out to the community. Some people are very receptive, but there's a lot of room to grow," he paused watching Mattie pick one of his wings up.

He made barbecue and spicy garlic flavored chicken wings; she was tearing the flapper apart to one of the hot wings.

“This Friday night I spend with my grandmother, if I came, she’d be with me…what time?” she bit into the wing.

“It’s gonna start about seven o’clock and please bring your grandmother. I teach the kids that our elders are to be cherished,” he said pausing watching Mattie’s eyes begin to water.

“Oh shit, I forgot to bring you something to drink, where is the nearest store?” he asked as Mattie fanned her mouth.

“I shoulda told you that those were hot too, damn my bad baby,” he stood from his chair.

“There’s a store inside…hold on,” Mattie said reaching for money in her front pocket.

“Honey I asked you to lunch, your money is no good with me, I’ve got it. What do you want to drink?”

“Oh, shit this is hot, Pepsi, this got my mouth on fire…they’re good just hot as hell.” Mattie said snatching a napkin from the bag he had brought the food in to wipe the sauce from her lips. Kendal had disappeared into the building and Grace was walking out.

"So that's the mystery man, I think I have seen him somewhere before?" Grace said approaching Mattie's table. Mattie shook her head affirmatively because her mouth was still hot.

"Damn I can smell those from up here, you got something to drink?" Grace asked as Mattie motioned her to sit down.

"He went to get me a Pepsi," Mattie said with her eyes still watering.

"Here he come I'm about to go back upstairs," Grace was attempting to say but Mattie grabbed her wrist to stay so she could be introduced to Kendal.

"Damn I get an introduction too?" Grace asked looking down at the container of potato salad.

"Girl eat some of that, it's got mayonnaise in it, it ought to help," she instructed Mattie as Kendal approached the table.

"I got you a Pepsi, but you may want to try this milk first,

I'm sorry I shouldn't have made em so hot," pausing as he acknowledged Grace.

"Hi, I'm Kendal," extending his hand to the older woman.

"Kendal this is Grace, Grace this is Kendal," Mattie said after drinking the milk down.

"I'm gonna have to back off these for now…I'll eat em later, do you want any?' she asked Grace who shook her head 'no'.

"Kim and I ordered some pizza. I'm gonna get out of here, but it was nice meeting you Kendal. I'll see you upstairs," Grace said excusing herself. Kendal stood slightly as well.

"Are you ok, your mouth still blazing?" he asked with concern leaning forward in his chair.

"I'm ok, they taste really good, the flavor, but they are smoking hot," she said sipping on the milk which was helping greatly.

"I'll cook something different next time, something southern, those lips should never be harmed," he paused

"That's my way of saying you have perfect lips, in fact you're more stunning in the sunlight because I can see 'you,'' he stated with the emphasis on 'you'.

Mattie was digging him; his manners and self-assurance were the cake, but his strong body was physically appealing like 'icing'. As the wind blew, she smelled his scent. It was the perfect fit for his personality; smooth, sexy and manly.

"Thanks, you've got a way with words, old smooth talker," Mattie said smiling leaning forward. For the next fifteen minutes he told her about a few of the kids that were realizing their potential at his center. Mattie put the food back into the bag and told him that anytime, after nine she'd be logged onto her computer, she hugged him, and he kissed her on the cheek. It didn't feel awkward to Mattie at all. As she walked away, she hoped that he was checking her every curve out. Mattie knew she had a dynamic body and a face to go with it, but she didn't flaunt it. As she rode the escalator upstairs, she saw Kendal sitting down on a motorcycle putting his helmet on.

She thought about the fact that she had never rode on the back of a motorcycle before, except with her father.

"But I'll let him drive me and just hold on," she thought

imagining her arms wrapped around him feeling the vibration of the bike under her. Mattie was horny for the first time in ages. Her panties were moist, and she could tell the inside of her thigh walls were tingling, she watched him ride away as he merged into traffic.

Mattie got back to her department where Grace was waiting at her desk with a slice of pizza on a plate.

"I want some of the barbecue wings, Kim had me order thick crust and I hate all this dough, it isn't even cooked all the way through," she threw the slice of pizza into the trash can.

"Mattie, if he's as nice as he seems, you gotta keeper," she paused taking a bite of chicken.

"He can cook too girl," she said licking the sauce off her fingers.

"I'm taking three of these," she finished. Mattie didn't have an appetite, for food. She was digging Kendal, his attention and concern for her seemed real and he wasn't overly sexual, although he had looked at her body a few times. She was going to take Grandma Redd with her to the award presentation, so she wouldn't feel awkward or out of place, plus it was a good way for her grandmother to get an idea of what type of man he was.

Grandma Redd's opinion counted the most next to her own, and Don Rojas was close. Mattie's phone vibrated from a text Geri sent.

"How was lunch tramp?" Mattie laughed out loud and replied.

"It was really, a really good lunch," Mattie told Geri about Sunday nights' conversation with Kendal that morning at the gym as they rode the stationary bikes. Geri felt that it was time for Mattie to open up and take a chance with someone. Instead of texting Geri again Mattie sent an instant message through to Kendal.

"Thanks for lunch and I look forward to seeing you Friday," she was getting over feeling embarrassed, if she was moving faster than what she had intended, she liked him. She thought how silly it was that they still hadn't exchanged contact numbers, although she did have his from his book. There were attractive women walking by when they were at lunch, but Kendal never let his eyes stray, although Mattie did, she had to see if they were looking at him.

"Really good ain't saying nothing, blah blah blah. I want details, what did he bring you to eat?" Geri text her again being adamant about being told more about her lunch date.

"Okay, he is fine, his eyes, his face…that ass. He's refreshing and oh my gawd I was tingling all in between my legs while I was trying to eat. I think he caught me looking at his dick too. He made some wings; spicy and barbecue flavored and potato salad…he cooked everything," Mattie was sending back to Geri when another text message came through. Mattie was hoping it was a reply from Kendal, but it wasn't.

"How was your little secret lunch date hooker? Me and Lala having our own lunch at Chipotle, don't be skimping on the details either," it was a text message from Cindy.

"Damn, your ass just couldn't wait to tell them about my lunch date, could you?" Mattie sent a follow up text to Geri. Mattie could care less about any of them knowing but it had been a long while since she was able to tell her friends about a new man. Mattie scrolled back up the list of her text messages sent to Geri and forwarded them to both Sheila and Cindy's phones.

"If y'all want details just swing by later, I've got to get back to work right now. Good bye hooker, hoe and tramp and you know which one you are," Mattie replied. She would tell them later, but she wasn't going to get into details about how she kept imagining Kendal laying up under her with his arms rubbing her hips and his strong hands gripping her ass. She was horny and needed physical contact with a man. She would exercise self-control until she felt she was ready emotionally. She had work to do right now if she was going to take another short day on Friday.

Mattie put her phone away and silenced it while she worked. She worked an hour and a half of overtime and was getting ready to leave when she heard her phone vibrating. She had two text messages both from Cindy asking if she wanted to stop somewhere for happy hour.

"Sorry mama, I worked overtime today, I'm just now leaving work. I'm going to head home to relax with grandma. Friday, I need you to go to an awards banquet, starts around 5:30." Mattie sent back. She knew Cindy would be late to her own funeral, so she gave her an earlier time. The second message was an instant message sent from Kendal.

"Lunch was perfect today; you were all the nourishment I needed. I pray my gorgeous lips aren't damaged," he had sent it twenty minutes after her original sent to him. She smiled figuring it had taken him that long to weave his way in and out of traffic on his motorcycle to get back to the center. Her lips were feeling better.

"If he keeps complimenting me, he gon see how hot they are," she thought but she wasn't thinking about the lips he was commenting on. There was an additional instant message from Kendal that was sent roughly two hours later.

"Tonight, is my turn just have patience if I'm not logged on by nine, I am headed downtown to the county to get one of my boys out of jail. I'll tell you all about it tonight…I enjoy you Madison," he finished.

When Kendal returned from lunch and parked his motorcycle, he noticed the white Ford Fusion with one of the local network's logo on the side and no one was sitting in the parked car.

He walked into the center and saw Marcie Mayfield, one of the morning show anchors, speaking with Frances at the large receptionist desk.

Marcie had dark, black skin and a head full of wavy, jet-black hair. She wore a green skirt with a matching blouse with orange and white mixed alongside the green. Her green sling back shoes showed the definition in her legs.

"Here's Kendal now," Frances said as Marcie turned and made her introduction.

"Mr. K, Kendal it is a pleasure to meet you and off the record I'm glad you told those assholes a thing or two. Is there somewhere we can talk?" she asked, after extending her hand.

"I told you you were going viral," Frances said, before excusing herself to help the children who volunteered their time for the awards banquet.

Kendal had no idea what to expect from this meeting, but he was certain he could use this platform to increase awareness of the program he wanted to continue building.

"Well Ms. Mayfield it seems I have time right now. We can speak outside, or in my office," he responded to her request.

"Actually, outside would be wonderful, I don't get to enjoy much of the beautiful weather lately." she replied.

Would you like bottled water or coffee?" He asked as he poured a cup of coffee from a Carafe sitting next to a Keurig coffee maker.

"Water would be great," Marcie said pausing.

“I remember when this was condemned, and the city wanted to tear it down. Now you are helping give back. Has this been your life’s ambition?” She asked as he handed her the bottled water.

Kendal knew he had to choose his words carefully with reporters. He had spoken out of turn in High School after a football game. It took him two years to live it down.

“I guess you can say that, but it took a few detours in life, the loss of my wife and traveling that has placed me where I am. What we do right now, for someone who wants a better life is the most important thing we can offer. Extending knowledge to those who need it most,” he walked Marcie through the game room and past the swimming pool and into the gym.

“This is amazing, and the children, the children have other outlets besides video games. They can learn and socialize at the same time. Phenomenal job sir,” she finished just as Kendal opened the back door to let out into a picnic area with six tables connected with benches on each side.

“Thank you.”

“So, Kendal like Frances said, the video has gone viral and my producer would like to have you on air tomorrow morning. The gist of it will be lighthearted, with a few tough questions on your beliefs that you told the white nationalists," she said before taking a sip of water.

"My brother, my brother would pay to be a fly on the wall right now. Older brothers you know. Tomorrow morning, I am available. One thing though, I would like a moment to speak about our community center," he answered.

Marcie looked very pleased and shook her head up and down. "That is not a problem, I saw the banner up about the ceremony on Friday, we can make sure to bring that up. You will have to be in the studio by seven and we will have a few questions ready for you to look over. I have been pushing for local coverage for every neighborhood, but for some reason even with the Urban Development League down the street this area is always overlooked. Here's my card if you need to get a hold of me," she reached into her purse for an ink pen and jotted her cell phone number on the back before standing.

"You can reach me anytime Kendal. I must depart for a press conference at city hall. After the fiasco yesterday, The Mayor's office is delivering a statement," she sighed not sounding enthusiastic as they walked back to her car.

"Marcie, thank you for coming down and giving us a chance to speak about what matters most. The children and their progress. I will be there fifteen minutes early," he replied as she started her car.

She rolled down her window and strapped her seat belt in.

"You seem to be a remarkable man Kendal, I am sorry for the loss of your wife. I'll have coffee waiting on you in the morning," she said as they bid farewell.

"So, you said yes," Frances said as a statement as he walked back into the center.

Kendal smiled and walked towards a small trash bin to throw the cup and empty bottled water away.

"Of course, we are going to do it. If that video can help get the message out and give us a larger reach, they can have me sit in front of a camera and ask me anything. Anyways it was never about me, but that young boy and his mother. Hopefully he isn't scarred. I gave them my business card and I really hope to see him again," Kendal explained. It was true it was about the young child in his initial response, but after everything else that had unfolded that morning coming to light, it was also about being funded by the city.

"Marcie's entire face lit up when she watched you walk across the room, from what I hear in these streets is that after her divorce was final, she dove head first into work and got the woman who had an affair with her husband fired. So be careful with that one. Everything that shines ain't gold Mr. K," Frances finished.

Kendal thanked her for that information and excused himself to his office. He had an additional reason for saying yes and he needed to make sure he watched the entire press conference that Marcie was on her way to. He needed to know what stance City Hall was taking, and how to use that to pivot in his morning interview for a second meeting, but this time with The Mayor himself.

Kendal could see the plan coming to fruition even after the minor setback. He watched the news conference and saw Marcie on camera when she asked the spokesperson why there was no protection against the mother and child caught on camera before a passer-by intervened.

The response given was a stock reply about first amendment rights and that even those who don't agree with the ideology of the white nationalists they had a right to congregate. When a follow up question was asked about whether they had even seen the video. The spokesperson said they had not.

Kendal saw that would be an opportunity he would take as an opening if any question was asked remotely pertaining to this news conference. He watched the video online twice more before walking back to his locker in the gym. He changed into shorts and t-shirt. He put on a pair of boxing gloves and started to hit the heavy bag followed by twenty minutes of jumping rope. Building a sweat helped him focus, and with everything moving fast around him, his thoughts circled back around to his earlier lunch date.

“The wings were too damn hot Kendal,” he thought shaking his head back and forth knowing next time he would tone them down. He walked back to the locker room and unlocked the entrance to the shower where only Mr. Litman and he had access. He undressed and started the shower and as the first bead of water hit his skin Kendal stared forward at the silver shower head as if coming to a grand revelation and he began laughing uncontrollably as he thought…“

Mattie looked right at my crotch at lunch,” vowing to bring it up when they were face to face again.

About the Author

A.V. Smith is an athlete turned writer. During the mid-2000's, he was a featured poet at the Columbus Arts Festival and also won second place during The Great Debaters poetry slam in Columbus, Ohio as Oprah Winfrey's movie was being released nationally. With a passion for storytelling, he paints with words that draw readers into the story. A.V. writes on an emotional level to empower readers to engage in deeper conversations about their past, their relationships, and their connection with The Universe. His first book is titled, "Madison God's Fingerprint 1.618." He currently has two more books in the Madison series ready for publication as well as a Fantasy Fiction series which is slated to release in late Spring 2020 under pseudonym J. B. White in recognition of his elders.

Through life and love, Andre' has learned our journeys are temporary, yet intensely meaningful. This understanding led him to donate a kidney to his younger brother. As the father of three children, his desire is to see his children overcome the fear of success by being the best version of themselves; therefore, he strives to lead by example, at times falling short, but understanding human beings are still a work in progress. When he is not engaged in his passion, you can find him with a fishing pole in his hand, coaching youth level football, or attending a local artist event.

For more information, please visit
www.warpedwritingandpublishing.com.

An Excerpt from Book II

Madison: In the Presence of God

The candles set on each corner of the kitchen counter top with a vase of flowers equidistant between the two. The amber and moss scent from the candles reminded Grandma Redd of her childhood growing up spending more days working in the field than relegated to sitting indoors staring at wireless devises like many youths of today.

Mattie listened to her as she discussed the topics the news was covering but when the newscaster mentioned progress in the human trafficking case her focus shifted.

"Several arrests have been made and we are hunting down the rest of this ring. Our nation, our city, this department will not tolerate such heinous crimes." A woman Mattie recognized as assistant district attorney Paulette Shields had given a statement on the steps of the courthouse after recent indictments. Mattie had set in on a few of her cases, witnessing a keen legal mind. She had been one of the few attorneys Mattie watched destroy Clayton Monroe III in a court of law.

"We need more people like that. She sho is passionate, and I feel sorry for anyone she gon go after or even try to get in that woman's way of giving out justice," Grandma Redd ran new yarn through the eye of her crotchet hook. She had taken two earlier naps and found herself up unusually later than expected.

"Yeah me too, grandma," it was that split decision made at the mall to do something that helped Paulette do her job, and Mattie found peace knowing that those responsible were going to face harsh legal ramifications for their actions. Although Mattie believed she could have served justice much swifter had she wanted, by ending them.

She moved from the love seat and walked into the kitchen and poured two glasses of sun tea before returning to the love seat, extending the second glass to her grandmother.

"Thank you honey."

Breaking News flashed on screen as the evening program

returned. The mugshot of apprehended felon Lucas Carson was shown on screen before the newscasters returned on air. Additional footage showed deputies had found him hiding in an old abandoned building that once prepared fresh baked goods near Columbus State Community College. Henry and his partner could be seen speaking with uniformed officers who had handcuffed the suspect who sat in the back of a cruiser with its lights still flashing.

"On a brighter note, arrests have been made in the armed robbery at Future First Bank where the bank manager was killed. The alleged shooter, Lucas Carson was apprehended from a tip called into the police hotline. Our streets have to be made safe again, so remember, if you see something say something." The female newscaster finished turning to her partner who signed them off.

"Tune in tomorrow morning for The Morning Jump Start with Marcie Mayfield for updates and a special surprise visit from a guest at the Columbus Zoo. I am Randy Carr and for Vanessa Jones good night and good rest."

Grandma Redd turned the channel to watch reruns of Good Times so Mattie took that as an opportunity to excuse herself to go train in her basement but first she needed to switch out her blue jeans and tank top. Changed into powder blue cotton shorts and classic black A shirt, she headed through the kitchen, tossing an empty Pepsi bottle into the trash.

Mattie lifted the lamp sitting next to the basement door to retrieve the key for access. She unlocked the heavy wooden door and replaced the key back under the lamp. As she pulled the door behind, she locked it from the inside, only to walk a few stairs downwards to flip the light switch on. Her eyes adjusted to the brightness as the light filled the room, reverberating off the mirrors spread throughout. She had a speed bag and heavy bag in one corner. In another, she had a Wing Chun Wooden Dummy to help develop her striking technique for close quarter combat. This was the piece of equipment proven most valuable in the confrontation helping David, her Colombian brother. Knowing where to strike and how to strike accurately had helped her break ribs and bones of men twice her size. Where she had once placed padding, it had been worn over the years from her repeated striking.

Mattie had weighted ropes and a dumbbell rack situated next to her squat bar. Different sized boxes were stacked in another corner, but the center of the room was covered by a mat covering a ten by ten area.

She had created this space when she separated the other side of the building into two units. She created an exit that let out into a floor space in her garage that was completely hidden, covered with a black tarp that she parked her vehicle over.

Mattie stretched and put her ear buds in as she began jumping rope. She thought about the times she double-dutched growing up when she still had her own family. Her mother had been her first teacher. She was drawn to memories of laughter and trips to the store with her mom, using food stamps purchased at discount when theirs ran out. The trips they took to Georgia to visit her grandmother and great aunts. She had flashes of swinging from a rope tied to a tree that overlooked one of the water holes on the family's property as she played with cousins and friends.

She thought back to being taught how to read and cook at the same time by her mother as she was forced to read while her mother prepared meals. Her father was in and out of the country in the military. When he was home, his purpose for his daughter was to train to be exceptional. Her mother balanced that with the softer things in life although while he was away, it was her mother who drove her to train. It was her mother always present in the tournaments. It was her mother who had protected her as a teenager. Mattie never understood why her letters were never answered or why her mother only relayed messages through Grandma Redd.

Mattie's fifteen-minute warmup had brought emotions to the surface. She walked to the wooden dummy and began to hit it with palm strikes and heel kicks. She thought about seeing her mom stand accused of false charges and torn down by career-oriented prosecutors who sought high conviction rates no matter the cost to the individual or family. Her mother was lied on, manipulated by law officials, forced to confess under duress while still in shock and without an attorney present.

Mattie felt the conflict rising as she put more force in her strikes, but she didn't stop. Every time she faced a new challenge in life, she fell back to wondering how different life would be had that chapter in her life been different. She would never know, and this was the source of her fury and sadness.

Mattie spaced out and had moved closer to the wooden dragon like she was applying pressure to an opponent and without realizing she put too much force behind alternating elbow strikes, until the blood splattered onto her forearms.

The pain shot through both hands and upward, but she knew within a few minutes it would pass.

"Pain is temporary, it doesn't last," her father's vice echoed in her thoughts as she paced the perimeter of her basement waiting for the pain to subside. She grabbed a kettlebell and sat down on her mat to begin her standard core workout; twelve separate exercises targeting different areas and each one was a set of fifty. She grew tired after the last set but pushed herself to the punching and speed bag for three rounds at two minutes.

The time had passed quickly. Mattie had worked up a sweat along with emotions she kept deep inside. This was a sort of therapy, a means to balance the conflict that had one time ripped her emotions apart. It had taken nearly two decades to accept the 'darkness of her youth' but she had come to an understanding that all her subcomponents made her complete. When she made her way back upstairs her grandmother had retired to her bedroom.

Mattie grabbed two bottled waters and walked into her bedroom. She could see the brightness of the moon as it set high above the tree line of the park. Nearly a full moon she wondered if her emotional outburst had been a result of the energies shifting. She laughed uncontrollably as she realized that was something Geri would attribute it to.

Mattie finished one bottle of water, throwing it away as she entered her bathroom. She started to run a bath but decided a shower would be sufficient, and she wanted to rest because her date with Kendal was tomorrow night. After showering she ate a salad and apple before turning Grandma Redd's television off when her phone rang. She smiled knowing the universe listened always.

"¿Mija, estas bien,Estás herido?" The voice from the only other woman she accepted as mother without the genetic makeup came through. Mattie assumed David had spoken with her about Ronald Jackson and now Senora Rojas was asking if she was ok or injured with genuine concern in her voice.

"Si, Senora estoy bien. No fue nada." Mattie answered in the same manner she had with Grandma Redd, all she needed to convey was 'I'm ok, it was nothing.'

Mama Rojas was how Mattie had hoped to hold her family together if she had one. She supported her husband even when her life was in jeopardy because she trusted in family. Her support for Mattie was just as deep as the children she had borne, and Mattie held no doubt that she would protect her as she did her own flesh and blood.

"Good, good. I had to talk Papi down from sending people, he can get a little loco." Senora Rojas said in English light heartedly, but Mattie knew how far-reaching Duvan Rojas would extend his power for his children.

Senora Luisa Rojas had been born in America but kept strong ties to her Colombian heritage. When she gave birth to David and his younger sister, she made certain it was in American hospital, so they could be afforded all the freedoms an American citizen had. Now with those freedoms they were taking steps to further legitimize the family.

"Tell Papi if I ever need help, he would be the first to know. David said everything was peaceful." Mattie said as a statement. She knew it was very likely that a third party was monitoring this phone call, she had to be selective with words.

"La paz es relativa," Senora Rojas paused before speaking in English again.

"Peace is relative. It has been quiet mija." she finished as her and Mattie talked about the next visit to Colombia. It had been almost four years, but Senora Rojas had spent a week with Mattie and David in Seattle about a year ago. Senor Rojas found that traveling abroad wasn't as open for him.

"Dije papi que lo extraño y mantenerse fuera de problemas." it was true that she missed him, and he needed to stay out of trouble. Mattie told Senora Rojas she loved her before ending the call. Even in this moment of joy from a woman she was proud to have in her life and a family that completely accepted her, she laid in bed struggling to find an answer to the noise that re-emerged from her recent workout. She fell asleep with ice packs on her forearms, wondering if her mother missed her as much as Senora Rojas.